THE
HOLLYWOOD
COLORED

**ALSO BY
ERIC WARE:**

THE HOLLYWOOD COLORED: BOOK II

THE
HOLLYWOOD COLORED

ERIC WARE

WAREWORD PUBLISHING

Published by Wareword Publishing
P.O. Box 9495
Montgomery, AL 36108
www.warewordpublishing.com

Cover and book design by *1106design.com*

Painting by *Kenjiartdesign.com*

Library of Congress Catalogue Card Number: 2003105498
Ware, Eric
The Hollywood Colored / Eric Ware

ISBN 0-9740704-0-8

SAN: 255-3635

Printed in the United States of America
First Printing

I thank my mother,
Jeri Ware,
for always making
creativity possible.

1

Luke Martin was a sharecropper who loved the movies.

"Look at him down there," Red said. He yanked the plow line off the beat down mule and threw it in the dirt. "Just look at him. Everyday it's the same damn thing. He gonna get to the end of that row he plowing, unhook that mule, and watch the sun go down. Just stare at it like a damn fool. Asked him why he did that one time and he say he like to — get this shit now — like to see the contrast of the colors in the sky. You believe that shit? Said somebody oughta take a picture of it and it's a shame don't nobody know how to make no picture show in color. That nigger crazy, I'm telling you. Always have been, even since we was kids. Look at that fucker. He better get his black ass back hind that mule and finish planting this white man's strawberries. Boss Man Braxton ain't fucking round with these berries, now you know that as much as me. Luke touched, man. I'm telling you. The nigger touched. I don't know why Benny fool with him. I really don't. Hey, you going down to The Joint to hear Benny play tonight?"

The other fella nodded.

"That nigger can sure 'nough play that guitar, can't he? Oh, uh, now remember, don't say nothing about Luke around Benny, all right? They pretty tight and shit and you know how crazy Benny can get."

The fella nodded again.

"Man, let get my ass home so this woman can make me some corn mush for I see these hos at The Joint tonight."

"Your woman don't care 'bout you going down there?" the fella said. Red scoffed at the stupid question.

"Do she care? Nigger, please. You new around here. I beat that bitch in her head she say something to me 'bout going to the club. I don't play that. I'm cool as Calvin Coolridge. I'm the president, nigger."

They laughed.

Red gripped the mule by the bridle with no concern for its comfort and yanked it along. He sneered at Luke one more time just because.

If Luke heard Red's baritone voice echo down the field he didn't let on. Truth be told, Luke didn't much care for red niggers in general. Just said there was something sneaky 'bout 'em like a snake or a bat or something. But Red wasn't lying. There Luke was, all six foot one of him, with a he-man's body and a girl's face, leaning up against that peaceful black mule like it was a bus stop, staring at the blue sky with his wide, brown eyes like he was waiting for something to happen.

Boss Man Braxton happened along checking over the fields to make sure things were just so. His saggy, khaki pants hung by one suspender since he always let the other one flop at day's end. He stopped when he saw Luke and let out a tedious breath.

"Howdy there, Luke."

"Hey, Mr. Braxton." Luke kept his eyes on his target and Braxton looked at the sky to see if anything new was happening there. But it was just the same thing he always saw. A sun, some clouds, a few birds.

"What you doing there, boy?"

"Nothing." When Luke looked at the sky, however, he saw a wide open canvas with a sea full of colors and too many possibilities. The cloud in the middle resembled a top-heavy woman if he thought about it just right and he wanted to meet her. He felt his nature rise against his overalls and turned to the side so the boss man wouldn't see. He took off his hat and propped his elbow up on the back of that contented mule like he was about to order lunch and noted how the sun would be more romantical going down into the creek if it had another coat of orange on it. Then he laughed like he was alone. He saw leftover images from the race picture played at the Bijou Playhouse last night. It flickered against the blue in black and white and passed through a cloud.

"Mr. Braxton, you think a fella could ever make a picture screen as big as the sky?"

"Can't see how such a thing'd be possible, boy." Braxton checked his watch. Luke formed an open rectangle with his stretched out thumb and fingers and squinted through the view box to check out the sky.

"They should still be bigger, don't you think? How's a fella suppose to look at life on the screen if the screen ain't as big as life?"

"All right, now. Good bye, boy. Have a good weekend." Luke recognized the tone and unhooked the lines. He gave the mule a light tap on the backside and the gentle beast followed him to the barn. Again, Mr. Braxton searched the sky for anything he might of missed.

Luke jogged the short distance home to the shack he shared on Braxton's property with his mama and daddy. He couldn't wait for Benny's show to be over tonight cause they'd be going to see *Within Our Gates*, a coon-free movie by Oscar Micheaux.

He read about the picture in *The Chicago Defender*. Luke and his daddy put their money together to keep up a subscription since there was no way in hell they could get a colored newspaper at the general store. According the *Defender*, Micheaux's movie was banned in southern states but, after all these years, the Bijou Playhouse snuck in the unedited version. He could have taken a date with him but didn't want to waste a picture show on no gal. Luke either went to the movies with Benny, to yell at colored folks on the screen, or by himself; because the theatre was the perfect place to be alone.

He smelled the sizzle of meat when he approached his home. He swung the door open, almost hitting Sarah, and ran straight to the plain, pine table.

"Hey Ma, hey Daddy. Ma, I'll just take a baloney sandwich and leave the crispy part on."

Mack tilted his paper down and looked at his son like a stranger.

"Don't come in here ordering your mama around like a waitress, you out of your damn mind?"

"Oh, leave him alone, Mack," Sarah said. "That all you're going to eat? A sandwich?"

"Yeah, Ma. Don't have much time. Riding to The Joint early with Benny then we going to the Playhouse."

Mack circled something in the paper he was reading.

"Never should of started you on them movies. You live at the goddamn Bijou."

"Aw, come on Daddy, that ain't true. Half the time I live at the club." Sarah laughed while frying the meat to her boy's specifications.

"What in the paper today, Daddy?"

"Nothing."

"Then why read it?" Sarah laughed again and Mack leaned back in his chair and looked at the cracks in the ceiling.

"I ain't in the mood for you today, son."

"Luke, wash your hands," Sarah said. She fished the meat out the skillet with a fork and Luke gave his hands a quick wash in the water bowl by the stove. Benny busted through the door without knocking and Luke shook his dirty hand.

"Hey, folkses!" Benny said. Benny was as big as Luke but his face was handsome instead of pretty and carried an edge. He spoke in a deep drawl that sounded like he was either teasing a friend or taunting an enemy. He took off his hat before kissing Sarah on the cheek and took a whiff of the skillet.

"Have some," Sarah said.

"Naw, thanks. I'm watching my boyish figure. Sides, baloney don't mix with brandy." Benny hooted and Luke laughed back while they elbowed each other. Sarah didn't think that was funny.

"Both a y'all act your age," Mack said without looking up from his reading. Benny strutted up behind Mack and stood there awhile with his guitar, Bertha, slung over his back. Benny had a funny way of standing like he was giving his private parts room to breathe. He stared over Mack's shoulder and waited for the whole thing to get on his nerves. Sarah gave Luke his dinner and watched him gobble it on his feet, trying not to laugh. Luke loved watching Benny kid his daddy since Mack scared almost everybody in town.

"Can I help you?" Mack said.

"Naw," Benny said. "Just reading the paper. What's that word right there?"

"You don't know?"

"Uh-uh. I skipped school that year." Benny slapped his leg and Luke laughed along like it was the funniest damn thing he ever heard.

"Naw, seriously though, Whatcha reading there, Mack?"

"Looking for a job."

"A job?" said Benny. "And leave the life of cropping berries? Nigger, you gonna hurt these white folks feelings." Luke stomped the floor in hysterics and Sarah looked at him like he was crazy.

"Some fellas in ReelTown talking about starting a sharecropper's union," Mack said. Need some folks to help organize. They call it the SCU. Might be a few years off but still."

"The SCU, huh?" said Benny. "Well, I'll see you running from some crackers if you talking 'bout starting a union."

"I ain't in the mood for you today, Benny."

"Be that way then. Wees got a prior engagement." Benny bowed in Luke's direction.

"Mr. Martin," Benny said.

"Mr. Raye," Luke said. Luke opened the door and Benny began his bowlegged march outside. Luke held out his hand and stopped him.

"Ladies first," Luke said.

"Forgive me." Benny slung his guitar off his back and held it in front of him like a baby. "Bertha," said Benny, "After you." Luke and Benny walked out the door like the two stooges after Bertha while Sarah shook her head.

"Grow the fuck up!" Mack said. Sarah ran to the door as the fellas were hopping in Benny's rusty truck. Luke had to kick the passenger door with his foot and pull up on the handle to get it to open.

"Be careful, son."

"I will, Ma."

"And don't fight with nobody. Folks getting killed in juke joints these days. Why just the other day, Maddie told me — " Sarah got drowned out by the engine revving up. "Son, if somebody say something to you, just ignore them. Don't say nothing back. No fights, please."

"Okay, Ma."

"Aw, come on, Miss Sarah," Benny said. "Somebody mess with Luke they's got to go through me. You knows that. Don't wait up." Benny let loose the clutch and they clunked on down the dirt road at top possible speed.

Sarah stood there with her hands on her hips. She closed the door and saw Mack with that look in his eye.

"Come here, Sarah," Mack said. He unbuttoned his shirt. "I want to talk to you." Sarah laughed.

"Mack Martin, I ain't thinking 'bout you." The newspaper drifted to the floor.

A row of weeping willows lined the curve of the road and the fellas were all right with being quiet for a minute.

"Does your dick ever gets hard when you looking at the sky?" Luke said. Benny laughed so hard he spit brandy on the windshield.

"Do what now?" Benny said.

"Today I was looking at the sky?"

"Uh, huh."

"Thinking 'bout this movie?"

"Big surprise."

"And my dick got hard. I think it mean something."

"Yeah, you got that right. What kinda movie was it? Was there fucking in it?"

"There was kissing in it but so what? That don't make my nature rise. And you know good and tee well you can't see no movie like that around here."

"Red said he saw one. Over in Birmingham."

"Red a lie."

"I'm just telling you what the man told me." Benny drained the brandy and threw the bottle out the window.

"Lorenzo Tucker," Luke said.

"Aw, man, I don't feel like playing this game."

"Lorenzo Tucker!"

"The black Valentino," Benny said.

"Slick Chester."

"The Colored Cagney."

"Bee Freeman." Benny had to think for a minute.

"The Sepia Mae West."

"There you go! And Ethel Moses?"

"The Negro Harlow. We done now?"

"I think I know what it means," Luke said.

"Huh?"

"That thing about the sky?"

"Oh."

"I want life. I want be with life. I want to make love to life. I want life all on top of me and life all up under me. I want all the life I can get." They rode by the cow pasture in silence.

"Nigger, I don't never know what the fuck you talking 'bout," Benny said. Luke leaned back in his seat, cradled in his own world, and liked it there just fine until Benny missed the turn on Junction Three.

"Where you going?" Luke said.

"Gotta pick up Red and them." Luke rolled his eyes and Benny pretended not to know what the problem was.

"Red? Man, fuck Red. Why you gotta go pick him up? He know the way to The Joint."

"Gotta support my fans, man."

"Fans? Nigger, please. This Red. I hate that nigger. Why can't it be just us?"

"Aw, come on now. Don't bitch out on me." Luke bitched out on Benny and didn't talk for the rest of the way.

They got to Red's place and him and two other fellas jumped in the back with some moonshine. Benny cracked his never dimming smile, Luke halfway spoke, and they was off.

Willa, Red's wife, peeked through the door of the shack to watch the truck ride off. She dabbed her bloody lip with her apron.

Red reached through the window from the back of the truck and passed the jug to Luke who ignored it.

"What's the matter Shakespeare? Don't drink no more?" Red said.

"Nigger, you know good and tee well you don't know who Shakespeare is so quit acting. Benny, don't forget about the show. We gots to leave at seven-thirty if we gonna be on time."

"Okay, man. Damn."

"How's that?" Red said. He poked his head through the rear window and looked back and forth between the fellas like a cop or something. Luke noticed Benny seemed a little embarrassed.

"Oh, uh, me and Luke gonna go see this, uh, kaleidoscope — "

"Picture show. A drama. "

"This dramatical picture show by some nigger name of Oscar — "

"Micheaux."

" — down there at the Bijou Playhouse." Nobody said nothing for a second while the wind whooshed over the truck. Then, Red said,

"That's cute. When y'all getting married." Benny stomped his foot on the break and only Red's broad shoulders kept his whole body from following his head through the back window.

"God damn, Benny!" Red said. The other two in the back laughed and pointed at Red while he struggled to regain his position and dignity but Benny had him in a head lock. "What's your problem, Benny?" Red said real loud. The two fellas in the back got up to help but Luke jumped out and snatched a bat out the truck's bed. Then he waved the two forward, daring them to try something, so they sat back down. Benny tightened his hold on Red.

"Nigger, I ain't beat your ass since we was kids. How's about a trip down memory lane?"

"Aw, come on, Benny. I was just joking, man."

"You ain't funny, though."

"Benny, I can't breathe, now. I ain't playing now."

"Bitch, I ain't playing neither."

"I'm sorry, man!"

"Now apologize to Luke."

"Luke, I'm sorry, man. Get this nigger off me, man!"

"What you say, Luke? Choke the shit out this freckle-face fucker or let him go? What the hell a nigger doing with freckles anyway?" Red's veins popped out on his head as he struggled to breathe.

"Please… Luke." Luke took the time to look at the sky and smiled at a star.

"Let him go." Benny released Red who fell back coughing, much to the amusement of the other two.

"Let's go!" Benny said. Luke jumped back in, the truck tore off down the road, and nobody spoke on that again. Red was back there gasping and getting himself together.

"Hey, Red," Luke said.

"What?"

"I think I'll have that drink now."

2

The Joint was a two-story dump, in a corner of the woods, on four acres of land, that only lived at night. Full of blues music and hootchy cootchy stylings. Homemade booze at prohibition prices. Overalls worn with shined, black boots. Back door open, screen door shut, letting rib, reefer, and cigarette smoke float in and out depending on the breeze. The funk of black men grinded on women's secret sweat; and bright moods lit up the dark dance floor where gin breath merged in hot, sloppy kisses.

Benny Raye was the star of The Joint.

"Baby got spare ribs, baby got thighs and legs.
Baby got spare ribs, baby got thighs and legs.
Papa got raw meat, ain't no need to beg.
Well, well.
Mama got dumplings, wanna stick 'em in her pot. Aw shuck, now.
Mama got dumplings, wanna stick 'em in her pot. Mmm. Mmm.
Papa got the ladle, gonna stir 'em up nice and hot. Aw shuck, now."

The blue light showed Benny in a trance with his guitar and the low beat kept the crowd hypnotized. Then he went off and played the guitar with his tongue, which was a hard trick to learn but a wonderful thing to master. All the men hooted and the women squealed.

"Stroke that thang, boy!" Red hollered from the dance floor. "Lick it!" Salt water gleamed off Benny's face and dripped in Bertha's hole. Then he threw the box in the air and waited. All the dancers halted to watch the instrument's hang time. Bertha spun in midair like a pin wheel and fell back in Benny's arms like a gal who hadn't seen her daddy in months.

He responded by hugging her with a strum and choked his baby about the neck with the affection of an owner. The crowd clapped their hands raw and stomped their feet. Luke raised his jar of beer at the bar and Benny gave him a wink.

"That's my boy," Luke said to the working girl. But the brown honey pot got tired of waiting for him to come around and didn't want to hear one more thing about the development of cinema. She decided to go upstairs with a nervous teenager who glanced back at his friends waving him on. The boy gave a slim pimp some money, who slipped him the key, and he was guided up to the second floor for the slaughter of his virginity. Luke looked down at his gold pocket watch and back up at Benny. It would soon be time for the newsreel to start and he knew how Benny could be. He surrendered his position to men elbowing for room at the crowded bar and pushed his way through stuck bodies on the dance floor. Benny was meditating in motion to the sounds of his solo when Luke finally traveled to the edge of the stage.

Luke waited, out of respect, and watched Benny's crazy fingers, all with little brains of their own, work them strings up and down Bertha's slender neck. All the while, Benny rocked his hips and bobbed his head as if engaged in prayer. Luke figured there was no right time to interrupt so he just jumped right in.

"I see you finally got that spin right. How ole Bertha hold up after you dropped her so much, I'll never know." Benny kept on playing with his eyes closed.

"Bertha the only woman who understands me. She let me stroke her when I feel like it, say what want when I'm stroking, and shut up when I'm done. I think I loves her."

Luke nodded his head like somebody who heard that a million times before.

"Yeah good ole Bertha so you ready?" Benny opened one eye to the second story of Ho Row and saw the brown honey slipping in a room with the virgin. He frowned at Luke.

"Nigger, how the hell you let that go?"

"I'm saving my money for the movies."

"As fine as that gal is? Braxton had you out in the sun too long today?" Luke didn't feel like discussing his sex life.

"So you ready?" He stepped away from the stage to cue Benny who ignored the hint.

"Man, you see all this money down here?" Luke glanced at the sweat stained hat Benny wore when he plowed that was full of hard and soft money. He knew what was coming next. "Didn't know it was gonna be this packed tonight. Past two weeks been kinda dry. Now, if I go to the picture show with you? I gots to give them money. If I stays here? Folks give me money. Name of the game is to get it. Not give it. See what I'm saying?" Luke's jaw got tight.

"Nigger, you ain't shit. How I'm s'pose to git there?" Benny shrugged.

"You can borrow my truck."

"You know good and tee well I can't drive. You messing me up, man, I'm gonna miss *Within Our Gates*! It's Micheaux's answer to that bullshit movie about the Klan. It's a cinematic debate! It's historic. And I'm gonna miss it! And it's your damn fault!" Benny yanked his hands off Bertha.

"Nigger, quit acting like a bitch!" His voice boomed through the frozen crowd and the only thing heard was Red's hawking laugh. Luke felt his face get hot. His whole chest thumped and his hands shook a bit. Benny picked up his jar of brandy off the planks of the saw dusted stage and eyed Luke like an overseer. Couldn't quite tell if he was mad or hurt. Then Luke hauled off and slugged Benny in the jaw and the jar of brandy hit the floor right after he did. *Yep. He mad.*

Benny tried to cushion Bertha from the fall as Luke snatched the hat full of money off the floor and dumped it in his face.

Aw shit. He hurt.

Some gal screamed, the bouncer approached, and Red laughed again. Luke was a big fella but the bouncer was bigger and proved it by grabbing him by the collar to escort him from the establishment. The patrons parted the way and Luke knew it was pointless to resist. He was pushed out into the cool night air which did nothing to stop the heat in his face. The bouncer shook his finger at him and slammed the torn screen door.

Benny got off the floor, still sheltering Bertha, and eyed the nigger who was looking at his money too hard. The quiet crowd watched in discomfort while he scooped money with sawdust into the beat-up hat. He got down on his hands and knees digging the coins out the grooves of the stage. A few men coughed. Then he jumped down offstage, got on his belly, and searched for any stray coins that might have fallen through the cracks. The bartender looked away. People shuffled in their seats while he was down there for what seemed like a good thirty seconds.

That's an eternity in stage time.

After while, he came back on up and dropped exactly one bent penny into the hat. He flashed a smile and held Bertha high over his head.

"That'll be extra for the fight." Everybody laughed and formed a line to put their two cents in. Benny sat on his stool, thumped Bertha, and gave the people what they wanted.

"Baby got spare ribs, Baby got thighs and legs…"

3

Luke reached the edge of town, weighed down with mud on his boots, with the Bijou Playhouse still a mile away. The Bijou had the distinction of being the only colored movie house in Braxton, Alabama. There was a rumor that it was going to close down soon and that sent Luke into a panic. He thought it would be bad for morale. Mostly his. He leaned against the seed store to rest.

Did they have enough money for seed or would they have to use credit again? Blacks mostly stayed on their side of town and only came into the square to buy supplies on credit from the same white man who owned the land they cropped on. It was a never-ending circle of debt that built the economy of the place.

The town of Braxton was quiet that night. A stray, gray dog tilted over a garbage can and the clanging caused Luke to jump. He hung his head at his fear and drove thoughts of Benny from his brain.

Benny ain't shit. He struck his heel against a curb to knock off red clumps of mud. *Ain't got nothing if you ain't got your word.*

Luke finally made it to the window at the theatre. The plump ticket taker smacked her gum and smiled at him. She leaned forward and looked down at the caked boots and the splashes on his dungarees. Then she let her eyes rest between his legs. Luke always pretended not to notice that shift in the eyes folks got when they spotted his swang so he eased closer to the glass to appear as a man from waist up.

"What happened to you, chile?" she said. "You look like a dog dug you up and changed his mind." She laughed and Luke smiled.

"Had to walk from The Joint," he said. He pulled out the last few bits from the bottom of his patched-up pocket.

"You walked all the way from there? Good twenty miles, ain't it?"

"'Bout that," Luke said. He slid the money closer. "I was hoping y'all still had the habit of a late show on Fridays?"

"That's we call it The Midnight Ramble. But, you couldn't find nothing else to do, honey? Walking twenty miles for Mr. Michaeux?" Luke put his hands in his pocket and bounced up and down.

"I don't mind," he said with a hint. She tried to peek below his belt.

"I wouldn't mind, either." Luke laughed to be polite. The clerk was the type of woman who needed a brick wall to fall on her twice. "You ain't got no girlfriend?"

"Naw."

"Uh-huh. So the position's open?" He gave her another polite laugh. She adjusted the ruffles on the stupid uniform management forced her to wear and leaned her face closer to the hole in the booth. "Fine thing like you couldn't get a date? That's strange." Luke sighed like a slave and looked away. This was the second brick wall for the clerk who pushed herself away from the glass with slow attitude. "You ain't got to get all salty," she said. Luke made a fist and forced his voice to sound like he wasn't getting angry.

"Will you please let me in?" She sat in her chair, kicked off her shoes, and rubbed her corns.

"No." Luke banged on the glass and made her jump.

"What's your problem?" he said.

"I ain't got no damn problem!"

"Then let me in!"

"I can't!"

"Why not?" The lobby doors flung open.

"It's over," she said. He watched with an open mouth while people burst out of the theatre. The clerked sucked in Luke's pain with the type of triumph only the rejected can enjoy.

"That was the best damn movie I ever saw," somebody said. "Make you proud to be colored."

Luke just stood there watching the procession of black and brown masses pouring out of the Bijou. Their happiness mocked him with knowledge of wonders he'd never see. He hung around until all were gone except the janitor and a few ushers picking up. He walked out into the middle of the street and stomped his hat. Then he sat on the curb and stewed. The clerk watched him sit there, like a child who couldn't go out to play, and felt sorry for him. But she felt sorry for herself too and was tired of everybody except ugly men turning her down. Fuck him. She picked up her shoes and walked back into the theatre.

Luke didn't have the will to move. How could Benny do this to him? He sat there and pondered all the evil things he could do to Bertha. Maybe hide her or break her. No, he couldn't break Bertha. Bertha was a good ole gal who ain't never done nothing to him but sing sweet songs to brighten his day. He looked into the lobby and let his eyes drift into the Bijou's bright lights.

*　　*　　*　　*

Luke's love affair with the movies began when he was little and his daddy had a fight with Boss Man Braxton. Luke was in trouble for wandering away into his misty magic land again. That was the boy's consistent problem. The thing he would always get whacked about. At school:

"Get your head out the clouds," Ms. Coleman said right before she whacked his fingers. At the market:

"Get your head out the clouds," his mama warned before he bumped into a white lady. The white lady hit Luke and Sarah hit her right back. The white lady did nothing about it because she was scared niggers knew voodoo or something. At church:

"Luke, pay attention," the Sunday school teacher said. Luke would wake up from his open-eyed dream to see the whole class laughing at him. At home, it was more of the same. What no one ever realized, however, was that Luke's head was never in the clouds because clouds were too dull to hold his attention. Luke was just thinking about the way things could be. About the way they ought to be.

"That tree oughta be closer to the creek. The water could reflect it and a fella could use it as a back rest when he's fishing. Wonder

ERIC WARE / 17

why God didn't think of that?" little Luke would ask. That got
him rapped in the mouth by Mack who had to hit him before he
laughed about it himself. He didn't want the boy to think blas-
pheming was funny. Then he'd look at the tree and wonder if his
son had a point. Luke had a natural fear of his father but a rap in
the mouth didn't quiet his opinions. "The sun should rise in the
west 'stead of the east cause our window face that way. Then Ma
could see better when she reads her bible 'fore a hard day's work."

His mama smiled and his daddy frowned. Mack finally got it
that Luke's view of the world was stronger than the fear of the
switch and let the whole thing go. Luke was a good boy. Who
cared if he was odd?

Boss Man Braxton, that's who. One time, Luke was looking at
a caterpillar going the wrong way on a vine. The fat, green worm
munched on the stem going down towards the root instead of up
to the strawberry. Luke had a problem with that. Benny hollered
and jumped around when he saw the thing. He normally handled
any manner of disgusting creature without a care. But there was
something about those big worms with them black eyes and
nubby, white teeth, looking like they might actually belong to
somebody human, that just terrified him.

Braxton watched Benny's antics in amusement and saw Luke
grab the worm that was responsible for eating a third of his crop
last year, and waited for him to kill it. Instead, the boy picked up
the worm and reversed its position on the plant.

"It should be going to the berry. Not away from it. Don't that
make sense? Look at that itty bitty green shooting at that big ole
red target like a arrow. Look, Benny. See how that worm looks like
a arrow shooting at a big ole red target? That make more sense,
don't it? That's the way it should be."

A shadow crept over the worm's corrected journey. Its new fate
was decided by Braxton as he gripped the worm and squeezed
all the jelly out while never taking his eyes off Luke. He wiped
the worm's remains on Benny's shirt who was just too horrified to
move. Braxton grabbed Luke's little arm and squeezed. Luke
yelled and feared jelly would ooze out of him too.

"Get your goddamn hands off my son or I'll kill you."

Boss Man Braxton spun around and came face to face with Mack. Braxton released Luke while everybody in the field kept working in a feverish attempt at anonymity. Two white foremen came along to see what the problem was. Braxton leaned into Mack.

"You know who you talking to, boy?" Mack shoved his nose into Braxton's which caused him to jerk his head back in surprise.

"I'm talking to the white man I'm gonna kill if he fuck with my son again. We sharecroppers, not slaves. The Yankees won. Sorry, 'bout that." The two white boys on the porch pulled out their guns but Mack wasn't fazed by that either. "Go head and shoot. See if you can replace me. And if you do, see if he gonna be a better line man than me. Fill more quotas than me. Move more product than me. Go head. I dare you."

The folks in the field could no longer pretend they weren't listening. They stood there unbent from toil, backs straight, sacs down, babies on side and hand on hip.

Braxton looked around at the audience and Luke was terrified he was about to see his daddy die. Benny was scared he would never get that dead worm off his body. Mack poked Braxton in the chest just to make his point.

"We sharecroppers. This a business arrangement. We ain't slaves. You touch my son again and I'll kill you, white boy."

Braxton's men looked at each other like they just saw a goat do math. A black goat. A cricket was the only thing anybody heard for a while. One oblivious, noisy cricket who hopped into the party late.

Braxton stayed still and wondered how to handle this. Maybe he should tell his men to shoot. But how would he explain that to the sheriff? Sure, it's just a nigra but it is broad daylight, after all, and there's a whole bunch of witnesses. Still, a white man's gotten away with worse. Aw, to hell with it.

"Just talk to the boy, Mack. And get back to work," he said.

"It's quitting time," Mack said.

And so it was. The bell rang across the field snapping the workers out of spectator mode. Women yelled to their children and a few folks hopped a truck, sharing space with pigs and bags of feed. Others, who lived further away, took the scenic route by necessity rather than choice. Mack, Luke, and Benny were among the walkers. Ace Simmons, Red's daddy, stepped alongside Mack while Braxton got in a huddle with his boys.

"Nigger, you best do something about that boy. Wanna get us all lynched?" Mack stopped in the dirt road and sneered at Ace's sweaty, light-rusted face.

"You handle your business. I'll handle mine." Ace huffed off mumbling something about uppity niggers while dragging Red along who shot a bird at Luke. "Never liked red niggers," Mack said. "Something sneaky 'bout 'em. Like a bat or something."

"You can say that again," Benny said. Benny never understood the boundaries between children and adults and was often told to shut up while grown folks is talking. Mack swatted Benny on the bottom and gave him a gentle shove.

"Go on home, Benny. Tell Maddie I'll give her money back Thursday." Benny ignored Mack and chatted with Luke as he walked on ahead. He took off the worm-stained shirt and threw it in the weeds.

"I'll see you at the creek, Luke."

"No, you won't," Mack said. "I ain't playing with you now."

"You ain't gonna let that boy fish?" Benny said like it was the stupidest thing he ever heard. Mack took off his belt and ran after Benny for show. In a time where neighbors beat other people's children as a sign of civic duty, Benny, often the point of civic pride, took off kicking. But Mack wasn't the type to hit another man's child no matter what he had done. Likewise, he didn't want nobody hitting his. Not even a white man.

They walked on with nothing to say for a while. The sun saw its twin on the way down the river and a thick bass teased Luke with a belly-flop. The cicadas just wouldn't shut up and complemented the sound of Mack's big boots thumping the earth. Luke kept in time with his father's wide strides even though he'd have to skip to keep up now and then. They stopped for Mack to take Sarah's orange head rag from his pocket and wipe the sweat off his forehead for all the good it did. It was hot as hell out there. Mack propped his foot against a flat rock at the river's edge and stretched out his stiff knee. Luke imitated his father and stretched out too. Without warning, Mack pulled Luke over his knee and started tanning that hide.

At first, Luke was surprised by the assault but that gave way to pain. Mack spoke not a word as he spanked his son. He drowned out the boy's cries with harder smacks and the knowledge it was for his own good. A good minute passed for Mack, and what seemed like forever to Luke, before he was plopped down on the road. Luke rubbed his ass and stomped away screaming with a strand of unbreakable snot coming out his nose the way kids get when their hides get tanned. Mack looked into the river until Luke calmed down.

"Why'd you do it, son? Why couldn't you just do your damn job and be done with it? You know there ain't no other place to share at round here, don't you?"

It was Luke's turn to look at the water while his daddy waited for an answer. Mack thought about how the boy's pretty profile came from Sarah's side of the family. He was too pretty and smart to be treated like shit by Braxton. But lessons had to be taught.

"Answer me. What was all that about? Why can't you just be like other boys and get along? What the hell you be thinking about anyway?"

"It just wasn't right, that's all."

"What the hell wasn't right?"

"The worm was going the wrong way. He shoulda been going up." Mack walked away and Luke rushed to keep up out of habit.

"Sometimes I think you crazy."

"I ain't crazy nothing!" Mack killed off a smile. The boy had spirit. Got that from his side of the family.

"Always something with you, Luke. The house the wrong way. The sun should be over there. The worm need to be going up. I mean, damn. You can't control the world. You got to live in it the way it is."

"I ain't trying to control it. I just want to fix it. I can't help it if I know how everything should be."

Mack flat out laughed. Luke got mad, in spite of the fresh whup-ing, and gave his daddy a pop in leg. Mack grabbed him with one hand, flipped him over his back like a bag of seed, and walked down the road again. Luke saw the plantation house get smaller and smaller and he giggled at this new view of life while the smell of dirt tickled the back of his nose.

Mack saw a truck and stuck his thumb out. Luke heard the truck stop and recognized the voice of Charlie, a man daddy fished with. They spoke a few words and Mack tossed Luke in the back and jumped in after him while the truck pulled off. The drive to town was a good half an hour and Luke noticed buildings he hadn't seen before. Then, there it was: The Bijou Playhouse.

*   *   *   *

"Hey! You can't hang around here all night!"

Luke snapped out of it and looked back at the big gal from the ticket booth tapping her foot. The ushers got their pay from the manager and hustled out into the street with talk of going to The Joint. The manager was an older man, a deacon, at Little Bethel Baptist Church, who prided himself on being the only colored man who owned something besides debt in the town of Braxton. Deacon Early was his name and a little thing like a wife, who was choir director, didn't stop him from propositioning the big gal at the ticket booth every goddamn night.

Luke stood up and stretched his knee on the curb. He took off down First Street and stopped himself from obsessing on Benny. He could hear the ticket taker loud talking as he left.

"Go on, now! I ain't playing with you now. I'm the kinda bitch to tell your wife!" Luke turned around to see if she was also the kind of bitch who needed any help. Wasn't her fault the movie was over, after all. Wasn't her fault Benny let him down again. Benny.

"All right, all right, keep your shirt on," Deacon Early said.

"I plan to, motherfucker." Deacon Early took one last look at her titty and limped off with three aching legs. She leaned against the wall and fanned herself from this latest assault. "Oughta be a law 'bout a gal getting hit on at work," she said. She spotted Luke down the block. "Hmm. That's a whole lotta man. Ain't that a caution? The cute ones don't notice you and the ugly ones'll give you the world. Well… I'm getting me some compensation for all this ducking and dodging I gotta do. Yessiree, folks. Big Flooty gonna enjoy the show. Uh huh. Big Flooty gonna have herself a time."

Luke waited for Deacon Early to turn the corner and told himself the ticket gal would be Okay. He decided this just wasn't his night and took off down the street again.

"Hey, come here a minute!" Luke turned back to see Big Flooty leaned up against the door frame of the ticket booth with a thick thigh exposed from the hiked up skirt. She wore a smile half teased and half asleep.

And then he knew.

He knew since he was twelve when some of his mama's acquaintances looked at him just a bit too long to be aunts anymore. Sometimes it was fun with the older women: Juicy discoveries of strange scents in pink flesh. The satisfaction of knowing a woman's pleasure was all because of him. Other times, it was an exercise in ugliness: His head forced down between the stench of neglected lips, the dormant desperation stretched awake, the strident commands in a grip of pathetic need.

He looked at Flooty's big leg and into the lobby. Then, he swayed up to his former adversary who smiled at every move of his pants.

"Hey, gal. What's your name?"

"Flooty. Big Flooty." She took one finger and traced down from the top of his chest to the tip of his belt.

"Why you got to tease a brother, gal? Acting all contrary for nothing. You gonna let a hardworking man watch a picture show or not?"

"I don't know nothing 'bout working no projector."

"Well, let me fiddle with it." He smiled with a confidence both presumptuous and true.

Big Flooty grabbed his belt and hauled him into the ticket booth. She squatted down and came face to waist with Mr. Martin.

"Ticket, please." Luke dropped his pants and Big Flooty was happier than a drunk with a bottle in her mouth.

4

Damn, what a show.

When "The End" appeared on the screen, Luke clapped his hands and smiled. No, it wasn't the best movie he'd ever seen. All silent movies were made with generous helpings of corn and this colored one was overacted in places and looked like it was made on the cheap. Luke liked William Foster better than Micheaux. But the subject matter was brave and right on time. *The Defender* said Michauex was the one to watch and Luke admired a black man who could be in charge. Still, he had this buzzing suspicion, like a whisper in his ear or a feeling in his chest; something just told him:

You could do better.

Luke pushed the strange thought back to the perimeter and continued to clap his hands. It was fun being the only one in the theatre. Just wrapped in cool dark, with one source of light showing folks how the world could be.

Luke's solitary applause was joined by the another set of clapping hands in the back. He jumped out of embarrassment as if someone had walked in on him pleasuring himself, and in a way, they had.

It was Benny.

He had Bertha slung over his back and one button on his fly was undone. Big Flooty clapped along beside him looking just a tad bit drunker.

Luke faced the screen and studied the rolling credits like a legal document. The projector ran out and the flickering of the empty reel hitting a flapping tail of film was the only sound in the theatre.

Luke jammed his hat on sideways and stalked up the aisle in wide steps. He ignored Benny and Big Flooty and pushed the swinging doors open like The Bronze Buckaroo.

Benny and Big Flooty looked at each other in shock before following him into the lobby. Benny wore a frown and Flooty had her arms folded.

"Oh, you welcome," she said.

"You too," Luke said without breaking stride.

Benny, far from being sensitive, still noticed Big Flooty's look of betrayal. He understood her unreasonable indignation the only way two whores could understand each other. He slapped her on the shoulder and tongued her quick.

"Aw, don't worry 'bout him, gal. He just mad at me is all. You take care."

Benny left the forlorn Flooty and strutted through the lobby with Bertha bouncing on his backside. He put his hand on the exit door and winked at his hostess. The lamplight outside, mixed with the leftover glow of the silver screen, found their perfect object of reflection on Benny Raye. He cracked a smile hinting at sexual secrets shared only by him and Satan.

"And thank you, baby."

"You welcome," she said. And had the nerve to blush. Benny Raye left the building. Big Flooty floated to the concessions counter and fed on hot memories with stale popcorn. Life was never dull at the Bijou Playhouse.

*　　*　　*　　*

"The Bijou Playhouse? Daddy, what we doing here?"

"Shut up."

Mack pushed little Luke off the truck and thanked Charlie for the ride. He shoved his son to the booth and slammed two bits in front of the nervous ticket taker who wore glasses thick enough to see a nigger's thoughts.

"Two."

Mack snatched the tickets from the teenager's hand and stomped into the lobby dragging Luke by the arm like a rag doll.

Luke knew not to speak lest he break the spell and wake up from his dream. His father was the type of man who got embarrassed doing loving things and would withdraw affection if one made too much of a fuss about it. Luke had no problems keeping quiet. He couldn't speak now even if he wanted to. He had only heard of this theatre and now he was here.

The designer of the Bijou Playhouse must have been quite a fella. Judging by the looks of the place, he was drunk and happy with a box full of darts and a map of the world when he started the job. For the layout of the Playhouse covered every possible demographic. The wall to wall carpeting had a Japanese design of a Swedish mountainside. The Roman archways were guarded by two African warriors pointing Civil War muskets. Brass knobs with chocolate colored tips held up the satin rope to the concession counter where a giant picture of a brown, Brazilian general shook hands with a mammy and pointed to popcorn.

"Eat up. It's fresh," the caption said over one of Santa's elves, even though it was nowhere near Christmas. The ceiling of the Bijou lobby was painted like a bright, blue sky holding pink clouds pregnant with the orange of sunset. Luke gazed at it while his daddy frightened the concessions cashier. He saw all kinds of birds hand painted with a genius level preschooler's abandon. Eagles flew with doves who chased after sparrows as they circled 'round vultures with dopey grins on their beaks.

"Now that's what a sky's s'pose to look like," said Luke.

"Shut up," said Mack.

He shoved Luke his popcorn and yanked him up the cheap, gold spiral staircase, leading up from the lobby into the theatre, which Mack grumbled about being unnecessary. Luke still had his head craned up at the ceiling and knocked into a few folks during Mack's rough ushering.

Then a strange and natural thing happened.

On the sky blue ceiling, a flock of egg white doves narrowed into a line pointing straight into the theatre. Once they hit the mahogany archway, the doves became a line of stars spreading out into a milky way on the now ebony ceiling with a crystal chandelier.

"Well, I do know," Mack said. He took a second to be impressed and held his son's hand while they stared at the fake night sky that managed to express something real. It was a tacky, overdone, joyous spectacle. Other folks swirled around them in a dash to get a seat at the only colored theatre in town.

"Come on, Daddy!" Luke took his turn playing the usher and pulled Mack down to an aisle seat at the front. The newsreel was just ending and the 1913 film was called *The Railroad Porter* directed by William Foster. Mack didn't like sitting so close but fuck it. Let the boy have his fun. There was no way Luke could control the world; so let him look at coloreds who could, in their way. Tomorrow it's back to the dirt, the crackers, and the heat.

*   *   *   *

"Nigger, quit acting like a bitch," said Benny. He drove next to his buddy at a mile an hour waiting for fatigue to kill off his pride. But Luke wasn't having it. "Aw, bitch, I know you tired. Gotta be. Working all day. Whiskey at the club. Walking to town. Blow job. That's a sweet bitch, ain't it? Big bitches suck dick better cause they hungry all the time. Then, sitting in that cool thee-ater. Getting all comfortable. Now you walking all the way back. Get the fuck in the truck." Luke said nothing. "Didn't I drive all the way down here just to get your stupid ass?"

Luke looked at Benny like he had never seen him before and kept on walking. Benny felt he had been compassionate long enough. He turned the wheel hard and cut Luke off. He hopped out the truck like he was gonna hit him but Luke knew that fake and didn't react.

"Nigger, we both know I ain't gonna say I'm sorry. I only 'pologize to bitches and I be lying then. Get in the truck."

"Benny, you'd fuck up a funeral. You know that?" Luke circled round the truck and kept on going. Benny cussed and pulled out a wad of cash.

"Made a killing tonight. Let me buy you a drink." Nothing.

"Aw shit, nigger. I'm sorry." Luke stopped. The road seemed longer than usual and there was a truck right behind him, after all. So he just hopped on in.

"That was a pretty good picture show," Luke said. "I wonder how people make 'em?" Benny spit on the street, got in the truck, and took off.

"I said I wonder how — "

"Nigger, I ain't talking to you."

5

"Well Water Woman, woman, can I have a sip?
Well Water Woman, woman, can I have a sip?
Cause I'm feeling kinda thirsty, gal, please let me
    take that dip."

The basic blues riff plucked through the air while croppers picked berries and swatted flies.

"I think you thirsty, baby, say you thirsty, just
    as parched as me. Aw, shuck now.
I say I think you thirsty, baby, say you thirsty,
    just as dry as me.
Aw, shuck now.
Rain come down from heaven but a whiskey is
    just as free."

Benny sat spread open atop a post by the field with Bertha providing balance and the beat. A few labor girls gossiped and sneaked peeks between his legs. Boss Man Braxton chuckled at the not so subtle song and checked some figures in the shade of his porch. Wet beads slid down the cold glass of lemonade when he rubbed it across his forehead. He swirled down some drink and crunched some ice.

Luke led a team of men clearing weeds where snakes had been spotted. A water moccasin bit a child there the other day and Braxton took his time getting her to a hospital since there was no colored doctor nearby. Luke threatened to lead a strike if something wasn't done about the weeds. It was an empty threat, of course, since no one belonged to a union in spite of Mack's hopes about the SCU. Nevertheless, Braxton feared Luke could slow things down for a day or two so he relented. Luke knew exactly what to do and how to do it as usual. It was his production and he expected folks to follow his directions.

> "Well Water Woman, woman, how deep's the
>   hole? Uh-huh.
> Well Water Woman, woman, how deep's the hole?
>   Uh-huh.
> If it's deep enough for fishing then, uh, baby, I can
>   bring my pole.
> Aw shuck, now."
> "You just a well water woman bucket on your hip.
> You just a well water woman wanna take that dip.
> You got cha head rag framing that pretty face.
> You got the finest black frame in human race.
>
> So come on gimme what I need gal!"

Bertha hit the climax as Benny crooned the conclusion.

> "You just a well water woman. Yeah!"

And that was that. No applause. No happy darkies with a song in their hearts tilling the soil as God intended. That was just that. Benny learned not to expect much more than a little extra loving from these mini-concerts Braxton agreed to let him take after lunch. It was nothing but a way for him to keep sharp for his juke joint gig. Most of this crowd didn't even come to The Joint and the men who did were over there working with Luke. These church-going women on his side of the field talked about him playing the devil's music behind his back while they smiled in his face. So this was a rehearsal on a break at a job he hated and that was that. It was no big deal and he didn't expect nothing. Still. The dumb ass niggers *could* clap. He hopped off the post and adjusted his balls without shame.

"Back to work, Benny!" Braxton said from the shade.

Benny took his time putting Bertha in the new case he just bought her out the Sears and Roebuck catalogue. Looked just like the picture, too. The money he earned last night, joined with the amount he'd been saving for almost two whole years, got just the right one. He leaned on the post and took a long look over the field of black folks and berries.

God damn, I hate this shitty ass town.

"Back to work, Benny," Braxton said.

A few hands looked up from their work while Benny turned his back on Braxton and considered his options. Didn't have much money. Mama left him a little but Maddie drunk that up a long time ago. Made some paper at The Joint but that wasn't nothing. The only work in the next county was more cropping. Had neither the money nor disposition for schooling. Maybe go up North. Niggers always talking 'bout going up north but up north for what? Only thing worse than a fucked up life down South is a fucked up life up North.

Benny hawked his throat and spit at a fly. Maybe… maybe out West. He watched a line of ants forming a carnivorous army of precision on an upside down June bug. Marching right through and hollowing it out.

Benny squinted his eyes against the sun. He felt a hand on his shoulder and turned around to meet the red, puffy face of Boss Man Braxton.

"You want to keep on working here, boy?" Braxton said.

"Bitch, my dick too big to be your boy." A few of Braxton's henchmen looked up to make sure they heard that right. Three of them got off the porch and advanced toward the scene.

"Benny." Everyone turned to the west and looked at Luke.

"Get back to work."

Benny gave Braxton a cocky look and walked through the henchman like he dared them to touch him. None of this could be backed up, of course. Benny was strong and a damn good fighter but he couldn't dodge bullets, now could he? Nobody but Luke would help him and then he'd be dead too. Still, every now and then, a fella had to let these folks know they couldn't push him around even if he ended up losing. Such is the beauty and the mystery of Black Male Pride.

Benny walked beside Luke and took a machete in hand. Luke scolded him with his eyes and, for a second, Benny felt ashamed, but only for a second. God love him.

"Where Mack and Miss Sarah?"

"Daddy stayed home on account of his knee and Ma stayed to look after him. Don't you worry about that. We got a job to do."

The clearing gang began hacking weeds in a three pronged attack to the river. Team "A" advanced with machetes swinging and stomping their feet from the east side of the river. Team "B" advanced from the other side, and then came Luke's team down the middle. Men with torches set a low, manageable ground fire at the river bank where the nest was suspected to be. Braxton offered to enlist his lodge (Klan) members, the county vet, and a few trappers who were experienced in this sort of thing. However, Luke said he didn't trust those people to handle it with the care these people deserved.

Benny knew that was a lie. Luke didn't even like these people. Even though Luke got a lot of mileage out of being the sensitive one, the good one, in the duo, while Benny got all that came along with being branded as Cain, the fact is, Luke was the one who always had to have his way. Luke wanted to be the point guard in this snake project so bad he could taste it. Maybe it was from all those movies where the heroes took charge of a dire situation.

Sarah always called Luke special on account of his views of the world. Benny saw it for what it was: an uncontrollable need to be in control.

"Light another fire!" Luke said. "And start stomping over there on the left side."

"Uh, look here, Luke," Benny said. "I don't know 'bout you, but I'm the kinda nigger that's scared a snakes. Exactly what we s'pose to do to this gang of moccasins once we get 'em all riled up?"

"Kill 'em. What you think?" Benny stopped swinging his machete.

"All of 'em?" Luke paused his work. He hadn't considered that. What were they going to do with the snakes? A good nest has about twenty or thirty in it. Luke got back to swinging and pretended it didn't bother him.

"Don't worry, man. Snakes more scared of us than we is of them."

"Yeah," said Benny. "Unless you mess with 'em." Luke swung his machete harder.

"Well, they bit that girl, Benny. All right? We can't just let these snakes go round fucking with people."

"Snakes don't go round fucking with people. Only people do that." Luke stopped working.

"Will you shut up? Huh? Will you? Will you shut the fuck up? Please." Luke got back to work while Benny looked at him a spell.

"I'm gonna beat your special ass after work. You hear me?"

Luke ignored him. The fires on both side of the banks flared up and spread.

"Watch that fire, boy!" Braxton said.

"Yes sir," Luke said. Benny laughed. Luke hated Benny when he laughed like that.

"You scared a that cracker, ain't you? Huh? Tell the truth now." Benny laughed again. Then he looked at the banks and stopped.

He saw men running and Red fell down and screamed like a baby.

A wave of black moccasins slithered over his body. Red lay there frozen, trying the best he could to swallow up air but his lungs wouldn't work. The snakes weren't really interested in Red, he was just in the way. Willa took off her head rag and waved it about.

"Help him, Jesus! Help him!" she said. Other panicked women screamed and dragged Willa away in spite of her protests. Some children were trampled in the stampede and Braxton was stuck to his porch watching the horror. His boys looked to him for advice but he had none to give.

Luke's plan was working like a charm. He wanted to drive the snakes out and he was.

He just didn't plan on about a hundred and fifty at one time. Men used their torches to burn the snakes who recoiled at the fire and balled up to strike. Mr. Jenkins got bit on the inside of the thigh right near his privates. He went down, clutching his leg, knowing his death was imminent. After all, who was gonna suck out the poison?

The nest was about eighty feet deep right on the edge of the river. The holes were hidden by weeds and ever wet soil. The crops didn't extend down to the water so there was no reason for people to see anything more than the occasional snake. Moccasins had no use for strawberries but the rodents who also thrived by the river did. Rats lived off crops, in spite of Braxton's use of useless pesticides, and snakes ate and bred thanks to the endless supply of berry-fattened prey. For over two decades, these snakes slithered, winded, and rolled atop each other only leaving the nest to feed and sun themselves. This secret bargain with the river worked out quite well and over time their numbers grew.

"They're all over the place!" Braxton said. Luke stood there with his machete raised in the type of calm only true terror brings. Benny was used to life being a bowl of shit so this was just one more thing.

"Any ideas?" Benny said.

"No," Luke whispered.

"Well. Why come we ain't running like everybody else?"

"I can't run. I started this. You go on if you want. Won't think no less of you." Benny looked at Luke like he lost his mind.

"I said you can run if — "

"I ain't talking to you," Benny said. They stood in the midst of pandemonium being bumped by rushing bodies on both sides. Benny raised his machete and waited.

Then they saw the second wave.

More masses of thick, muddy bodies crawled over each other in a wide arc of hissing straight towards the big house. The field was black with snakes. Luke knew striking out against such odds was a waste of time. They were now only a few feet away.

"Don't move," Luke said.

"Bertha!"

"I said, don't… Benny!"

Benny took off like a shot to the post where he left Bertha and cussed himself for leaving his baby. Red always said Benny cared more about that damn guitar than he did about people and he was right. Course, Red couldn't talk right now.

The snakes followed no leader but, like a flock of birds peal to one side in the air, so a flank of snakes turned to the vibrations of Benny's feet.

Luke stayed still while the snakes crawled over and between his boots. Just don't move. Don't look at them. They ain't gonna bite. Just don't move. Luke didn't know how he knew that. What's to stop a snake from biting just because he felt like it? What if all this talk about snakes being more afraid of people was just nigger talk? Like if you eat a watermelon seed, a melon'll grow out your ear. He felt a big one wrap around his leg like a whip, stay there a moment, and go on. Just don't move.

But Benny was moving.

He got his hands on Bertha and kissed her. Then he turned around and halted when he saw the black tide spreading his way. He threw a rock into the middle of them and jumped up the post just in time. The multitude slithered right on by, but then, much to his surprise, some of them stopped and winded their way up the post.

"Luke! Get me out of this, boy!"

"Hit 'em with Bertha!"

One look from Benny and Luke felt shame in the middle of panic. A few of Braxton's boys finally woke up and shot into the run of moccasins. Snake heads popped open and scattered their numbers but that was hardly enough. Braxton lit a wagon of hay on fire and some croppers helped him tip it on over. This scorched more and scared them away. The workers huddled on Braxton's porch which was as close as they had ever been to the front door.

"You niggers get away from my door!" Braxton said. But nobody moved. Luke was now clear to help Benny who kicked at four snakes who wanted him bad. They dodged his boot and countered with strikes.

"Hang on, Benny!"

Luke's weak legs pushed him forward. If he'd ever run faster in his life he couldn't remember. He saw the things stretching up with wide open mouths to get a nick at Benny. Two of them kept trying to wind their way up the post. The other two stayed coiled and waited on a sure thing. Benny balanced himself with one foot and looked for a safe place to jump.

Luke was almost there. If only Benny would just use Bertha as a weapon. But he wouldn't. Benny might be fighting for his life but he had his priorities straight.

Then he fell. And Luke screamed.

6

Benny's mama died in childbirth and his daddy took off later so all he had now was Aunt Maddie.

"Crazy ass bitch. That's what he called me. A crazy ass bitch. That boy got the devil in him, I'm telling you. Thinking 'bout putting his little grown ass out."

"Maddie, you put that boy out we gonna call the white folks on you. I'm telling you that right now," Sarah said.

"Well, I ain't got no man like you. I'm tired and I'm old. Told my sister not to mess around with that mullet head but couldn't nobody tell her nothing. Now you know that for yourself. Nigger got outta here so fast when that bastard was born I thought he had wings. She dead and now this. Doctor told that girl she couldn't have no baby but couldn't nobody tell her nothing. Never could. And I can't be doing this by myself, now. I'm serious, now. Everybody ain't got no good man like you, Sarah. I ain't count on this shit this late in life."

"Just let him hang around Luke, that's all. He's got a calming influence on the boy. And keep your hands off him for two whole seconds. And pass the peas, we running behind."

Maddie stopped griping long enough to pass the wooden bowl with fresh peas in it. The door to the shack was open, letting in a cool evening breeze, while the hoot owl kept up a gentle fuss in the distance warning of the coming moon. Two giant sacks of peas had to be snapped and shelled by morning if the ladies were going to get the two extra dollars from Deacon Early. Maddie started those little huffing sounds she made when she wanted to say something but didn't know how to say it. The habit got on the easygoing Sarah's nerves.

"What, Maddie, what?"

"Huh. Luke. Huh. Well, no offense, Sister Sarah, but that boy ain't touched, is he? Always got his head in the clouds. I heard your man almost beat up Boss Man Braxton just cause Luke was out there playing round with the worms 'stead of killing 'em. No offense, now. But I don't know If I'd call that influence calming."

"You heard, huh? Well, who'd you hear that from, Maddie? Ace Simmons? Mack say Ace always gossip like a woman while he's cheating on his own. I heard his wife was a little bit touched herself so any woman messing 'round with her man better watch out she don't get buckshot in her bottom. No offense, now. I'm sure that ain't you. That's just what folks say. I'm so glad I don't pay chatty niggers no mind. Ain't you, Maddie?

As for Luke, well, I don't think my boy is odd, I think he's special. He's got a way of looking at the world that folks can't appreciate. You know, Maddie, they say if all the stories about Jesus were written down, the world wouldn't be able to contain them. Know what that means? That means there's a whole lot of stuff about Jesus we don't know. Now, I wonder if a little boy Jesus, who knew he was the son of God when he was running round Nazareth being a carpenter's son, ever looked at the world in a different way? And I wonder if his little brothers and sisters ever made fun of him being different the way Luke gets made fun of now? I wonder if Jesus was ever made to feel like there was something crazy 'bout being special?"

Sarah sipped cold tea from a jar and rubbed her aching fingers. She took note of the setting sun and wondered why Luke wasn't home yet. She didn't voice her concerns to Maddie, though. Different friends are good for different things and you don't give your spirit away on folks who couldn't appreciate your insecurities. Sarah knew not to cast her pearls before swine.

"'Course now, I ain't in no way comparing my child to the son of God. My boy is special, true 'nough, but I really doubt he 'bout to die for my sins and come back a few days later. All I'm saying is, I understand him enough for the both of us and all the rest of these gossipy back wood niggers 'round here. And that's good enough for me. 'Course now, if you want to keep on running 'round after Benny by yourself then you go right ahead. But just remember: You beat that boy like you beat him last week… I'm gonna call the white folks on you."

They continued snapping shells and letting the round peas patter into the bowl. Maddie took a swig of gin from a jar and swirled it around in her mouth before she let it hit her throat. The hoot owl continued its pacifying song while the sun got a little bit sleepier.

"One of these days, I'm gonna shoot that damn bird," Maddie said. Sarah ignored her. "Well, I sure ain't mean nothing by it, Sister Sarah, you know I love your child like he was my own." Sarah stopped herself from replying to that one. "Yeah, you right, girl. You right." Maddie thought about Ace Simmon's nutty wife for a second. "I don't be paying no attention to no nigger talk neither." She took another swig of gin and got up to go to the outhouse. "Yep. Benny and Luke. Luke and Benny. I guess it's for the best." Sarah wondered where the boys could be.

"Come on, Luke," Benny said. He pulled him along with one hand while holding his guitar with the other.

"Stop. You getting me dirty."

"We already dirty. Who cares?"

"My mama care. We gotta go. It's getting late. I'm gonna get a whupping."

"Stop acting like a girl."

"You gonna get a whupping, too."

"That crazy ass bitch put her hands on me again, I'll put rat poison in her gin. I swear to fucking God."

"We ain't supposed to be down here. We gonna get in trouble."

"Shh. Shut up. They gonna hear us."

A group of laughing men and loud women walked up the wooden steps of the club. The boys hid under the raised stairs going to the elevated house that Deacon Early ran as a juke joint on the side. The Deacon had recently been widowed by his third wife, God rest her soul, and that little bit of life insurance Boss Man Braxton sold him was now allowing him to expand his horizons.

Luke thought the platforms should be raised a little higher because if a flood came, and they came every year, two feet off the ground would be nowhere near high enough. He thought about sharing this with Benny but stopped himself. Benny often made fun of his observations which hurt Luke's feelings. If Benny saw his feelings were hurt, he'd smell blood and keep on digging. So Luke kept the renovations to himself. His mama always told him not to cast his pearls before swine.

Benny elbowed Luke hard and pointed up through the steps. Luke rubbed his arm and looked straight up into the pantied crotch of one of the loud women. Her man kissed her long and the boys enjoyed the show. Seeing panties was just about the best thing that could happen to two eight year old boys. Sometimes they'd see panties hanging out on a line of wash and laugh about it 'til they dropped. But it wasn't funny to Benny this time. Seeing these particular panties made him feel kind of funny down there. It was the first time Benny wanted panties of his own, so to speak. The couples went on inside. Benny grabbed Luke and they scooted underneath the center of the structure. Benny knew there was a trap door or something somewhere around here. There had to be.

The blue light from the club seeped through the floor boards and cast shadowed bars across the boy's dirty faces. The stomps of the crowd, cutting a jig, pounded saw dust onto them through the cracks. Luke made an attempt to brush off his clothes. His mama was going to kill him for sure.

Benny smelled fried pig skins with hot sauce coming from above. He put his nose up to the cracks and sniffed hard. The sawdust tried to make him sneeze but he fought it off. So many scents rushed his nose. He smelled sweat but not the sweat of the fields. Smelled smoke but smoke that smelt kinda funny. Perfume and Barbasol. Spilt beer and whiskey. All things familiar but so much better. He had to get into that club.

There. A trap door. Benny rested his guitar against a rafter and scrambled in the dirt to shove up against the trap. He stood up as much as he could in the cramped space and put all his little weight against the door like Atlas.

"Luke, stop staring at them damn rafters and help me!"

Luke's assistance amounted to nothing and both boys gave in to fatigue. Benny dropped to his knees, all out of breath, and clutched the earth in anger. For some reason he felt like crying but didn't know why.

He didn't want Luke to see him like that because Luke would get the look everybody who felt sorry for him got and he didn't need all that. It made him feel weak. Then he'd have to do something to show folks they were feeling sorry for the wrong person. That got him in trouble with Braxton, other kid's mamas, or whoever was around at the time. That's how he got a reputation.

Benny saw a picture of his daddy one time. The man with big hands who left his guitar behind. How come his mama was smiling in the picture but his daddy wasn't? His aunt told him a man ain't supposed to smile but he didn't trust anything she said. Benny noticed in other pictures that neither men nor women smiled. Just the way people took pictures, he guessed, and most folks didn't have teeth they wanted to show anyway. Benny made a promise with himself then and there to always take care of his teeth.

Still, it bothered him that his mama would smile when his daddy would not. Was he mad at her about something? Maybe she was the reason he went away. That made Benny hate her for a minute but then he felt real bad about it. His mama seemed like a good ole gal and he didn't believe a word his aunt said about her. One day, he was gonna put rat poison in her gin and run away to join the circus. This much he knew for sure. Nobody was gonna lynch him over the likes of Maddie.

Another thing he was sure of was that his daddy left this guitar just for him. Maddie said he just left it cause he was in a hurry to get out of town, but what did she know? Benny wouldn't leave his sling shot or something important like that laying around no matter how much of a hurry he was in. But his daddy forgot this big, pretty guitar? Didn't make no sense.

"I'm telling you he just left it like he left everything else. That's it. That's all. Now go out and play," Maddie would say.

Benny knew that was a lie. It was his and his daddy left it for him. His daddy was a man who didn't take nothing off nobody, just like him. Maddie, or Braxton, or one of the other white folks in town did something to him and he had to go away. He wouldn't leave just because his mama's belly was big. You could tell from the picture he was braver than that.

Cause he hated this town as much as I do. And he left this guitar as a signal that he didn't just leave me cause he felt like it, but cause he had to.

"Maybe if I learn how to play it real good he'll come back," Benny said when they were skipping rocks one day. Luke agreed. He couldn't imagine not having a daddy. He always fought along-side Benny every time one of the other children, boy or girl, called him a bastard. Sometimes they lost but most of the time they won. Luke didn't care when he got a whupping for fighting since it was for a good cause, just like Robin Hood at the Bijou Playhouse. The other kids learned not to mess with them when they were together and they were always together. That's how they got a reputation.

"But I got to learn how to play real good so he can hear the music. It'll go way across the water and bring him back to me. Like that story you told me 'bout with the Greek fella and the sirens."

Once again Luke agreed. It sounded like a perfect plan. Benny took to picking and plucking on his own and even surprised Maddie with how accomplished he had become. But months passed and his daddy still didn't come home. Benny concluded it was because he wasn't good enough yet. As hard as he tried, he was just a boy, and needed help.

He got through the calluses on his own and held it like he had seen people do in pictures. He figured out certain sounds would change into other sounds if he squeezed the neck when he stroked the belly. But he couldn't make it say what he wanted it to say and the frustration of that almost made him break it more than once. Only the knowledge that it was a gift from his daddy stopped him from swinging it against the wall. Maddie laughed, of course, when Benny asked for money for guitar lessons.

"You spend too much time with that thing as it is," she said. Benny thought he would have a better time asking when she was drunk.

However, unlike other adults he had witnessed, Maddie just became more like herself when she drank. Figures.

"That boy got talent," Mack would say. Benny liked Mack and often fantasized about being his son. The arrangement would have worked out just fine since Luke was his brother in spirit. After a while of that, though, Benny forced himself to stop the fantasy. He didn't think it was fair to his daddy to think about another man that way.

"Because my daddy definitely left me this here guitar," he said loud enough for Maddie to hear one day. Benny wondered if there was something wrong with him because he didn't miss his mama as much as he missed his daddy. He finally worked it out that his mama was in heaven and ain't never coming back but his daddy was still out there somewhere. Naturally, he would think more about him being down here with the living and all. Yep, Benny had gone as far as his natural talent, eight months of practice, and swollen fingers would take him. Now, he needed a teacher.

Then, the other day, Luke sprinted up to him with a flyer in hand. He was so out of breath he couldn't speak and waved the paper in Benny's face while struggling for composure.

"Nigger, you know I can't read," Benny said. He got Luke some well water so he could pull himself together. Luke gulped the water but was still shaky from excitement and stammered through the flyer as best he could.

"Rastus P. Jr. Blues Man Extraordinaire. One night only."

Benny stood still as Luke rambled on about the particulars.

Rastus P. Jr.? Everybody knew Rastus P. Jr. One of the men in town square snatched the flyer from Luke's hand and went yelling to the people in the general store about it. The whole block was humming with the news.

"Rastus P. Jr. is coming! Rastus P. Jr. coming! Ooh, child, Rastus P? That's a whole lotta man. That nigger can sure 'nough sang!" And so it went.

So anyway, that's what the boys were doing there. Although, Luke didn't count on it being this late and Benny didn't count on it being this hard. Now, the only thing between Benny's dreams of getting Rastus P. Jr. to teach him how to play the guitar and get his daddy back was this stupid trap door.

"This shit ain't gonna work. Come on!" They crawled out from under the house into the back yard of the club. Oil drums had been converted to barbecue pits and Deacon Early was in charge of the meat. The sizzling juice of ribs, seasoned with vinegar and pepper, hit the white-hot, powdered coals. Flavored smoke lifted into the air, wafting through the crowd who had their money out. Deacon Early never missed a trick for a man of God.

Torches were set up to provide additional light since it was now night. Luke knew he'd be getting a beating but going back now wouldn't make the pain any less so he stayed.

A few couples were on the porch rubbing one another's legs and kissing deep. Half the black folks of Braxton made the scene in their Sunday best on a Friday night. A light-skinned gal faked disinterest as a toothless field hand with a fat roll talked her up. Colored college boys, from the next county, were at the dominos table getting a higher education in losing from the locals. A card table was set up next to that with an almost violent game of spades taking place. Some wall flowers held up the back of the porch watching the wet couples slow-dragging on the grass to a Bessie Smith record on the phonograph.

Every now and then, an ice cool woman, who looked like a slim man if you eyed her quick, would come up and talk to one of the wall flowers. She'd then introduce them to some teenage girls, who seemed just hair afraid of the dike, and they'd take the wall flowers upstairs. Folks pretended not to look but they always did. The colored college boys shouted encouraging profanity but they were outsiders so nobody really cared.

Luke stayed close to Benny who was stalking around the back yard, moving in between people, looking up at faces, with a mission in mind. Luke feared someone would recognize him but no one gave much thought to the boys. Homeless children were wandering around all the time, begging for this or getting into that, so nobody paid them attention. Benny made several revolutions around the back yard to no avail. He stood off to the side in disgust and tried to block out the forest to study the trees. Nothing.

"This ain't getting us nowhere," Benny said to Luke like the whole thing was his fault. Luke patted his growling stomach and eyed the barbecue chicken Deacon Early just slammed on the grill with flair.

"What you getting mad at me for?" Luke said.

"Well hell, you the one s'pose to be the smart one. Why don't you think of something?"

Luke didn't let Benny get to him. He knew not having a daddy was driving him a little crazy and he had a point. Luke knew he was smart because his mama always said so. And they couldn't stay out here all night, after all.

"Let's go over there," Luke said. He pointed to the wall flowers.

"Why?"

"Cause people who stand over there get to go inside. Rastus P. Jr. ain't gonna hang around out here, is he? He a star. He inside. Folks who lean on that wall get to go inside after that skinny man come up and talk to them. That's where we need to be. Inside. We outside. That ain't no good."

Benny considered Luke's words for a minute. He watched the skinny man talk to a wall flower and, sure enough, he was escorted inside by a pretty girl.

"Well, it's about time you said something made some sense. Come on."

The boys squeezed their way through the thick crowd by the barbecue pit. Benny tried to snatch a rib but Deacon Early swatted his hand without even looking. They pressed on through the musty bodies in the dance section and ran a little as some big fella told them to take their little asses home. They were ignored by the colored college boys and local card players as they leapt onto the porch. The necking couples likewise paid them no mind. Only the wall flowers seemed a tad uncomfortable when the boys leaned up against the wall and casually took their place on Ho Row.

The boys stood there for about three minutes until the eight or nine men felt too funny about staying. They wanted to chase the boys off but this would have drawn attention to themselves and most of the men were married. So one by one, they all just kind of filtered away. Some acted like they had a sudden urge to play dominoes or go to the outhouse. Others became hungry for no real reason that had anything to do with food. Only one stubborn old man in his seventies stayed in his corner of Ho Row. He was a regular customer who had paid his dues in this game called life and wasn't about to let a couple of kids stand between him and his bi-monthly piece of tail.

Another fifteen minutes or so passed. Luke wondered if he would ever recover from his certain ass whupping. He pondered whether his mama and daddy would beat him as a team or take turns. He hoped they used a switch. They thought it hurt him more and he cried like it did. But, quiet as it's kept, Luke had built up an immunity to the switch. The belt was still fearsome but if he twisted the right way, without looking like he was trying to dodge, he could take the belt without damage. It was his daddy's hand on his backside that frightened him the most. Or his mama's hand across his face that wounded him most. His daddy's hand. Hard as a brick but moved like the wind. Or his mama's unforgiving slap that hurt his feelings as well as his face. God, please don't let them use their hands.

Luke's stomach growled and Benny's answered. They looked at each other and laughed. Then Benny farted. This made them laugh more since nothing in the world was funnier to an eight year old boy than fart. That did it for the old man. He had paid his dues in this game called life and wasn't 'bout to stand up here, on his bunions, on a Friday night, smelling a strange child's fart. He was out.

The dike came out and was shocked by the absence of customers. All she saw was two giggling, dirty children wrestling with each other.

"Where everybody went?" she said.

The boys were startled out of their horseplay and stared at the dike without manners. She was a skinny, little thing of about five feet one with copper skin and a square jaw line. She wore colored glasses and smoked thin cigars. She had on a porter's hat and dungarees with a shirt and tie. She faintly smelled of reefer and stank of gin.

"What the fuck y'all doing here? Go on home to your mamas."

"I ain't got no mama and I do as I please," Benny said.

"Well, please your ass on down the road. You kids chasing away business."

"Hey! You a woman. I thought you was a man," Luke said.

"Same here. Now beat it."

"She a dike," said Benny who was never scared of adults. Benny didn't know exactly what that meant but had heard Maddie say it once and knew it was something about being a tomboy.

That Pimp slapped Benny so hard spit came out his mouth. Benny drew back and punched her right in the mouth and made her lip bleed. The colored college boys looked up to the porch to see what the trouble was. She grabbed Benny by the shirt and slammed him against the wall.

Luke kicked her in the shin, and it hurt her like hell, but she didn't cry out. She grabbed Luke by the throat and slammed him up next to Benny. Benny was about to go for the lip again but she whipped out a knife. One of the colored college boys rose to intervene but his friend put a hand on his wrist. He sat back down without a word. The locals at the table didn't even acknowledge what was going on. Deacon Early was too far out with the barbecue and music to be aware a child was about to get cut on his property. The boys were still at the sight of the blade. She leaned in close and leered in their faces.

"I'm gonna cut your little asses six ways 'til Sunday," she said.

"Your breath stank, dike," Benny said. One of the young prostitutes came on the porch and tried to help.

"Come on, leave 'em alone. They just kids."

"Get your hot ass back up them steps!"

"What's the matter with you? They kids," she persisted. The Pimp lashed out and sliced her on the arm. The girl cried out and grabbed her bleeding cut while two other hos hustled her upstairs. That broke the mood for the couples on the porch and they moved away in a rush.

"Let's go," one of the colored college boys said. They got up and left while the locals teased them with a chance to get their money back. The Pimp took a quick look around to see if anyone challenged her. No one, not even the biggest man, made a move. They all avoided her eyes or found engrossing conversations to engage in. Deacon Early was still caught up in thoughts of profits to be of any use. The couples in the dance section cared only about the groove. She turned her attention back to the boys.

"Now you see what I just did to my bitch?" The Pimp said.

"Well, I love her. And if I did that to her, what you think I'm gonna do to your little asses?"

She caressed Benny's throat with the blade. Benny remained defiant but nobody had ever tried to kill him before. Sure, Maddie talked about it but this woman really would. A tear ran down his face and The Pimp laughed at him. Luke grabbed her arm.

"Stop it," he said.

"Boy, if you don't get your hands off me, I'll cut you first."

"But you don't know what you doing. This is Rastus P. Jr.'s son!" The Pimp froze. The disinterested men at the game tables couldn't pretend they didn't hear that and rose as one unit to approach Ho Row. The Pimp saw an army coming her way. The Big Man, who avoided her eyes before, now marched at her with determination. Even the Old Man hobbled back for duty.

"Get your fucking hands off Rastus P. Jr.'s boy, dike," the Big Man said.

"Messing round with a child. Crazy ass pimp," the Old Man said.

The Pimp had a fast decision to make. Was this one of Rastus's kids for real? Could be. Nothing spread faster across the land than the sperm of Rastus P. Jr. Nigger had more bastards than a law firm. At least he took care of them, though. He was good for that much. That's why he was on the road everyday 'cept Christmas and New Year's. Then he got drunk and made more babies. An angry mob was bad for business, all right. Fans of Rastus P. Jr. were more devoted than monks.

"Aw hell, I'm just playing with the boy, that's all. I didn't know who he was." She gave Benny a hug and a kiss. He wiped it off and pushed her away.

"This dike say she gonna cut me six ways 'til Sunday," Benny announced to the crowd. "Yall gonna let her get away with that?"

"Bitch, we will kill you," the Old Man said. "The music of Rastus P. Jr. make my nature rise." Everybody looked at him and wasn't sure what to say. He sensed their discomfort and refused to care. He'd paid his dues in this game called life and could talk about his nature if he wanted to. The Pimp couldn't let this get out of hand. There were some things not even Deacon Early would tolerate. Assaulting the star's progeny would be at the top of that list.

"Look here, now. Everybody all hopped up over nothing. What say we settle it with a little free snatch and call it a night? One time only, though! And don't say I never gave you nothing." The men cheered and the ones who were too embarrassed before rushed Ho Row. "Get in line, motherfuckers! Get in line! And no repeats! You get in, you get out!" The Pimp struggled to organize. Luke stepped forth and tapped her on the shoulder. She suppressed the urge to backhand him and smiled. "Yes, sugar?"

"Excuse me, ma'am, but we here to see Rastus."

"Well, Rastus busy right now." Benny had enough.

"Busy doing what, dike?"

"Busy minding his business!" Almost getting lynched and giving away pussy was getting on her nerves. She settled down when a few men gave her the eye. She grinned and tried to stroke Benny's hair but he swatted her away. "Your father's taking a little… nap. But you can see him after the show. One of my… assistants will bring him down. You have yourself some barbecue and watch the show. My treat."

"Yay!" said Luke.

"Not you," snapped The Pimp. "You ain't Rastus P. Jr.'s son." Benny stepped forward with vengeance. He still remembered she made him cry.

"Watch it, dike," Benny said. He put his arm around Luke. "He's my best friend." Luke smiled. The Pimp peeled four dollars off her roll like she was shedding skin. She almost snarled at the boys and slunk away. Luke and Benny were lifted to the shoulders of the men and cheered.

"You boys a good luck charm, that's what you is," the Big Man said. "You put your money away, Rastus the third, it's no good here. You boys want chicken or ribs?"

"Yes," they said together. Everybody laughed and the Old Man said something about getting them babies out the night air before he was taken away for a free fuck. The boys were whisked inside the juke joint with food and drink in front of them before they knew it.

Benny was introduced as Rastus P. Jr's boy and folks said how he looked just like him. Luke chuckled between mouthfuls of chicken. He gulped down a cold cup of water and let out a self satisfied sigh.

"If my brain was any bigger, I'd have to carry it in a bucket," Luke said. Benny nodded while he sucked on a rib bone. No doubt about it. Luke was the smart one, all right. Benny had no problem with that. The place was filling up as more folks came in from the yard.

"Here you go, Rastus the third. Put some hair on your chest," the Big Man said. Benny took the jar by both hands and had his first sip of beer. The taste shocked him because he thought it was a soda or something. But he held it in his mouth and let it leak out his bloated cheeks and down his throat. Of course, he got a buzz right away. Benny had never been this happy in his life. Luke spit out his beer and said something about throwing up. Just then, the lights dimmed more than they already were. The room hushed and a spotlight appeared on a small, empty stage. Deacon Early's voice boomed from the back of the room.

"And now, ladies and gentlemen, for your total and complete entertainment pleasure: Rastus P. Jr.!"

Luke didn't have to throw up no more. Benny took another swallow of beer and grinned at the stage in a happy haze.

7

Benny was in a haze, weak and feverish, on the sweat-soaked bed. Voices bubbled through the hot air with sad importance.

"Help me, Rastus," Benny said. And he was out again. Luke pulled the sheets up around him.

Mack was determined to go get that woman folks talked about.

"I don't want that devil mess in my house," Sarah said.

"God gave people different talents and it's a sin not to use them!" They had another fight.

Sarah yelled something about Saul and the witch of Endor before he stalked out the house.

"Superstitious foolishness, that's what it is," Sarah said. "Man get on my nerves. Luke, get me another compress. Hurry. And rinse out your mouth again."

Luke brought Benny to his house after the snakes attacked because Maddie was useless, as usual. Over the years, she had gone from a mean drunk to a sad one. Her decline was something one could set a watch by.

The Martins had spent half the night sucking poison out of Benny. Sometimes together and sometimes in shifts. Benny was in and out of consciousness saying things the family was embarrassed to hear. They didn't say nothing about it and avoided each other's eyes when he went on talking about his daddy, his mama, and Luke being the smart one. Something about his guitar and how he wished Mack was his daddy. Crazy talk. Sick talk. Snake bite talk.

It all happened so fast when Benny fell off the post. The first snake dug in his side and the other clamped on his thigh. Benny laid

Bertha down with care while the snakes hung from him like fruit. They stuck to him like scabs glued on with teeth and he pried them off as best he could. He threw them on the grass just as Luke arrived to beat them into mush with a stick. There was something especially wrong with these things. The third one bit Benny's hand when he swung at it a hair too slow. The fourth one struck at Luke's leg but got a boot on the head for his trouble. Luke couldn't understand why the group on the porch, even white boys with guns, wouldn't come to assist.

"Help! Help us!" But they didn't.

The last snake was still jammed in Benny's hand. Luke pinched the corners of the mouth to make it let go while it stared at him with its dry, black eyes. Benny cussed and that's when Luke knew it was bad. That's when he heard how frail he was.

Luke grabbed the thing by the tail and swung its head against the post. The skull made a loud knock and left a mark on the wood. He slung it over with the rest and beat them into a blob while everybody on the porch just watched.

Red arose from his coma with Willa's prayers guiding him back to the light. Didn't have a mark on him.

"Benny!" Luke said. "You all right, man?" Benny didn't answer so Luke ran to the porch.

"We need to get Benny to a hospital."

"Go right ahead," Braxton said.

"State General's the closest."

"State General don't allow nigras and you know it."

"That's why I need you. They'll listen to you."

"Can't help you. State General don't allow nigras."

"Nigras? What the fuck is a nigra? Either say colored or nigger or shut the fuck up! You think I get a warm glow inside if you call me a nigra?" Everyone was stunned, including Braxton, who opened his mouth wide enough to take a leak in. One of Braxton's boys, who always thought Luke was uppity, cocked his rifle. Luke stepped on the porch and got in Braxton's face. "This never would have happened if you took care of the weeds in the first place. Red, get your ass up, ain't shit wrong with you. Look at y'all. Always talking 'bout how much pussy you get at The Joint but when you had a chance to be real men, you locked up on me. Fuck all y'all! Mr. Braxton, your family been living off the backs of colored folks for years. Why don't you do the same thing you'd do for a damn mule?

Everybody stared at Luke.

"Now, look here, nigger. I don't make the rules. They don't let niggers in State General for no reason at'tall. I don't care if he was having a baby. He still couldn't get in. Take him to your own people in the next county."

"He'll be dead by then," Luke said.

"He's good as dead now," Braxton's boy said.

Luke charged the white man with the gun in the invulnerability of Black Male Pride. The white boy raised his gun to shoot and bullets ricocheted by his feet. All whipped around to see Mack with a riffle in the back of Charlie's truck. Boss Man Braxton couldn't believe it. He descended the steps of his porch and stared at Mack.

"Are you crazy, boy? Don't you know I'll kill you for this?"

"And I'll kill anybody who fuck with my son. Told you that a long time ago. Luke, get Benny in the truck." Luke ran back to Benny who was out cold.

"He dead?" Mack said. Luke checked for a pulse while the whole porch waited.

"I feel something. Yeah," Luke said.

"Then hurry up." Luke grabbed Benny under the arms and pulled him to the truck.

"Thanks for nothing, Braxton," Luke said. Braxton just laughed for some reason.

"I see dead niggers," Braxton said. Charlie drove off while Mack guarded the rear.

So anyway, that's what happened in the afternoon that decayed into a hateful night. Sarah reasoned the ride alone would kill Benny and ain't nobody had time to drive to the next county looking for no colored doctor. And who knew when the Klan would come a calling. But Sarah had a good relationship with Braxton's wife. She'd appeal to her and buy them some time. As for now, they would have to help Benny themselves.

Luke took the side, Mack the leg, and Sarah took the hands. Benny was unmindful of Mack's hunting knife, sterilized with whiskey, cutting across his leg. He remained unconscious when Sarah took her pruning knife and freed the puss in his hand. But he jumped when Luke cut him with the fishing knife.

"What the hell you doing *now*?" Mack said.

"Mack. Don't start. Luke, just slice across, baby. Across." Luke followed his mother's instructions with a nervous hand. Then the family fed on Benny to save his life.

"I think I got it all," Luke said after while. He gargled with ginger water and Sarah scooted around to make the inspection. She gargled and dumped the spittoon full of spit, venom, and blood out the window. Sarah formed a tight seal with her lips on Benny's side and sucked the blood in one good draw. Luke turned away as her cheeks sunk in. Mack kept his eyes on Luke as he feasted on the leg. Sarah tapped Luke on the shoulder and shook her head. She spit and returned to her burden without a word. Luke got back to it and more time passed. The family took a break. Benny's cords were loosened and adjusted so the limbs could get fresh blood. Sarah didn't know if she had done the right thing or not. She just thought Benny must hurt in a dream somewhere and would probably appreciate it.

The Martins ate plain bread to soak up poison that ginger water might have missed. Maddie came in and asked some dumb questions. The family ignored her so she decided to leave. She looked at Benny like she might touch him but she just left. The hoot owl started its routine melody and Sarah jumped. The hoot owl made her realize just how long they'd been at it and Benny wasn't getting any better. He'd stopped talking in his sleep and was now plain quiet.

The silence had Luke worried the most. Noise was the symbol of Benny's life force: Cussing, fucking, whining, laughing, arguing, bragging, snoring, burping, hollering, mocking, crunching, guzzling, singing, with plucking, strumming, and wailing on Bertha to round him out. But a quiet Benny was against all nature. It wasn't the way things should be.

Bertha leaned in the corner of the shack like a relic of war abandoned by its knight. After being quiet for so long, Benny's body shook and his teeth clenched. They jumped back in fear and then held him down so he wouldn't hurt himself. Mack reprimanded himself for thinking Benny was always trouble. The convulsion passed. Something had to be done. That's why Mack left. To go get that woman.

"We done all we can do for now," Sarah said. "Let's pray together." She covered Benny with a blue blanket and put a wet, white cloth on his forehead. She took Luke by his hand and they sat by the window.

"You go first," she said. "You love him the most."

"Don't say it like that."

"Oh, don't be silly. There's nothing wrong with you loving a man. You love your daddy. David loved Jonathan, didn't he?"

"I don't know."

"'Course, you do. I think that poison's making you a little crazy." Sarah leaned over from exhaustion.

"Mama, you all right?"

"'Course I am. Don't get jumpy. You go first. Pray."

"I don't know what to say."

"Just say the first thing that comes to mind. Nothing you say will be wrong to Him."

Luke looked at Benny. He had really swollen up bad now so Luke looked away. He looked away for the same reason he never went to funerals now that he was a man and nobody could make him go. The people never looked like themselves. He didn't care how good the undertaker was supposed to be. The people never looked like themselves. Ever.

"Pray," Sarah said. Luke closed his eyes.

"Dear God..."

Then he burst into tears more bitter than the venom in his mouth. Sarah rubbed his back the way she used to do when the other children made fun of him. She looked out the window, listened to the hoot owl, and prayed for all concerned.

8

"And now, ladies and gentleman, for your total and complete entertainment pleasure: Rastus P. Jr.!"

The crowd applauded. No Rastus. Then,

> *"Get back from me!"*

Silence.

> *"Whatever you are. Get back from me."*

A guitar strummed.

> *"Yes, Lawd.*
> *As east is to west. As worst is to best.*
> *I'm passing the test.*
> *Get back from me."*

All the people in The Joint jerked their heads around to the voice at the back of the room. They looked up to the shallow second story, and behind the banister, with the door open behind him, with a half dressed, worn out gal in view, was Rastus P. Jr. He spanked his guitar.

> *"Get back from me! (Silence)*
> *You sweet motherfucker. Get back from me.*

A guitar strummed.

> *Help me, Lawd.*
> *As short is to long. As right is to wrong.*
> *I'm sanging my song.*
> *Get back from me!"*

Rastus sang about the kind of shit folks wanted to hear about. Shit they had been through. Shit they understood. Shit they were ashamed of thinking 'til they found out other folks thought the same shit, too. They clapped their hands to the acoustic gospel-funk of his legendary guitar: Jeraldine.

Deacon Early shined the spotlight up to Ho Row, illuminating Rastus in his shaman blues-man glory. He wore blue alligator boots tipped with brass. Size thirteen. He sported form-fitting dungarees on tree trunk thighs. Instead of a belt, he had a black rope holding up them pants that was woven from the hair of an Indian woman. One time, Rastus turned out this little Indian gal before escaping her tribe who was holding him hostage. She killed herself rather than be betrothed to the brave who was supposed to have her. The brave promised he wouldn't rest until Rastus was as dead as his intended bride. Or so the story went.

Rastus wore an open red shirt he didn't bother buttoning up since everybody knew what he was doing on the second story. His nappy, balled up chest hair was decorated with a silver dollar worn around his neck. It was twice the size of a normal silver dollar cause Rastus's great granddaddy stole it as a Freedman from a Confederate convoy headed up to Washington. Them crazy rebels was gonna try to flood the Yankee economy with this pseudo money so folks would have to depend on slaves forever. Only after the Freedman robbed the train, did the plot to assassinate Lincoln go full force. Or so the story went.

He sported a full beard with no mustache. He had a kind, dark face but eyes with a warning. His white cowboy hat was cocked to the right. His white bright smile was cocked to the left. Jeraldine was feeling herself tonight. And Rastus descended the stairs.

"You came into my life, unannounced, uninvited.
"Love got out of hand. Spilling over. Too excited.
Hurt too many people just to show how much we
    care.
Now my eyes is open. So be gone and beware!

Get back from me.
You sweet motherfucker!
Get back from me.
Over there.
As wet is to dry.
As laugh is to cry.
Please don't question why.
We gots to say, "bye."
So get ye behind me.
And don't try to find.
I can't let cha bind me.
Get back from me."

Rastus P. Jr. had now reached the floor. Benny and Luke had never seen such a thing. It was like something from the circus, revival, and hell. They loved it. Jeraldine launched into her solo and Rastus predated Chuck Berry by doing a head jerking stalk to the stage. He eyed the yearning women and winked at the grinning men. He glanced at the boys and if he wondered, or gave a damn, what two children were doing there, it didn't show. And The Pimp took note of that. So she hugged the shadows and watched the show.

Rastus P. Jr. was now on-stage playing Jeraldine with his tongue. The crowd went crazy. The boys jumped up and down in their chairs tipping over the beer.

"Do what cha do, boy, do what cha do!" the Big Man said.

"Play that thang, boy, play that thang!" the Old Man shouted from his room.

Deacon Early almost felt like he was in church with all the testifying, music, and the Holy Ghost going on. Yeah, the Holy Ghost made the show too. Word on the street was the music of Rastus P. Jr. made barren women fertile and a weak man's nature rise. Deacon Early wondered if it could possibly be true when women fell out after screaming something 'bout Jesus and having Rastus's baby. Jeraldine reached a crescendo and Rastus matched her in a scream of blue ferocity. He stomped two times on the stage and stopped.

"Get back from me." The silence went on for two or three beats before the thunderstruck crowd jumped up and cheered. Luke yelled and whistled but Benny was quiet and just stared at Rastus. He gripped his guitar so tight in his trembling hand, a drop of blood slid down the string. Rastus was drawn to the only still body in the crowd and stared back at Benny. Contact. He tipped his hat at Benny who looked around to make sure the god on the stage was looking at him. When he realized he was Rastus's intended point of view, he got all goofy and bashful the way boys did. He laughed and put his head down on the table.

"What's the matter with you?" Luke said over the cheers. "He's looking right at you. Wave at him or something, stupid." Benny waved. Rastus winked. Then he fought to quiet down the crowd.

"All right, all right, now. That's enough. Y'all keep clapping for me this hard, I'm gonna have to fuck ya." The crowd laughed. "And I'm tired. Been fucking all night." More laughs. "Where that Pimp at? Come on out here, Pimp, you hear me calling you."

The Pimp appeared from the shadows. The boys looked at each other.

"I love you, pimp. Y'all give this dike a big round of applause or I'm leaving. Give it up!" The crowd put their hands together for The Pimp.

"I declare, I declare. That dike's dick bigger than mine." Everybody laughed, including The Pimp. "And that's saying something." Women screamed. "Yes, lawd. I love that pimp. One day I'm gonna pay her." The crowd fell out. He had them all in the palm of his easy hand. The Old Man shouted from the banister,

"Rastus P. Jr., you make my nature rise!"

"Don't smile at me when you say that, partner." The crowd hollered again and the Old Man had a coughing fit of laughter.

"It ain't that kind of show. Maybe the dike can introduce you to her brother." A fella spit his beer out on the back of a woman's head and got his face slapped. "Let me introduce y'all to my favorite gal. I think you know her. Meet Jeraldine."

Rastus played a perfunctory riff on Jeraldine as folks stood up to applaud and this time Benny joined them. Could his daddy's guitar look that pretty if he shined it up some?

"Yeah. I'd just be another nigger with a complaint if it wasn't ole Jeraldine. That's Jeraldine with a J. Get it right, now. Jeraldine's a special ole gal. Her hair's from the strands of a master's whip but her body makes nothing but music. Just like the blues."

"Well, all right!" somebody said.

"Y'all know something 'bout the blues?" They claim in unison they do.

"I say any you niggers know something 'bout the blues?" They assure him, even louder, that they do. He took time to study the captive crowd like he was trying to figure out if they were lying or not. Nobody breathed.

"Then know this."

He patted Jeraldine and together they wailed a tale of woe about a man who just wanted to get away from it all. This time Luke really did have to throw up and said something to Benny about the outhouse before he left. Benny didn't even hear him. It was one of the few times he felt comfortable if Luke wasn't around. All that existed for this eight year old boy, with a bad reputation, in this house of blues, with a bad reputation, was Rastus and Jeraldine.

Benny wasn't old enough to experience the loss the adults in the audience had, but the song made him feel kinda funny anyway. Like someone had peeped in his window, when Maddie was snoring one off, and seen him crying about his daddy. Like they had watched him soaking his pillow in the dark and slipped off to write a song about it.

Rastus sang about a man who went away because the life he was living wasn't good enough for him. He figured if he could just go away for a little while, he could make life better than it was. But once he got to this promised land, he realized things were just as bad, if not worse, than the place he left.

The man who went away hung with a certain crowd, doing all the things they did, to make his pain go away. He thought these new people were his friends and gave up time and money to keep them. He even thought he might be in love. He found out the folks he thought friends were no friends at all. And the love he thought he felt was just a pleasurable way to avoid his task in life. The pleasure faded, along with his money, and the man who went away wanted to go home now.

But home was filled with people who expected him to succeed. Home was full of people he had ignored for a very long time. Home wasn't home anymore and the man who went away felt God punished him for a mission he had failed to complete.

Benny looked around at the crowd. They were different from before. No one yelled. Men stared at their drinks without drinking or looked at the ceiling. Women still wanted to be with Rastus but this time out comfort instead of lust. Other folks just closed their eyes and rocked with respect to Jeraldine's rhythm.

The man who went away was driven mad with confusion and never went home. He cursed God on his death bed for giving him a mission impossible to understand. He died alone with no money, no friends, and no glory.

Benny knew two things as the song reached its conclusion. He wanted to move a crowd just like Rastus P. Jr. And his daddy was never coming home again.

Luke joined Benny on wobbly legs amidst the screams of the grateful audience.

"Look here, y'all," Rastus said. "I'm 'bout to wet my whistle and shake my weasel. Don't kill each other 'till I get back."

The audience laughed and applauded as Rastus ended the convenient two-song set. Rastus was a big believer in putting the audience on his schedule. If management didn't like it, then fuck 'em. The crowd was there to hear him sing and look at *him*. He sang and looked better if he was allowed to indulge himself. So the management, of whatever venue he played, let him get away with murder. The trip to the bar and the outhouse was slowed by a load of people who rushed the stage. Rastus took the time to speak and flirt with the masses. The bartender walked some moonshine cut with orange juice to him.

"Look here," Luke said, "I'm way past getting a whupping now. These people gonna kill me. Go on over there and ask him to help you play your guitar so you can get your daddy back. We gots to go." Benny looked Luke dead in the eye and said,

"My daddy ain't coming back."

"What you talking 'bout?"

"My daddy is the man who went away. He ain't coming back. That's it."

Luke noticed something sad and strong in Benny. He knew Benny wanted a daddy real bad and didn't know why they were here in the first place, risking his death, if it wasn't about getting him one. He started to talk Benny out of his depression, like he usually did, but Benny wasn't really depressed. It was something else. So Something stopped Luke from disputing.

"Nope. My daddy ain't coming back. But I don't care. I'm still gonna learn how to play this here guitar. Come on."

"Come on where? We can't get through all them people. If you ain't trying to get your daddy back then we needs to go. I ain't kidding. My mama ain't like Ms. Maddie. She care where I am and what time I get back."

"I told you in ain't about my daddy, fool. It's about my guitar."

"Damn, your guitar. I'm gonna get a whupping." Luke walked off but Benny grabbed him by the shoulder and spun him around. Luke jerked away and almost knocked his jar of half finished beer over. Benny strapped the guitar on his shoulder.

"I thought you was my friend," Benny said.

"I thought you was mine. I'm gonna get a whupping."

"Stop acting like a girl. Hell, you act like you ain't never got a whupping before. I gotta talk to a man about a guitar."

"I don't act like no girl and you say that again I'm gonna punch you in your damn nose. Get somebody else to teach you to play your stupid ole guitar."

"Somebody like who, motherfucker? Ain't nobody else and you know it. Its gotta be Rastus. Nigger, stop being selfish."

"Selfish? Nigger, I ain't talking to you. I'm gonna get a whupping. Bye." Luke turned to go and bumped right into The Pimp.

"Problem, boys?" she said. Benny and Luke started looking crazy.

"Naw, dike, we ain't got no problem," Benny said. He poked his chest out a little.

"Well, that's good," The Pimp said. She took her knife out and they froze. She took an apple out of her baggy pocket and smiled. She peeled the apple and looked at the boys a spell before she spoke again.

"Hope there ain't no hard feelings about earlier."

"Oh, uh, no ma'am. We forgot all about that. Ain't we, Benny?" Benny didn't answer.

"What's all this "ma'am" stuff? You making me feel old, boy." She laughed and Luke laughed with her because he didn't know what else to do. She stroked his pretty face. "I just love little boys," she drawled. She took a giant bite out her apple and took her time munching on it before she swallowed. One big bite was all she wanted and she put the apple back down. She picked up the half finished beer and finished it. Then she fixed her eyes on Benny. "Well. Let's go say hey to daddy." She grabbed the boys by the shoulders and steered them towards the stage. They made a slight move of resistance but she gave them a squeeze that chased any thoughts of escape from their minds.

"Excuse me, please. 'Scuse me," said The Pimp. They sifted through the crowd and Benny looked to Luke for guidance. However, Luke's big brain was all thought out. Could anything be worse than this? First, this crazy lady was gonna kill him and then he was gonna get a whupping.

"Excuse me, please. 'Scuse, me. Hey! Get the fuck out the way. Thank you. 'Scuse me, please. 'Scuse me. Son of Rastus P. Jr. coming through. 'Scuse me, please."

They were now one person away from Mr. Jr. The Pimp saw Rastus putting the moves on a female fan with too much make up and a whole lot of back side. She couldn't help but check out the made-up woman herself. Maybe later. Gals coming in here all hot over Rastus, and not able to get him, could make the switch if they're liquored up just right. The Pimp looked at the boys and tightened up on their shoulders. Her smile faded for the first time since she walked to their table.

"All right, sugar, you stick around now," Rastus said. "I'll talk to you after the show." The made-up woman whispered so close to Rastus that lipstick got on his ear. He chuckled at whatever she said. "Aw, no you won't, will ya? Aw, shuck now." He laughed loud and a few other women in club, who had their turns whispering in Rastus's ear, made a note to give her a dirty look. The made-up woman moved off after making a show of adjusting her bosom. She caught The Pimp checking her out.

"Don't even think about it," the Made-Up Woman said. And walked away.

"Bitch."

"Aw, don't be that way," Rastus said to the Pimp. "You gotta leave something for me."

"Nigger, I leave something for you every time you come around. Ain't it 'bout time for a brother to settle up on a tab?"

"Aw, come on, sugar, you know I'm good for it."

"Forget the charm," The Pimp said just a little too loud. "All I want out of them pants is your money. If you got any left for once."

Rastus saw a few patrons pretending not to listen. Sure, he had money problems and, yeah, he had a lot of kids, and had to take third rate jobs, like the one from this greedy ass deacon. But the last thing he needed, or would tolerate, was somebody throwing up the point in front of the fans. Fuck that. Who cared if he really did owe her money and she had a legitimate point? The illogical glory of Black Male Pride was deeply rooted in Rastus P. Jr.

"You want to keep it down a bit?" he said.

"You want to pay me my money? You know. Just a bit." Rastus's eyes flicked a little which gave The Pimp the only warning she would get.

"Bitch, I ain't got your money, and the little bit I got, I'm gambling with. When my dick gets hard, I'm gonna fuck another one of your hos for free fore I go off and slam that other bitch you want so bad. Now what the fuck you gonna do about it?"

The boys stood there like ducks who walked into a hunting lodge asking for directions. They tried to squirm away on the sly but The Pimp just clamped down harder without looking at them. There was a long silence. And then:

"Aw, woman, you know I love you," said Rastus.

"Come here, fool," said The Pimp. Then they kissed like two enemies who always wondered what the other one tasted like. The boys scrunched up their faces at each other and a few shocked patrons giggled. The Old Man soliloquized from Ho Row.

"Rastus P. Jr. The only man who could get a dike wet."

Rastus and The Pimp broke their strange truce and eyed each other like one of them still might try something funny. Angry about the money, but satisfied with the respect, such as it was, The Pimp pulled back to her starting position.

"I brought you a visitor." She released the boys and put her hand in her pocket by the knife. Rastus looked down at the boys and waited for them to speak. No one did. She cocked her head at Benny.

"Well?" she said.

"Oh, I saw you in the audience," Rastus said. Benny said nothing before his god. Luke, Mr. big brain, chirped up through his fear.

"Oh, please. Like we was gonna miss it."

"Uh, huh," Rastus said. He wasn't quite sure what to make of Luke. But the other boy reminded him of himself at an early age. The Pimp tightened her grip around the blade. "So how you doing?" Rastus said to Benny. Benny didn't speak. The Pimp didn't know what to make of that since Rastus personified casual. Hell, he'd greet his own mama like a poker buddy. So did he mean, "How you doing, son?" or "How you doing, boy I never seen before?" She could have just asked, of course, but The Pimp was the kinda cat who liked to play with her food. She zoomed in on Benny who looked to Luke for direction. Luke jerked his head over towards Rastus. The Pimp shot Luke a look that cut his pantomime cold.

"Oh, you know him," Luke said. "Quiet as ever." Luke grinned like he was visiting on Sunday Morning.

"Uh, huh," Rastus said. He couldn't decide weather he liked Luke or not. And he didn't know what to make of Benny. He decided to make the boy's guitar a topic of conversation. "Brought, your guitar along, huh?"

Nothing.

"Oh, please," Luke said. "Like he was gonna leave that behind. I mean, it's in the blood. Right?"

"Yeah, you got that right," Rastus said. The Pimp was still confused. Did he mean, you got that right, like father like son? Or did he mean, yep, any fool playing guitar for a living just can't help himself? She waited. Benny continued to look at Rastus with his mouth open.

Rastus decided to have pity on Benny. He figured the boy was one of the retarded children Deacon Early brought up from the church to show a good time or something. Poor little re-tard. Probably didn't even know what a guitar was. Probably just using that thang as a pacifier or something. It just broke his heart. Deacon Early ought to be 'shamed of himself bringing this sweet little moron to a place like this with that pushy kid in charge. Made him sick. He pulled Benny to him and gave him a hug.

"I bet you don't get out much, huh?" Rastus said.

"No, he don't. But he had to see you. Naturally," Luke said.

"Naturally," Rastus said. The Pimp was on full alert. "Well, let me see what you can play on that thang," Rastus said. For the first time in his life, Benny feared an adult. He positioned his deadbeat daddy's guitar and strummed in hesitation. The nearby crowd turned to listen.

"That's right. Play it like your daddy taught you," the Big Man said. The Pimp noted no discernible reaction from daddy. Rastus listened for a while and thought it a double shame that this child was retarded and had a daddy who couldn't play guitar worth a damn. The crowd clapped along out of courtesy but it didn't take them long to realize that Rastus P. the Third better find something else to do for a living. Luke could tell Benny was in trouble and knew he better do something quick. He addressed the crowd.

"'Course, he's much better when he's warmed up."

"Boy, do you ever shut up?" Rastus said. Luke saw The Pimp staring at him hard and he backed towards the door. She followed.

He tried to yell but nothing came out. Benny's hand shook and his playing suffered for it.

"It's okay, Rastus," The Pimp said as she advanced on Luke. "Children can be such a disappointment."

"What's that now?" Rastus said. She backed Luke into a dark corner and slid out her knife.

"I said — "

At that moment, Benny came alive. He ripped out a riff he heard on Maddie's phonograph. Maddie wouldn't let him touch the thing and beat him bad one night when she caught him playing it. But Benny started spiking Maddie's tea so she'd be double drunk when she drank on purpose. Maddie passed out a little bit sooner and Benny used that time to listen to the unknown artist sing a song about catfish and dogs. Benny got his first callouses through his trial and error method of playing what he heard about catfish and dogs. He accepted the fact that his daddy was long gone. But his best friend was right there. So he played.

The Pimp jerked around to Benny and Luke almost collapsed from relief. The disinterested crowd figured Rastus the Third really did need some time to warm up after all. They clapped to the beat out of joy instead of obligation. Benny smiled at all the attention while Rastus checked him out.

His fingering's all wrong. His hand's way too heavy and the guitar's out of tune. But damn, that re-tard sure can play.

The Pimp was disappointed. She eyed Luke with one last threat before sheathing her blade and noticed Rastus seemed proud of the boy. He whipped out Jeraldine and accompanied Benny who was thrilled by the gesture. Luke danced a jilly, to the amusement of the crowd, and the three-ring circus was in full effect. A working girl, with a bandage on her arm, danced with Luke and the floor filled up after that. The Pimp looked over the happy crowd and walked away by herself. The Made-Up Woman searched for a partner but all the men were taken. The Pimp saw the woman's dilemma and tipped her hat. The Made-Woman shrugged her shoulders.

"Fuck it," she said. She joined The Pimp on the dance floor and a good time was had by all.

9

Only the appearance of Rastus P. Jr. at Mack and Sarah's shack saved Luke from the worst ass whupping since slavery. Sarah and Mack couldn't believe their eyes when the boys showed up with him. They were worried sick, of course, and scolded Luke for being in a place like that.

"No offense, Mr. Jr.," Mack said.

"None taken. It's a fucked up place, all right. And call me Rastus. All my friends do. And I hope I can call y'all friends."

"You certainly may," Mack said. "Have a sit down."They sat and Sarah made do with some stew while apologizing for meager offerings.

"Aw, go head on, now. I was raised on this stuff and ain't had home cooked hot food since I was in Canada. Knew a little gal down there what could cook a bit. I thank you kindly."

Sarah couldn't believe a black man had been anywhere as far away as Canada and Rastus explained how blues gots plenty of appreciation outside the states.

"Love us more than our own people do seem like to me."

"That's a story now, Rastus. Don't nobody love you more than we do." Mack said. He poured him a glass of brandy full to the rim. Rastus said another reason for going to Canada and overseas was to escape the black face routine.

"I ain't putting that shit on my face. Don't care what nobody say. Fuck Bert Williams. 'Scuse me, ma'am."

"You a real man, Rastus," Mack said. He filled Rastus's halfway empty glass.

"Well, far be it from me to dispute my husband in front of company — "

"That's a good woman you got there, Mack."

"Don't I know it."

" — but I don't think Mr. Williams doing that cause he enjoy it."

"Aw, hell, sometimes I talk too much. Fuck Bert Williams. Don't even know the nigger. And lord know he got more money than I'll ever see. I'm just saying. It ain't for me is all. I'm a blues man. Not a clown. Being black hard enough without playing at being black. That's all I'm saying."

"Let me get you some more bread, Rastus."

"Aw, thank you ma'am, but I can't eat ano — "

"What the women like in Canada, Rastus?"

"What the hell you care?" Sarah said.

They all laughed and the boys reacted from hearing Sarah cuss. Rastus dazzled the folks with adventures in travel and the boys ate supper in the corner on the floor. Luke was way past relief at his stay of execution and Benny catalogued Rastus's every move. So they didn't have much to say. An hour or so had passed and Rastus, who regarded himself as nothing more than an ordinary man with extraordinary talent, began to ask Sarah and Mack about their own lives. They spoke of how they met as children and were only two generations removed from slavery.

"Hell, who ain't?" Rastus said. Then he remembered he wasn't talking about himself no more. They continued about how they made the trek to Braxton from Montgomery and sharecropped because it was pretty much the only game in town where you could have a home and raise a family. Rastus then told them how his grandmother was a sharecropper and they all bitched and moaned about how it was no way for a black man to get ahead.

"But what you else you gonna do?" Mack said.

"Something else," Rastus said. "Anything else. Cropping drove my mama to an early grave."

"Aw, come on now, Rastus," Mack said. He poured his guest the last drop of brandy. "Everybody ain't got talent like you." Rastus slammed his hand on the table and made Sarah jump.

"Now I'm 'bout to get my ass beat and insult my host," Rastus said with drama. "You a lie, Mack! Everybody ain't got talent like me but everybody got talent. All God's children got something they can do that can help them get out of something they don't want. Everybody got talent. Everybody. Even motherfuckers you don't like got that one thing they can do."

Sarah and Mack were silent and nothing could be heard but the breathing of the sleeping boys.

"Well," Mack said. "If you find out what it is, you let me know."

"Oh, it's probably too late for a broke down nigger like you, Mack." They all laughed and Mack punched Rastus in the arm. Rastus got out of his chair to play-box with Mack while Sarah squealed,

"Get him, Mack" and clapped her hands. Mack collapsed in his chair from laughing and Rastus pulled out his private stash of brandy, much to the host's delight. They even persuaded Sarah to have a little sip.

"But I tell you one thing, though. It ain't too late for them kids." Rastus said.

"Yes, Jesus," said Sarah.

"Well, Benny's good at the guitar, for a kid," Mack said. "And Luke's good at... Luke's good at..." Rastus waited while Sarah rolled her eyes.

"Luke's good at noticing how things should really be," Sarah said. "He's good with words. Know how to open up his mouth and talk to people. Motivate 'em. Get 'em to do things or look at life in a certain way." Everybody paused.

"Yeah. Luke's good for that," Mack said.

"Hmm. Sound like a artist or something," Rastus said. "Well, I don't know how much help I could be to Luke. But I got several more trips to Braxton as I criss-cross this great land of ours and I'd be more than happy to help the re-tard play that guitar." Mack laughed so hard no sound came out.

"Oh, uh, Benny ain't retarded," Sarah said. "He just crazy." Sarah agreed to talk to Maddie for Rastus about Benny. She would have gone down the way to get her but they were all having such a nice time and she didn't want Maddie fucking it up with her foolishness. Rastus agreed to come back at least once a month or every other month to see how Benny was coming along.

"And your boy can hang out with us too, of course. To tell us how life should be," Rastus said.

Mack was silent with gratitude. He grabbed Rastus's forearm and just sat there a minute. Sarah almost cried. But she believed in emotion over sentiment so she stopped herself. She knew they were going to be tired as hell to go pick them strawberries tomorrow but she didn't care. It wasn't everyday a star ate dinner at your shack. Sarah straightened up the place and Mack went outside to try one of Rastus's cigars and talk men talk.

Sarah got on her knees and covered Luke and Benny with a soft, blue blanket. She caressed them both and pondered where Luke's vision of life and Benny's guitar playing would take them.

10

The HooDoo Woman had arrived. Sarah had strong objections to her presence. After another argument with Mack, she left to look after Maddie. She wanted to get away for herself as well. She'd done all she could do for Benny and had prayed herself out.

"You did a good job, sister," the HooDoo Woman said. "If it wasn't for you he'd be dead already." Sarah hesitated at the door. She detested everything the woman stood for but she was a guest in her home, after all.

"Thank you." She slammed the door hard on her way out.

If the HooDoo Woman had a name nobody ever called her by it. She was just the HooDoo Woman. She looked like they all looked. White hair, a shawl, and oily skin etched by age and secrets. Some folks believed in her and some folks didn't. Deacon Early, who had done more reading than most folks, said it was all the power of the mind. Red swore the woman helped him win a bet for five hundred dollars but Red was a fool so that wasn't much comfort. Luke wondered why anyone who had magic powers would hang around Braxton, Alabama. The best advice Mack had about the HooDoo Woman was from his fishing buddy Charlie. And Charlie wasn't no liar and Charlie wasn't no fool.

Charlie was once messing around with this gal who he knew was no good for him but he couldn't leave her alone. The woman spent up his money, talked to him like he was nothing, and wasn't nice to his mama. Charlie was convinced she was also sleeping with Ace but never called her on it. That wasn't like Charlie. He wasn't scared of nobody and didn't avoid necessary confrontations. The more Mack tried to talk some sense into Charlie, and tell him the whole town was talking about him, the deeper he dug in the relationship. The whole thing almost ended their friendship one time so Mack didn't bring it up no more.

Sure the sex was great but Charlie was a grown man who had great sex before so he couldn't figure the whole thing out himself. He tried to break up with her once or twice, maybe three times, but he always fell sick with fever. Now, Charlie was a healthy man. He figured he was heartsick for the bitch which was proved when his fever vanished when they got back together. Couldn't live with her, got sick without her. Then one day he announced he was going to marry the woman.

His family and friends thought he was crazy but had learned by this time not to say anything against her. A wedding was planned with Mack as best man and that, as they say, was that. Everybody waited for the day of doom to culminate in a week.

Then, one day, Charlie went to dig some bait in his favorite spot. No one, not even his best friend Mack, knew where he dug those thick, special worms guaranteed to catch bass. It was a secret. So naturally Charlie was surprised to see the HooDoo Woman standing right on the spot where he planned to dig. The HooDoo Woman walked up to Charlie and rubbed her hand on the back of his neck.

"Somebody put a fix on you," she said without greeting. "Somebody put a fix on you."

She told Charlie that if he chased away some kids that was coming up to her window making fun of her, and gave her a dollar, she'd remove the curse. Charlie thought the woman was crazy but he knew that gang she was talking about and thought somebody should stop them from messing with an old lady. He left the bait spot and followed her to The Joint and told the gang of teenagers that if they fucked with her again he'd shoot 'em in the leg. He wasn't really gonna do that but Charlie had a reputation so they apologized to the woman and left her alone. Money was tight but Charlie figured if a crazy old lady out in the woods by herself needed a dollar then who was he to deny her. He reasoned the Lord would supply his needs and forgot all about it.

That night, Charlie woke up at two-thirty in the morning with a raging hard dick. He hadn't had one like that since he knew what a dick was for. Dick hard as diamond. So hard it hurt. Damn thing just wouldn't go down. He even put cold water on it but that made it harder. He decided the only thing he could do was to abuse himself so he could get back to sleep. He did just that and busted a nut that went clean up to the ceiling. He couldn't even shoot that far when he was a boy. Then he passed out and slept like he hadn't slept in months. He had a dream about a dead fish floating down the river. The fish banked on the river's edge and his secret worms ate it from the inside out.

When he woke up at his regular time, with a regular erection, he realized he had no love for the woman whatsoever. He rushed over to her place in his boots and long johns to tell her so. She just assumed Charlie was in one of his moods and thought she could seduce him since she could see through his long johns he had a regular erection and all. But that didn't work. Then she cussed him out and said all manner of hurtful things about him and his family. But that didn't hurt.

Charlie told the bitch the wedding was off and if she tried to make up with him he'd shoot her in the leg. He walked away with his hard dick bouncing and was never sick another day in his life.

Now that's a miracle. Mack knew that for sure. And Charlie wasn't no liar and Charlie wasn't no fool. So that's why the HooDoo Woman was there.

She had Luke and Mack clear a space in the center of the room and place Benny on the floor. Benny was as good as dead but not good enough. He was swollen all over now and not just on the snake bites. She adjusted his stiff limbs so he was spread eagle and told them to think about the reasons he should live. Then she went to boiling juniper in a kettle. The baby Jesus was hid under a juniper tree when an angel warned Joseph to stay away from Egypt since Herod would try to kill the child. Now juniper was good for warding off evil spirits. Least, that's what folks said.

Mack thought long and hard about how it was just plain wrong for someone as young as Benny to die. Luke thought about how he and Benny would race through the fields in spring, how they were best friends, and how good a guitar player Benny was. He got Bertha out of the corner and placed her on Benny's chest.

"You don't have to do that," the HooDoo Woman said.

"Yes, I do."

"Boy, why you got to know everything? Listen to what the woman saying."

"That's all right," the HooDoo Woman said. "That's all right. Leave it be."

"You think it's my fault, don't you? You been itching to say that all night so just say it!"

"You better watch your tone with me, boy."

"I *said* leave it be!" The HooDoo Woman gave them both the spooks and the last thing they wanted to do was piss her off. She lit four candles and put them in a circle; North, South, East, and West, around her patient. She spread salt around the room and lit a wad of frankincense. Frankincense was good for warding off evil too since it was a gift to the baby Jesus. Salt was good for keeping away witches but that didn't include the HooDoo Woman. Besides, everybody except Sarah and church folks knew that hoodoo wasn't witchcraft. It was hoodoo.

She pried Benny's mouth open and took a deep swallow of juniper water. Then she gargled and spit it down Benny's throat. She told Luke and Mack to hold hands and the hoot owl began to sing. Luke and Mack hesitated and then held hands without looking at each other. She knelt down and gripped Benny's pus filled side while she reached her other hand skyward. She chanted in a mumble and Luke concentrated to understand her. Then, he swore to God, he heard her say:

"Get back from me. Whatever you are, get back from me. As east is to west, as worst is to best, we are passing this test. Get back from me."

Luke didn't allow himself to consider the implications of that and just kept on thinking good thoughts. The HooDoo Woman kept chanting for a good thirty minutes. Benny sweated and she kept on.

"As wet is to dry, as laugh is to cry, as live is to die, get back from me."

The song took on an ancient African tone in her mouth. Something that was part of the earth alone. Luke couldn't figure out if she stole the song from Rastus or if he stole it from her. Then he decided the song belonged to no one but itself. Humans could borrow it as long as they gave it back.

Now Benny began to shake. The hoot owl got excited just as Sarah and Maddie walked in the door. The men looked up but the HooDoo Woman ignored the intrusion. Sarah looked at her stuff pushed up against the walls, and her men clutching their hands, like some kinda voodoo warriors, and promised herself to have Deacon Early arrange an exorcism just as soon as this mess was over. Maddie shrank to the floor, right there in the open doorway, and cried.

Sarah couldn't stand women who cried at the drop of a hat. She accepted the fact that women have to be stronger than men because a man was always gonna fuck something up. How could we be here for our babies after our men fuck up if we go around crying all the time? Sarah despised weakness more in a woman than she did in a man.

She looked at her man, Mack. He was a good man who hadn't fucked up yet. Maybe he wouldn't. Who knows? Mack treated her right and loved her right. He was the undisputed head of the house but didn't treat her like property. Sarah decided that if it was all the power of the mind, like the well read Deacon Early said, then they would need all the help they could get. Mack smiled at her a little and she went to join her men in their pagan circle. The HooDoo Woman glanced her way but Sarah avoided her eyes. Maddie got up off the floor and attempted to join them but:

"Not you," said the HooDoo."This is a circle of love." Maddie's jaw's got tight but not even she was crazy enough to cuss out a hoodoo. Sarah wondered how the woman could speak on such things before reminding herself that Maddie's treatment of Benny was common knowledge. She decided to just concentrate on the healing. The hour was late now and either this thing was going to work or it wasn't.

The HooDoo Woman stood up after while and went to get the boiling juniper water off the fire. She stood over Benny's body, raised the pot over her head, and poured the scalding liquid on his side.

"Stop it!" Sarah said. She lunged at the woman and Mack pulled her back.

"You crazy? What you doing?" Luke said.

"Sometime a person need a shock to live. Put him back in bed. He be fine now," said the HooDoo. She gathered up her things.

"Get out of my house, devil. Get out!" Sarah said. The Hoodoo sat herself down at the table next to Maddie and waited. A few seconds later, Maddie got up and found something to do at the fire.

"I said get out."

"I ain't going nowhere 'till I get my payment."

"Your what?"

"Doctors get a salary. Preachers get tithes. I ain't no different. I want my pee-cans and my dollar." Sarah looked to Mack for clarification. He cleared his throat and began.

"I told her you'd pick her fifty pounds of pee-cans and we'd give her a dollar if she helped."

"Nigger, you out your damn mind? I ain't picking no pecans for this demon."

"You watch your tone with me, woman."

"I'll pick 'em," Luke said. The room was quiet. The HooDoo Woman raised herself up and looked at Luke.

"Don't cheat me. It wouldn't be good if you cheated me."

"Bitch, don't you threaten my baby."

"Shut up, Sarah. He ain't gonna cheat you, ma'am. He'll pick 'em for you day after tomorrow."

"Pick 'em tomorrow. Y'all ain't gonna be here that long." How did she know about Boss Man Braxton? Then Sarah reminded herself that this was a small town and people talk. "Now what about my dollar?"

"We ain't got no money, Mack, why'd you tell her that?" Mack turned away and shrugged his shoulders. Sarah sighed as she realized that Mack was fucking up. She wasn't afraid of no hoodoo but she didn't relish the idea of cheating or owing nobody. Then, Maddie reached into her bloomers and pulled out a pint of store-bought bourbon.

"It's all I got," Maddie said.

"Then it's worth so much more," the HooDoo said. Maddie gave her the bottle. The HooDoo took a sweet sip and seemed normal for a second. "Our business is concluded. I'll be waiting on my pee-cans, Luke." He nodded and tried to remember if he ever told her his name.

The HooDoo Woman left the shack while the hoot owl provided exit music. Maddie broke down again but this time Sarah didn't judge her for it. She hugged her friend and got ready to fix her some food.

"That was a good thing you did, Maddie, a good and selfless thing. God gonna bless you for it too. Now you just hush up that crying and I'm gonna fix you something to eat. Luke, wash that devil spice out my pot real good so I can fix Maddie something." Luke got the pot and ran out of the house to the creek to hide fresh tears that were coming. Mack picked up Benny and plopped him down on the bed.

"Well, I done all I could," Mack said. He let out a grunt.

"We all have, Mack," Sarah said. She banged a pot. Mack decided to get out of the house before he hauled off and slugged his wife or something.

"I'm going to The Joint. I'll be back when I get back."

"How you going to The Joint if you ain't even got a dollar?" Sarah said. Maddie reached into her utility bloomers and ripped out a dollar.

"Thanks for everything, Mack. You a good man. Go have yourself a drink." Mack took the dollar by the corner, nodded at Maddie, and left.

"Well, ain't you full of surprises," Sarah said. Maddie giggled and rested her cheeks in her hands like a little girl. Sarah thought it best Mack was out of the house since it had been a hard day all the way round. She decided to think about Braxton tomorrow and prayed they could make it through the night without a visit from the Klan. She hoped her appeal to Mrs. Braxton would work. Mack done pulled a gun on a white man. Lord have mercy.

She thought about Mack going to Ho Row but reasoned he couldn't get too much tail with a dollar. *If he's that easy to lose, I probably shouldn't want him.* Another thing not to think about right this moment. She decided to dress Benny's burns before she started Maddie's dinner. Crazy old woman. Benny was in the hands of the Lord now. Then, Sarah screamed when she examined his side. There was no burn, no swelling, no fang marks, no nothing. Benny was fast asleep with a smile on his face.

11

Rastus decided to do a benefit for the local colored school. He told little Benny he could play along with him if he was good enough by show time. That would be in about two months and Benny had been practicing under Rastus's tutelage for just over a year.

The routine was always the same. Rastus would roll into town with great fanfare to do his gig at Deacon Early's joint. Then he took up with one of the gals after he paid on his tab to The Pimp. After he got his fill on Ho Row, Benny and Luke brought him up his barbecue and liquor. Sometimes he'd let them take a sip depending on what kind of a mood he was in.

"Don't you tell your daddy I did this, boy," he said to Luke.

"I'm glad I ain't got no daddy to tell me what to do," Benny said.

"Shut up," Luke said.

"You shut up."

"Both a y'all shut up or get out. This ain't no goddamn nursery. Luke, you better not tell your mama I cussed at you."

"I'm glad I ain't got no mama to — "

"Benny, shut the fuck up! If I wanted to listen to fussing kids, I'd go home." Benny plopped down on the bed face first in a pout. He jerked his head back up with a scrunched-up nose.

"These sheets stank," he said.

"Them sheets don't stank nothing," Rastus said with a full mouth of ribs.

"Yes, they do too. Luke, smell this." Luke buried his head into the bed and took a deep whiff.

"Pee yew, something died in your bed Rastus," Luke said. He and Benny laughed and pointed their fingers at Rastus. They repeated 'Stanky sheet, stanky sheet, smell like shit stuck to your feet' until Rastus got tired of hearing it.

"I thought y'all was men," he said after they collapsed in laughter from the umpteenth verse.

"I *am* a man, nigger, I'm nine," Benny said.

"I'm a man, too. Been working in the fields since I was five. If that ain't a man, you tell me what is," Luke said.

"A man somebody know what pussy smell like," Rastus said. He grabbed the sheet in his sauce covered fingers and mashed it into his nose, smelling it like it was the most beautiful bouquet in captivity.

"Ahh. Smell like a rose and taste like chicken. Hey, I think I'm gonna write that down. Luke, fetch my paper." Luke went over to Rastus's bag and dug out his scratching pad and a nubby, chewed-up pencil. Benny laid his head down on Rastus's lap, who used his back as a desk, and everybody was content to be quiet for a while. After about twenty minutes of that, Rastus handed the paper to Benny. "What 'cha think of that, boy," the proud Rastus said. "This my masterpiece for sure." Benny waved the paper out his face.

"When we gonna start my lessons?" he said.

"Why, you hateful little bastard. Here I go to all the trouble to write you a epic and all you can do is sit up here and think about yourself." Luke rolled over to take a nap. Rastus and Benny were about to get into one of their squabbles again.

"Man, I don't feel like waiting on you to get drunk before we starts. I got chores to do."

"Like your lazy ass ever do what Maddie tells you anyway."

"Oh, yeah. She asked about you again. Might come up here to see a show. You gonna marry her and be my uncle?" Benny laughed and poked Luke who giggled along.

"Shit. You keep thinking that. Only way I'd fuck that bitch is if God blackmailed me." They all laughed and one of the working gals opened the door on the party. Luke recognized her as the woman who got cut trying to save them from The Pimp.

"It's time for your freebie, Rastus," she said. She was eighteen years old, or so she said, and Rastus never had the heart to call her a lie. She was black as night and tight all over with four handfuls of top and six hands of bottom. Her hair was always hot-combed no matter what time of the day or night it was. She was completed with bright white bright teeth and a skinny waist. The boys were virgins but after hanging out at The Joint they knew what hos were and what they were for. Luke lived in a shack with two young parents and wasn't always asleep when they thought he was. Maddie had visitors and Benny had ears. Older children talked and they were surrounded by animals so they wasn't exactly stupid, for crying out loud.

"Aw, shit," Benny said. "I ain't never gonna get my lessons now."

"You boys run off and find something to do. I'll start your lessons in a couple of hours, Benny. Bye."

Six hours later, Benny's lessons began. Luke took off because it was getting late and not even Rastus could save him from disobeying his folks again.

Rastus took Benny to an open field where cows fed on hay and the sun relaxed into the horizon. There was nobody around and that suited them fine. The lesson plan consisted of Benny doing Rastus's songs. Some were famous, some he was working on, and some were just for him. He taught the boy how to hold a guitar proper and drilled him on riffs until his fingers bled. They'd take a break and Rastus would soak Benny's fingers in the stream. Then he'd hold the boy's fingers between his big, soothing hands with a blue kerchief until the bleeding stopped.

Benny wasn't used to anybody tending to him and he liked it. Maddie's crazy ass would pour gin on a scraped knee and tell the boy to walk it off. Rastus took time to make sure the child was okay and Benny appreciated the difference. Sometimes Benny would cry from the pain of the drills. However, Rastus preferred real emotion over sentiment and didn't go all wobbly over a child's tears.

"You wanted this, remember? Now play. The blues ain't nothing but blood and tears so you doing just fine. Now play, goddamit, play!" Then he rolled himself a reefer and listened to the boy's technique. Rastus would be gone for a month straight, sometimes two. So it was imperative that Benny practiced daily when Rastus wasn't around so they wouldn't waste time going over old ground.

He always did.

Benny came to the conclusion of Rastus's early hit, "I Can't Wait Till Payday Come," and waited for critique. Rastus took a deep toke, held it, and released it through his nose. Then, he offered Benny the reefer. Benny took it, inhaled, and near 'bout coughed his lungs out. The cows mooed in complaint and Rastus laughed while patting his pupil on the back.

"Boy, it pains me to say it, but you just as good as I was at your age. Maybe a little bit better. But just a little bit, mind you."

Benny grinned and dropped his head the way he did when he did when he was avoiding dealing with something heavy.

"You know what, Rastus?"

"What?"

"If Luke wasn't my best friend, you could have the job." Rastus took a long toke and put his arm around Benny.

"You know what, Benny?"

"What?"

"If I didn't go broke supporting fourteen hundred chillun, I'd be happy to make you fourteen hundred and one." Benny rested his head against Rastus and they watched the sun get a little bit sleepier. "You coming along good. Real good. Now let me show you a trick. Go on over to that far post over there and sing that sad song I taught you."

"Why I got to go way over there?"

"Nigger, don't question me. Who the star round here? Get your black ass over there 'fore I spit on you or something." Benny took another hit off the reefer and grumbled about how stupid it all was as he left. He stepped in some cow shit, cussed, and kept on traveling the ninety feet to the post while Rastus laughed. He climbed on up, and got his guitar into position, then cranked out the sad song.

"Not so loud," Rastus said from across the field. One of the cows mooed at all the noise and Rastus hit it in the head with a rock. "You better shut 'fore I eat your ass, cow."

"What?" Benny shouted.

"I ain't talking to you. Start again. Lower." Benny sung a few bars before Rastus interrupted. "Lower." This happened about eight or nine times before Benny could continue without incident. "I can't hear you," Rastus said. Benny lost it. He cussed up a storm of old cuss words and new ones he learned at The Joint. He hollered about how stupid this was, how mean Rastus was, and how hungry he was.

"Lower," said Rastus. Benny sat there and huffed in anger before hopping down on the ground. "Get your black ass back on that post 'fore I hit you in the head with a rock." Benny climbed back up and complained about the futility of it all when it hit him: Rastus wasn't shouting but he could hear everything he said.

"Hey! How come you don't have to shout when you talk and I can hear what you be saying from over there?"

"A few reasons," Rastus said. The sun was just about in bed causing Rastus and the cows to look like silhouettes to Benny. "For one thing, I'm aiming at you with my voice and squeezing my belly when I talk. For another, sound bounce off this ground and these trees so I don't have to do all the work. And most importantly, I really mean what the fuck I'm saying."

Benny pondered that for a while and the cow mooed again.

"Don't you hear that cow just fine? But he ain't mooing his melody like he crazy is he? Don't try too hard. Make ya look weak."

After while Benny said, "I don't like sad songs, Rastus."

"I noticed that about you, Benny. You get into the songs about women and partying real natural like. But you bullshit your way though them sad numbers. You can't be no blues man if you don't like sad songs. Just remember, when somebody else hear them songs, and think about how fucked up they own life is, it actually make 'em feel better when you sang. It's funny, I know, but you kinda providing a service, boy, like a doctor or a hoodoo man. No sir, you can't be running way from no sad song if you gonna be a blues man. No sirree."

"But what if they make *me* feel sad?"

"So what? What if it do? You'll get over it. Don't nothing make a gal hotter than for her to see you really know what you talking 'bout on that stage. Don't nothing get the crowd in your corner more. Don't you think Ma Rainey really mean what the fuck she be saying?

"Yeah."

"Don't make you lose respect for her, do it?"

"Nope."

"Well, all right then. Now talk to me, boy."

Benny kept everything in mind. He took deep breaths and squoze his belly when he sang. He didn't try too hard because he didn't want to look weak. Especially not in front of Rastus. He aimed the sound like a gun and let God's amphitheatre do the work. And he really meant what he was saying. The song was about the man who went away. And Rastus heard every word right before Benny broke down and cried.

Rastus took his time walking the ninety feet and the boy's crying gave way to wails. Rastus finished his second reefer before he scooped Benny off the post and took the guitar in hand. Benny hid his face in Rastus's shoulder and couldn't stop his tears while he was carried up the dirt road leading back to The Joint.

"You gonna be a big ole star one day, boy. Bigger than me. Bigger than everybody."

The sun was now asleep.

12

"**R**un, Luke, Run!" Mary said. She was five feet eight with a good, strong body and the face of a starlet. But to everybody in Braxton she was just good ole Mary.

"You gonna make somebody a good wife someday," Mack said.

"Now, Mack, let's stay out of the girl's business," Sarah said. She silenced him with another sandwich from the picnic basket.

"Another, pig ear sandwich, Mary? They got a special sauce. They're Luke's favorites. I could show you how to make them." Mack rolled his eyes at that one. Sarah caught him and stuck out her tongue. Mary was one of those girls who wasn't scared of eating and accepted the sandwich with gusto.

"Mmm, delicious, Ms. Martin. I sure would love your reci… run, Luke, Run!" Maddie came up and plopped down on the blanket spread out in the field without invitation.

"Hey, folkses! How y'all doing? Ooh, pig ear samiches." She tore into one and smacked with her mouth open. "Damn, this good! Mmm, 'scuse me. I sure wish I could… Benny, don't you let that nigger catch you!" Sarah looked at Mack in dread. He chuckled and pulled her closer to him as they settled back and watched the baseball game.

Benny almost got tagged out stealing second but Red couldn't catch him. The Big Man and Red had an argument about how Red should have thrown the ball instead of running it. But Red had to prove he was faster than Benny.

It had been almost four weeks since Benny was healed. He helped Luke pick the pecans and played the HooDoo Woman a song when they dropped them off. The HooDoo applauded with true appreciation and munched on her reward. Luke invited her to the game but she said she didn't mix well with town folk and that was that.

"You should be playing a song for Jesus," Sarah complained when they were leaving for the game. "He was the one who really saved you."

"Aw, hell, Ms. Sarah, where was Jesus when them snakes was biting my ass up?"

"Benny!" Sarah said.

"Nigger, don't cuss round my mama. You out your goddamn mind?"

"Luke!" Mack said.

"Benny, I'm ashamed of you," Sarah continued. "In the bible, Job lost all his children at once. He was stricken with illness and lost all his wealth. And he still refused to cuss God to his face."

"Yeah, well. Did he ever get bit up by a whole bunch of snakes?"

"Luke laughed, Mack tried not to, and they all headed off to the game. Luke gave the town folk attitude when they reached the baseball field so they were all uneasy around him. He hated these back wood niggers and couldn't wait to get away from them. Someday. Somehow.

Benny got a hero's welcome, though. The men lifted him up on their shoulders and carried him around. Luke told Benny everything so he knew they were full of shit. But Benny loved attention so he let them soothe their guilt by idolizing him. He made plans to sleep with some of their wives and decided to let sleeping dogs lie. Not Luke, though. Nope. Not Luke. Luke could carry a grudge longer than a woman with child. Then he could nurse that grudge and watch it grow.

It wasn't just the snake attack but everything about his so-called neighbors. Luke had ignored little comments when he was a child but now he was a man and didn't feel like pretending not to notice things. Even though most of the coloreds in Braxton were poor, the Martins always seemed to get along a bit better than other folks because of the way they managed themselves. Yeah, the Martins were broke sharecroppers like everybody else, but Sarah made it her business to make her talents visible. She developed her sewing skills and got Luke to read her books about dressmaking that Mack got from the Salvation Army. Sarah let it be known to Mrs. Braxton that she could do something to a dress besides just hem it. One day, Mrs. Braxton gave a worn out dress to Sarah because she liked the way she handled herself.

"You're not always gabbing instead of working like your friends," Mrs. Braxton said. Oh, hell, but niggers talked about that one for a while. Never mind that Sarah really did work more than talk. She had been complimented by a cracker at their expense. So they pretended not to hear her when she spoke for a few days. But what really got them talking was when Sarah brought that dress back to Mrs. Braxton, looking good as new, with scraps of material she saved over the years. Only her natural determination and Luke's disinterested reading from those dress books had been her help. Mrs. Braxton couldn't believe it.

"Well, I declare, Sarah, what can't you do?"

Oh, child, niggers hated that. And they really had rocks in their jaws when Mrs. Braxton got her white friends to send their mending to Mrs. Martin. Sarah and her family were still as poor as everybody else but maybe their credit had been extended sometimes, or maybe the missus convinced Braxton to drop a debt here, or maybe they got a few leftovers from a holiday table, or maybe Mrs. Braxton found things for Sarah to do in the house on a hot day. Now, Sarah was way too black with hands way too rough to be called a house nigger and didn't have to prove her work ethic to nobody. Still, these things added up over time and, like they say: A nigger likes to see you do well as long as you ain't doing better than him. Luke picked it up, over the years, that the same women who smiled in his face were the same ones who resented his mother. Sarah was indifferent.

"I ain't stopping nobody from learning how to sew," she said as she went on 'bout her business.

Then there was Mack. Mack was the type of man everybody respected but there was a catch. Respecting Mack meant admitting he had qualities they didn't possess. So he could only be admired with a penalty. One day, the men were all talking on the steps of the general store.

"Mack done put his foot in it this time," Ace Simmons said. Everybody but Charlie chimed in on the subject. "Pulling a gun on a white man like that. Shit. He think he the only nigger in the world who care about his children or something? You lucky you was just driving, Charlie, and Braxton don't hold you responsible. This time." Ace laughed but Charlie didn't. "You getting mixed up in that union Mack be talking about, Charlie?"

"I'm thinking 'bout it. A union guarantees a man's rights."

"Uh-huh. The right to die."

"Yeah, I like ole Mack," this yella fella named Grady said, "But pride goeth before the lynching." He laughed and took a sip of Pepsi Cola.

"You ever noticed how Mack be acting too holy to go on Ho Row. Hell, we *all* married," Ace said. He laid the checkerboard out on a barrel. "Nothing wrong with a man enjoying himself after a hard day in the field, is it?"

"Where Mack get that watch from? That real gold?" Grady said.

"Now, nigger, you know damn well that ain't real gold. You think Braxton gonna give him a real gold watch?"

"Mrs. Braxton gave it to Sarah for fucking around with them clothes," Red said. "I be seeing Luke with it now. You know they always taking the Braxton's leftovers." The men grunted in agreement and Charlie got up to leave.

"Ain't nothing wrong with a little pussy on the side. Hell, I go to church too," Ace said. "And Sarah think she know everything 'bout the bible."

"You ever read it?" Charlie said. Silence.

"Nigger, you know I can't read," Ace said. He spread the red checkers out. "But Deacon Early say man is put here to have dominion over the earth. Don't that mean hos? Shit. Mary Magdelene was a ho from the way I heard it."

"They done spoiled that boy. That's the problem." Grady said. "Remember how Mack used to take that boy to the movies every weekend?" He spread the black checkers out. "Niggers ain't got no money for no movies. That's white folk shit."

"The Bijou mostly play race pictures," Charlie said. "You know.

Pictures with a all-colored cast?" They took a moment to let that sink in.

"Well, it's still white folk shit," Ace said.

"How the fuck it gonna be white folk shit when there ain't nothing but niggers on the screen?" Charlie said. The other men on the porch looked away. The subject was dropped since everyone was beginning to get it that Charlie was the wrong one to talk about this around. Mack was confused when Charlie didn't invite the other fellas to the fishing hole anymore but just figured they must have had a fight about something.

And then there was Luke. The one who was special but nobody knew why. The one who was good with words so maybe he would be a senator or something.

"Aw, please. You ever hear of a nigger senator?" Ace said after Charlie left. Somebody was sure they had heard of one from Mississippi but no one could remember his name. Luke was good at taking charge, so maybe he would be a overseer or something.

"Shit, I wish a nigger would try to tell me what to do," Red said. "He ain't no better than me. How come I can't be foreman? Huh?" Luke had a special way of looking at the world so maybe he would be a preacher or something.

"A preacher? After all the hos him and Benny done had? Shit. That nigger can't tell me nothing 'bout Jesus," Grady said. Luke, like his daddy, commanded something people respected and like his daddy was resented for it. But Luke was odd. Strange. Some other quality that wasn't adding up.

"The nigger touched," Red said.

But Mary didn't think Luke was crazy and wasn't threatened by his ideas of the world. Instead, she was inspired and entertained by them. She completely saw the logic in the sun being over here instead of over there. She didn't know why. Who cared why? Certainly not Mary.

She never joined in on backbiting about the Martins. She would see how the gossips smiled in Sarah's face and it made her sick. Mary hated two-faced niggers more than Jesus did.

Her faith in Luke's mental faculties were proved just last week when she fell in the creek on an errand for Mrs. Braxton. Mary was balancing a basket of laundered clothes on her head and walking on stones forming a dotted bridge across the creek. A fish startled her and down she went into the creek while the laundry floated away. She screamed from the shock of cold water and scrambled in her wet, heavy dress to chase after the wash. And down she went again. Then, she heard somebody call her name and turned around to see Luke rolling on the grass in laughter.

Luke paused in his chuckles long enough to notice how the water sealed the dress around Mary's firm body.

"Help me, fool!" she said. Luke ran down the bank far ahead of Mrs. Braxton's bloomers. "Luke, don't you leave me! I'm gonna tell your mama on you!" However, Luke wasn't leaving but executing a plan. He picked up a long stick he knew to be by a tree a few feet down because, even at that age, he and Benny would use these sticks for playing at sword fights like Zorro. Folks said Luke and Benny should start acting like men now that they were twenty-something but they never gave a damn about how folks thought they should be. Luke picked up his sword and used it as a fishing rod to catch all the clothes. He progressed to plop them all in a soggy pile on the ground.

"Not like that," Mary said. She shivered in her wet dress and waddled in his direction. "You gonna get 'em all dirty again." She scooped the mess into her basket and sat on a stump all forlorn. Luke laughed without guilt since he had done his bit to help her and it wasn't his problem. That dress sure was fitting right, though. Little Miss Mary sure has grown. She had it with Luke's mocking and snatched the stick away from him and whacked him on the behind with it.

"Gal, you crazy?"

"Don't call me gal," she said. She swung, Luke dodged, somersaulted, and came back up with a new stick that he held like a sword. Mary was bored. "Did it take all that?" she said. Luke just assumed she was pretending not to be impressed and ignored her cynicism.

"Have at thee," he said on guard.

"Have what? Boy, I ain't playing with you now. I got to — "

"Have at thee, strumpet!" Mary didn't know what a strumpet was but she knew she didn't like it. So she decided to do something about that. Although she had never seen Zorro, she had seen picture books with sword fights in them. She was the only child in her family who used to get schooling on a regular basis since all the men-children stayed out to work the fields.

She extended her stick into a sword and stretched her free hand behind her and up at an angle. Sunlight warmed her chilled bones and the dress clung to her breast as she spread her back leg out behind her like a track star and bent her front leg forward like a... like a swordsman.

Luke was through. Never had he seen such technique from anyone other than himself. Benny couldn't be bothered to get all the details right and resisted Luke's constant direction.

"Hey, you look like you know what you doing. A whole lot better than you was doing in that creek." He cracked into fresh laughter and Mary's amazon spirit was ignited by male ridicule.

"Have at thee," she roared and took a vicious stab at Luke.

"Whoa, now!" He barley dodged that one in time. He parried her attack and struck her at her four o'clock position. She met his telegraphed thrust with ease and struck him hard at one o'clock. He spun and made all kinds of swashbuckling sounds he heard Fairbanks, and sundry other white boys, make in the movies.

"Aha! Ho Ho! Arrgh, foul villain!"

"Shut up and fight!" She circled her sword above her head with a jungle yell and struck six, five, and two o'clock right after the other. Almost got him that time. Luke was forced back toward the creek. This was the first time Luke played with somebody who really wanted to hurt him. He had to take the offensive. No way in hell was the black Douglas Fairbanks gonna lose to a girl. However, this was a girl who grew up in a family of eight brothers. And being underestimated is a wonderful weapon.

Luke swung wild at her head. She ducked and threw him off balance.

"Wait!" he said.

"Have at thee, foul bastard!" She gave him a simple push and down he went into the creek. It was her turn to laugh and she did so with glee. "Let's play it again," Mary said. Luke stretched back in the creek and let the water wash over him with a pretty girl's laughter in the background. This was the way things should be.

Mary studied Luke for a while. She was enchanted and jealous at his ease with the elements. She was all right just watching him before she remembered this game was the result of her tragedy.

"Oh Lord. Help me, Luke." She ran to air out the lumpy mass of clothes. Luke forced himself out of the perfect bed of water and watched Mary spread out Mrs. Braxton's bloomers on a pine branch. He picked up a pair but she slapped his hand.

"Well, you told me to help."

"Not with that. That's all we need is Boss Man Braxton happening upon a colored man handling his wife's underclothes."

"Well, word on the street is he wouldn't recognize them." Mary laughed and gave Luke the corners of a blanket. They smiled at each other while they wrung out the cloth.

"You sure can sword fight for a woman."

"And you lose like a man." Luke liked Mary. There was something about her that separated her from the gals he was used to relieving himself on. He tried to touch her down there one time, when they was kids, but she socked him in the eye. It swoll up real big and he told his daddy Benny did it. They flapped the blanket up and down to air it out.

"Let's make a parachute!" Luke said.

"What?"

"Come on!" Luke climbed up on the Old Crook Tree. The Old Crook Tree got caught up in some barbed wire when it was a stripling. But instead of dying, the Old Crook Tree just kept on growing up, and around, and between that wire. That was sixty or so odd years ago. One day, Braxton took the barbed wire down when he expanded his land past the creek. By that time, the Old Crook tree had a fat trunk that went up, made a sharp turn, then straight up again. It formed a perfect "L" shape. It was as big and normal as any other pine in the forest outside of that. It was everybody's favorite tree since it was easy climbing for young and old. Some newspaper folks came and took a picture of it one time.

Mary watched Luke climb onto the Old Crook Tree, with his corner of blanket, and just kinda got pulled along when she started thinking about the folly of her position. Here she is done dropped all this white woman's clothes, got work to do, and wet to the bone. Instead of picking up this white woman's clothes, getting back to work, and drying herself off, she out her gallivanting in the woods with a grown man, who might be touched, playing swords and parachutes. Yeah, that's what she started to think. But then, Luke pulled her along into his world where chores and bosses didn't exist.

"I don't know what I'm gonna tell Mrs. Braxton," Mary said. She hopped the "L" and up a high branch.

"Tell her you fell."

"That won't help. That'll make it worse."

"Tell her some Klansmen rode by and stole all the sheets. You tried to fight them off but all you had was a sword." Mary laughed. "Then, one of them Ku Klucks chased you up a tree. And the only way you escaped was by parachute. Jump!" She screamed and they jumped off the limb together. The blanket puffed out just like a real parachute. It didn't hold, of course, but it was good for a quick thrill on the way back to earth.

They landed on their rumps and giggled in the grass. Luke thought about how he's not used to laughing like this with anybody besides Benny.

"Well, that didn't help," Mary said. She took a halfhearted swipe at the dirty blanket. "But that's Okay. I'll think of something."

"I gave you something," Luke said. Mary laughed yet again. Luke wasn't used to hearing a gal laugh so much without it getting on his nerves.

"No offense, Mr. Martin, but I don't think they'd buy it. It was sweet, though." Luke rolled his eyes.

"Sweet?"

"I mean it was good. You know. Great. You got a wonderful imagination, Luke." He was stunned. Nobody ever told him that before and he didn't know how to take it. He wasn't touched. His head wasn't in the clouds. He wasn't kinda peculiar. He had a... wonderful imagination.

"Thank you," he said. "Thank you very much." Mary saw Luke getting big down there but this time she didn't sock him in the eye. As the sun reached it's zenith, and the creek eased by, they decided it was a good time to dry their clothes.

So anyway, that's what she was doing at the game.

The bases were loaded with Benny safe at second and Luke a hugging third. Charlie squatted at first base and Deacon Early was up at bat. Mack would've played but was content to sit with his wife and the food on account of his bad knee. Sarah watched Maddie down a third pig ear sandwich and fought the temptation to say something cute. She was Christian, after all, and Jesus said something 'bout how you got to be nice to motherfuckers you can't stand since it ain't no trick being nice to somebody you like.

Sarah observed with pride that Mary couldn't keep her eyes off Luke so that helped dull the pain. Deacon Early tested his swing when The Pimp, who was pitching, let a sizzler fly over home base.

"Strike one!" the Umpire said. Folks rose like smoke in protest of the call.

"Nigger, you blind?" the Big Man said. "Deacon wasn't even ready!"

"Can't a man warm up?" hacked the Old Man across the field. Deacon Early raised his hand to calm the crowd. They were eased by his confidence and the game went on. The Pimp frowned at the working gal, who served as the catcher, and ignored her signal. Benny nodded for Luke to get ready to run since he was about to steal third. This didn't go unnoticed by Red.

The Pimp wound up her arm like a wind mill and let that go on a bit too long before the crowd laughed at her. This time the Deacon was ready and the Pimp let it fly. The crowd was astounded.

"Strike two," the Umpire said. The field was silent except for the Deacon's chuckle of nervous bravado and cheers from the team of working gals.

Charlie was standing off first base, and without warning, The Pimp spun around and threw that ball like a bullet from outer space. Red wasn't ready for such power and ducked. Half the crowd cussed and half of 'em laughed when Red ran after the ball that tore through the grass. Charlie took off toward second while

Benny raced for third and Luke headed home. Red caught up with the ball while The Pimp yelled all manner of embarrassing things about his manhood and general appearance. Charlie couldn't run as fast as he use to since his new woman fed him better. The prospects of success weren't bright as he huffed on home.

"Run, Charlie, run!" Mack said. He jumped up and down with a sandwich in hand and everybody joined him. Luke was bent over on the batter's bench sucking air. He looked over to see if Mary was enjoying the game and saw her watching him instead. He kinda smiled at that. Benny made it home and did his best to encourage poor Charlie.

"Run, you fat fucker! Run!"

Red threw a curve to The Pimp with desperate speed just as Charlie was rounding third. The Pimp drew her arm back and let it whip. The ball flew to the catcher like a bird. Just then, Charlie recalled his youth and went for the slide. Meanwhile, Deacon Early, who was still in shock because he never had two strikes before, was just standing there in the way. Charlie's slide created a dusty cloud of confusion and the baseball entered around the same time. Some folks said they heard a thump. Some said they heard a crunch. However, there was no argument over what they heard next:

"Sweet motherfucking Jesus!" the Deacon said. The crowd gasped as the dust cleared. Deacon Early was balled up on home plate clutching his ankle with Charlie parked on top of him.

"Safe!" the Umpire said. The working gal said something about cheating and threw the ball back to the seething Pimp. Charlie hefted himself off the Deacon and tried to help him up.

"Don't touch it, you dumb motherfucker! Shit! Jesus fucking Christ, take this Goddamn pain away! Motherfucking Moses!" Folks looked at each other sideways while the Deacon continued his colorful marriage of the holy and profane. He kept holding his ankle and rolled face down on home while snot, slob, and tears watered the dirt. Then he just kind of laid there and moaned. Folks didn't quite know what to do next. As usual, when things got quiet and uncomfortable, Benny decided to say something helpful.

"You dumb ass dike. You did that shit on purpose!" The Pimp whipped out her blade and mothers hollered.

"You must like being laid up," she said. Benny picked up the bat and waved it in the air.

"You must like getting your head beat in." She let loose a pitch and the knife thunked in the bat with an accurate danger. It wiggled there a while as folks looked on in dismay.

"Strike one," said The Pimp. Benny closed his wide open mouth, dropped the bat, and charged her. But he tripped over poor Deacon Early on his way.

"Holy goddamn God!" screamed the Deacon. A few folks laughed and others mumbled something about not going to that church no more. But that was just talk since it was the only colored church for miles so where else was they gonna go? Luke ran to help Charlie hold Benny back from attacking the laughing Pimp. That ole Pimp was throwing the ball up and down like she hadn't a care in the world. She winked at her gal who waved at her in admiration.

"I like this game," said Maddie. Sarah couldn't believe she had the gall to finish the last pig ear sandwich.

"Why somebody always got to ruin something? Benny, stop acting like a fool!" Sarah said.

"Aw, leave 'em be, Sarah. The dike had it coming," Mack said.

"That woman the wrong one to fool with, Mr. Martin. Stop it, Benny!" Mary said. Folks chimed in from their picnic blankets with varying opinions of attack and restraint. Some of the working gals, led by Red, ran in from outfield for a fight. Luke and Charlie were losing their grip on Benny who had lost his grip on himself. The Umpire pulled a pistol out his pocket and shot in the air. The hostilities ceased.

"Play ball," the Umpire said.

"Play ball how?" Luke said. "You see we got a man down."

The Umpire yawned and pointed his gun at Luke. "Baseball is a tough game. If you can't handle it, go home to your mama. Clean up on home base!" The teenagers, who used to mess with the HooDoo Woman, ran out and roughly lifted Deacon off home base while he whimpered in the pain of blasphemy.

"You got a replacement hitter?" the Ump said. All the men on the batter's bench looked at the switch blade sticking out of the bat and found something else to look at.

"I'll do it," Luke said.

"No you won't," Benny said. "That dike belong to me." Luke took Benny aside.

"Benny, what the hell you think you doing? I'm a better hitter than you."

"Yeah, that's true. But I'm meaner than you, man. Always have been. Sides, don't you want to spend some time with your future wife?"

Luke looked at Benny like he told him Lincoln had titties.

"Wife? Man, please. We only did it one time. I ain't thinking 'bout getting — "

"Aw, shuck, now, I know you, nigger. You won't shut up 'bout this bitch."

"Don't call her — "

"See there, see there? That's what I'm talking 'bout. Now, after all the pussy we done shared, when the hell you ever cared 'bout me calling a bitch a bitch?" Luke looked at Mary who was smiling at him and, as always, he was surprised by her attention. He waved at her while Sarah and Mack beamed behind her. "Yeah," Benny said. "Look at Ms. Sarah. Look at ole Mack. Think they finally 'bout to get the chance to make love out loud."

"Nigger, don't you talk about my mama like — "

"Aw, hush now, nigger. Quit acting like a bitch. I'm just playing." Another gunshot went off in the air further spooking the crowd.

"Hey, lovebirds, y'all done? Folks want to see some ball," the Umpire said.

"Keep your shirt on. I'm coming."

"Well come on." Benny gave the Ump a look and tried to figure out how many shots he had left in that gun. He decided he could only take on one fight at a time and squeezed Luke on the shoulder as a sign of dismissal.

"Go head on now. I'll take care of this." Luke could tell Benny was in that mood where he couldn't be talked out of nothing. And Mary was looking sweet over there. And he was kinda hungry. He looked forward to one of Sarah's pig ear sandwiches. Luke trotted off to Mary and Benny took the bat in hand. He yanked the blade out, spit on it, and tossed it on the ground.

"I keep a spare," said The Pimp. The catcher sashayed behind Benny and squatted on home plate. She stuck her tongue out at him.

"Yeah, remember that for later," Benny said. He tested his swing with fury.

"Play ball," said the Ump. The Pimp bent down over the pitcher's mound and let one fly with disdain. Benny swung hard.

"Strike one," the Umpire said. The catcher returned the ball and The Pimp liked the signal that time. She let it rip.

"Strike two!" Benny tried not to lose his cool and did his best to ignore the murmurs of the crowd behind him.

Please, Lord. Please don't let me lose to this dike. I'd rather you kill me than that.

The Pimp stretched her arm out and lit up a cig.

"It's always been something between you and me, ain't it... Junior?"

"Fuck you, dike," Benny said. His grip on the bat was tight and sweaty. The Pimp wound up windmill style. This time folks didn't laugh.

Lord, you ain't never done shit for me. Please don't let this dike beat me in front of all these niggers. Please.

At that moment, gunfire rang through the air. It wasn't gunfire from the Umpire, though. Everybody turned around to see Boss Man Braxton and the Boys on horseback. Behind Braxton, all in white and fifty strong, were the Knights of the Ku Klux Klan.

Benny made a mental note to never pray again.

13

*"Happy Birthday to you. Happy Birthday to you,
Happy Birthday, dear Luke. Happy Birthday to
you."*

Benny strummed out the song on his deadbeat daddy's guitar.
Rastus had bought him some brand new strings.

*"How old are you? How old are you?
How old are you? How old are you?"*

The song eased out in the transmuted power of a blues melody.
Benny now had a solid reputation and would be debuting at the
school benefit tomorrow.

"I'm ten years old..." Sarah cried a little and Mack patted her
with impatience. Rastus downed a shot of brandy and pretended
he didn't notice Maddie lusting after him. All the children from the
field were in attendance.

They crooned a blues harmony chorus of "Happy Birthday"
with Benny Raye singing the lead. They had been assigned their
parts by Benny and rehearsed within an inch of their lives. Red led
a protest but got hit in the head with a rock. Rastus saw Benny's
rough behavior with the children but was glad to see the boy take
initiative. They rehearsed every day for a week, after chores, when
Benny would ditch Luke with an excuse about this or that. At first,
Luke was hurt by Benny's sudden distance. But when he came

through the door and saw half the community crammed in his shack, he understood and smiled. Mary was there too.

> *"Happy Birthday to you. (Oh Lawdy.)*
> *Happy Birthday to you. (How old you is? Forty?)*
> *Happy Birthday to you. (Gonna be a man soon.)*
> *Happy Birthday to you. (No more licking the spoon.)*

Benny went off on an improvised solo.

> *"Hell yeah, Hell yeah, I say, Hap-hap-Happy*
> *birthday to ya. Slap-nap-bappy birthday to ya.*
> *Yap-wap-Happy birth — "*

"Benny, shut up! Damn. Let's eat!" Mack said. All the children attacked the cake and Rufus gave Benny a wink.

"Open my present first," Benny said.

"It ain't time to open the presents yet, Benny," Sarah said.

"Hell, woman let 'em get it over with." Mack's mood suffocated the room like an odor and Sarah had her lip out as well. Rastus studied them both.

"Well, you heard him. Get it the hell over with," Benny said.

"Boy, I'll pop you in your mouth you don't stop that cussing," Maddie said.

"Your drunk ass have to catch me first."

"Benny, what I told you about talking to Maddie like that?" Sarah said.

"Folkses, folkses. Everybody calm down," Rastus said. Luke stood there looking lost at his own party. He saw Mary looking at him and turned away.

"Benny, come here," Rastus said. Benny walked to Rastus who pulled him over his knee and gave him three hard swats before yanking him back up.

"Now apologize."

"I'm *so* sorry," he said to Maddie with all the sarcasm in the world. Rastus pushed him back over to the table with the other kids who laughed in their taskmaster's face.

"Why thank you, kind sir," Maddie said. She smiled at Rastus in the bewitching lack of sex appeal that all drunks exude.

"Uh, now, Luke, open your present," Rastus said. He propped Jeraldine on his lap and she provided a little mood music to get this party going. Benny gave Luke a lopsided brown package tied with frayed, white string. "From Benny" was written across it real neat in pencil.

"I wrote that cause Benny don't know how to write his name too good." Mary said. Sarah smiled.

"Didn't nobody ask you all that," Benny said. Luke opened his present a bit too slow for Benny who snatched it out his hand, ripped off the paper, and threw it back to him.

"Oooh," all the kids said. They climbed off the table dropping crumbs on Sarah's clean floor.

"What… in the fuck… is that?" Maddie said.

"It's a turtle!" Luke shouted with joy. "A magic turtle." And so it was. It was the most beautiful magic turtle anybody ever had or ever will see.

Benny explained like a boastful engineer to the attentive crowd how the turtle was formed and Jeraldine underscored his speech. The body of the turtle was a round, smooth rock with a flat under-side about as big as a man's fist. Benny always kept a pile of rocks handy since he never knew when he felt like hitting a cow or an enemy with one. Perfect circles of smaller rocks comprised the head and four feet of the turtle.

"You'd be surprised how hard it is to find a perfectly round rock," Benny said. The children ran their hands across the turtle's back and even Red was impressed. The lecture went on with a description of how glue completed the operation to form the basic shape of a turtle. After that, it soaked in green paint for two whole days, dried in the sun, then soaked in shellac for two whole days.

"Just where you get all these supplies from, you little heathen?"

"Getting that turtle outta that shellac was rough though," said Benny ignoring Maddie's interruption of his seminar. After he got it out, he polished it at least half an hour a day until it gleamed like a mirror in the creek at noon. And with a teeny paint brush, and some black paint, he drew little squares and triangles to give the turtle a shell. Two eyes and a little black smile finished it off. A magic turtle.

"You gonna like this better than anybody else present in here," Benny said.

"That's beautiful, Benny," Sarah said. "Luke, ain't you gonna say thank you?"

"Thank you."

"You welcome." They would have hugged each other like they sometimes did but Red would have called them sissies and got hit it the head with the magic turtle. That would have ended the party so it was best for everybody that they just shook hands.

"Now eat cake," Mack said. Luke enjoyed the first piece of his own cake and licked the chocolate icing off his fingers while he got his other presents. Each child gave him a penny and Maddie gave him a dollar while Rastus gave him two. His mama gave him a new shirt she fixed up from the Salvation Army and his daddy put his name on it too. Benny was right. Luke did like his present best. However, he loved it not because of the craftsmanship, which was exquisite, or the effort, which was considerable, but because of what the magic turtle really was.

The other day, Luke and Benny were out fishing in the hot shade of the Old Crook Tree. They had cane poles and bait that acted like fish repellent.

They did what men always do when they fish: Talk about life.

"I'm gonna miss Rastus when he goes away," Benny said.

"He always come back," said Luke. He pulled up his line to see if the worm was still there and dunked it back in.

"Yeah, I know. But he got fourteen hundred chillun. He they daddy, not mine. He getting to be a real big star across the water. And one day he ain't coming back. I know he ain't." Benny checked his bait and began to wonder if there was any such thing as fish.

"I thought you was glad you didn't have no daddy so couldn't nobody tell you what to do."

"I am." They fished in silence.

"You done learned everything he can teach you on that guitar," Luke said. "Gonna be playing for the school benefit soon."

"Man, fuck that benefit. I don't go to no school. I'm doing this for the blues."

"So, Rastus said you can be a big star, huh?"

"Yeah, yeah."

"What's the matter, don't you want to be star?"

"How I'm gonna be a star around here?

"You got to leave, stupid. You got to go to Hollywood Land." Luke looked at the sky. Hollywood Land. He and Benny saw the sign on newsreels at the Playhouse.

"Who I know in Hollywood Land?" Benny said. "Where I'm gonna stay? What we gonna eat?"

"We'd live off bugs in the desert. We'd build a shelter and rob banks to stay alive." Benny realized Luke was going to his special place and yawned.

"Hey," Benny said. "Look at that.

"What?"

"That. Over there." A beautiful turtle made it's slow way across the bank. The sun sparkled off the wet, green shell speckled with black dots. The boys left their poles and Luke picked the turtle up. He tried to pet the head before it retreated into its shell.

"Never seen a turtle like this before," Luke said.

"Me neither. Must not be from round here."

"Where else he gonna be from, stupid? You think it drove into town or something?"

Benny felt that hot ball in the center of his chest which forecasted something mean.

"Don't do that," Benny said.

"Do what?"

"Act like you better than me. And stop calling me stupid."

"Then quit acting stupid," Luke said. He was absorbed in the turtle's unusual shell and regarded it like a piece of gold. It was a unique thing in a common place just like him. He tapped its shell and peeked inside.

"Come on out, magic turtle." Luke said, "I won't hurt you." Benny snatched it away.

"Hey, give it back!"

"This turtle don't belong to you."

"Give it back. I ain't playing with you now."

"Make me." Luke tackled Benny and the turtle flew off in the distance. It bounced on the ground upside down wiggling about. They tore into each other, rolling over and over in the direction of the animal, with each having a brief turn of dominance in the battle. Just then, Benny rolled Luke on top of the turtle and the fight was halted by the sound of a crunch. They didn't move. Benny's mouth was wide open and Luke's eyes got wet.

"Shh. Shh. Don't cry. Don't cry," Benny said. But it was too late for that. Luke felt the remains seeping through his shirt and bawled like a slapped girl. Benny hopped off him and tried to think of something to say. He helped Luke up, so he could get a look at his back, and it was just as bad as one might expect with the turtle meat squishing out the sides and all. The creature's home was now it's casket since the owner didn't live there anymore. Benny knew he had to clean his buddy up somehow and the thought of that made him vomit all over Luke's back. Luke let out a holler and stormed new tears. Benny wiped vomit off his mouth and dropped to his knees.

"Shit," Benny said. "Why do everything happen to me?" Luke hiccuped his tears while Benny looked around for something to clean him with. He saw a dangling branch off the Old Crook Tree. He gave it a heave and went to work on Luke.

"Turn around," Benny said. Luke did like he was told and felt chunks of turtle scrapped off his back. It was clumsy work since Benny had his eyes closed.

"Hurry up! Hurry up!" Luke said. Benny dug his fingers into the turtle's carcass and flung it to the ground in disgust.

"There," Benny said. "Now come on. And don't look. It'll make you throw up." It was good advice. Benny guided the dazed Luke to the creek and ordered him about.

"Sit down. Yeah, that's good. Gimme your shirt." Luke just sat there like he was in a coma so Benny had to unbutton his shirt.

"I declare, I declare. Like having a fucking child or something. Lift your arm out. I told you not to call me stupid, didn't I? Well, didn't I? Gimme your other arm. I can get that shit off anybody. Things supposed to be different with us, ain't they? Well, ain't they?"

Benny dipped the shirt in the creek in shame. He didn't know much about laundering so he imitated the way he had seen women do it on a rock. The stain disappeared but Benny kept on washing. He was trying to scrub away something that wasn't in the shirt.

"All right," Benny said. "I'm done. He smiled at Luke who didn't bother to acknowledge him. He ached to make things right between them but didn't know how to do it without looking weak.

Then, the cane pole jiggled. Benny jumped to his feet unsure of what he saw. Sure enough, it happened again.

"Luke! We got a bite!" Luke glanced at the pole but it wasn't moving anymore.

"Leave me alone," Luke said. Out of the blue, the pole took off down the bank knocking into rocks and twigs on it's way. Luke leapt out of his depression and after the catch. The pole accelerated and Luke was behind it pumping fast with the rough soles of his bare feet absorbing the impact of uneven ground.

"Don't let him get away!" Benny said. The pole snagged on a tree thirty feet down the bank. A great weight from below pulled the tight line, bending the pole, and Luke feared all was lost. He was just about to grab it when he heard the crackling cane.

"Get it, Luke!" The pole broke in half, sprinkling splinters on its way to the creek, and Luke dove in the dirt. The ground ate his stomach and chest as he slid. He stretched out his hand and grabbed the pole right before it was swallowed by water. Relieved, he rolled on his back and smiled while the fish jerked below him. Benny ran up breathing hard. "You got him," Benny said. "Oooh, look at your chest, man." Luke looked at the white meat on his body while holding the line with confidence. He laughed like he didn't give a damn and Benny joined him. Then, the fish dragged him along the bank on his back.

"Help!" Luke said. Benny made a dive for his foot and grabbed it just before Luke went into the creek. The waves thrashed in a vicious tug of war.

"The line's gonna break!" Luke said.

"Ain't nobody gonna believe us!" Benny said. He climbed on Luke's back and grabbed the piece of cane with him. They worked their way to their feet, falling down, and scrambling up again. All the time, their arms yanked at their sockets this way and that way.

"We gotta end this quick," Luke said. "Help me work it over there by that stump. Give it a little slack!" Benny followed Luke's directions and they let up a little, giving the fish the illusion of freedom.

"Now!" Luke said. They ran around the stump and yanked the fish to a stop. The water churned in anger and splashed the boys from quite a way. Benny grabbed Luke by the waist and dug his heels into the helpful earth.

"Stop wasting time over here with me and kill it! I got this!"

"Your better not drop that line, boy!"

"Hurry up!" Benny released Luke and jumped to the bank. Luke slid a little but managed to hold on with his tired knuckles begging for a break.

Benny whipped the knife out his pants and raised it in the air. He searched the bubbles for the best place to strike. He settled on the middle of all that fuss and, mindful not to cut the line, he stabbed three hard, quick times. Benny stuck his hand into the water but pulled it out with a shout. Blood dripped from his fingers.

"What happened?"

"Bastard stabbed me back!"

"Must be a catfish."

Benny plunged his knife into the water while Luke held the line. Benny was bold enough to sink his hand in the water again and grabbed the thing by the tail.

"I got him! Keep pulling!"

Luke braced a foot against the stump and pulled with all his might. Benny grinned and stabbed that fish like he was beating a drum.

Then the line broke.

Luke fell and Benny lost his grip on the tail.

"Damn!" Benny said. Luke looked at the blood trailing away from the bank and simply said,

"No." He ran straight at the creek and dived right in with a cannonball splash. Benny stared at the water like a minstrel man. He tucked the knife in his teeth, held his nose, and jumped in too.

Bubbles arose from deep below and vanished in the quiet wind. Brown waters reflected the afternoon sky inhabited by one cawing crow. Ripples bounced off the lonesome banks and washed away into nothing.

Then: "BA-WOOSH." The boys broke the surface heaving for air. A flock of black birds took refuge in the sky and their wings provided the sound of Mother Nature's applause. For those rascals had caught that damn fish.

Somehow, they out swam the battle worn creature and spotted him trying to hide in the bush. Someway, they beat the thing down in his neck of the woods and managed to hit air before they swallowed up death. They hauled the giant catfish out to the bank and Benny kicked it in the side just because. Luke picked up a heavy rock and bashed it in the skull.

Benny gutted and cleaned it while Luke gathered twigs to make fire with two rocks like his daddy taught him. Benny sharpened a long stick and ran that whale through. Luke held one side, Benny held the other, they turned it till it looked right, and dinner was served. Later, they rubbed their bloated bellies and laughed about their adventures.

"Man, I thought our asses was drowned for sure."

"No way I was gonna let that fish get away."

"You smart as hell, Luke." Luke paused as he remembered the turtle and Benny felt the shift in his mood.

"We better bury your little friend before he start stanking." Luke was surprised he addressed the topic directly and decided to reward him for the effort. To keep holding a grudge at this point would be like kicking a toddler for trying to walk.

"Okay." The boys dug a hole a foot deep and just as wide. They buried the body while Benny hummed the blues and Luke quoted something from Ephesians.

"Sit here for a minute," said Benny. He climbed the tree with his knife and got to work.

"What you doing?"

"Nothing, man."

"Well, if you ain't doing nothing let's go."

"Just a minute. Damn." Benny made several more master strokes. "Come here, he said." Luke climbed the tree to see what the fuss was about.

"Luke and Benny. Friends till the end," the carving read. Luke smiled.

"That's nice. Real nice. You good at that." Benny put his arm around him.

"I love you, man."

"I love you too."

"I'm sorry 'bout that dumb ass turtle."

"That's Okay." They balanced themselves on the branch and hugged. They climbed down the tree, kicked dirt on the fire, and walked back to the shacks.

"I'll make it up to you, man."

"Sure you will, Benny."

And that's the story of the magic turtle.

Things were winding down back at Luke's birthday party. Sarah finally got all them screaming kids out her house so she could commence to cleaning.

Rastus was doing his best to ward off Maddie's advances without coming off rude. Mack was in a corner doing a bad job of pretending nothing was bothering him by reading a newspaper over and over. Maddie accomplished the impressive task of being absolutely drunk without falling down. That might not seem like much but it's very hard to do and takes decades of practice. She waddled over to Rastus to make her move. Rastus saw her approach out the corner of his eye and concentrated harder on playing.

"Hey. Fine ass nigger. Hey. Hey. I know you hear me. You... you fine ass nigger. Come here. Get up, goddammit. I wanna talk to you. Put that guitar down, sweet pea."

Sarah would have done something to intervene but her feet hurt.

"Rastus P. Jr. Yes, sir. All the ladies want them some Rastus P. Jr." She put her arms around Rastus and clamped her hand down on Jeraldine's neck to still the strings. Lord, what she want to do that for? Rastus's eyes flickered and Maddie sobered up enough to realize she did something stupid. His voice dropped as low as the devil's in a library.

"Now, Maddie? How would you like it if somebody put their hands on your neck?" Maddie was used to getting knocked around by her gentleman callers and they all had the same look he had now. "You wouldn't like that, would you?" She shook her head. "Well, all right, then," Rastus had a hard time calming down. His deep voice trembled like he was telling a good friend his mama died. His skin warmed up and he worked real hard at taking normal breaths. Mack looked up from the paper he was pretending to read while Rastus ground out his last words. "Get your hands… off Jeraldine. And don't you never… long as you black and drunk… ever touch her again." As luck would have it, Maddie's hand was cemented in fear on Jeraldine's neck. "I said, get your hand off Jeraldine!" Rastus mistook her immobility for a challenge and did something he had never done before: Strike a woman. Sarah moved in too late and Maddie hit the floor from the back of his hand. Mack jumped from his chair and got in Rastus's face.

"Rastus! You crazy?"

"Rastus, how could you?" Sarah said. She knelt down to wipe Maddie's bloody nose. Then Benny ran in the room. The other children were behind him and peeked in the door.

"She had her hands on Jeraldine."

"So what?" Mack said. "Can't you see she's drunk?"

"She always drunk. What's the difference?"

"Nigger, if you don't know the difference, I can't explain it to you!" Maddie put her head on the floor and wailed while Sarah rubbed her back.

"She had her hand on Jeraldine." Mack looked at him like he was something in a zoo.

"It's just a guitar." Rastus looked at Mack and realized something special was over.

"I think I better leave, now."

"I think you better." Rastus grabbed his white cowboy hat.

"I'm sorry, Maddie. But you shouldn't have had your hands on — "

"Get the fuck out."

Rastus turned towards the voice and was mortified to learn that it came from Benny. Mack and Sarah didn't reprimand Benny for cussing like they usually did. He appealed to the boy with hat in hand.

"Now look here, boy. She touched Jeraldine. You know what that means." Maddie grabbed Rastus by the leg and prayed.

"I'm sorry, I'm sorry, I'm sorry," she whispered. Rastus reached down to touch her but Benny ran forward and slapped his hand. The boy moved Sarah aside like the attending physician and curled on the floor next to Maddie. He rubbed her tears away with his dirty sleeve as if he had done it many times before.

"You all right, Ain-tee?" he said. She clutched him close. Her tight hug hurt him but he hugged her back tighter. "It's all right, Ain-tee. It's all right."

"I didn't know," she said. "I was just playing, Benny. I was just playing."

"I know you was, Aintee. I know you was. Luke, get the brandy."

Luke knew where his daddy kept the brandy and looked at him for permission. Permission was granted and he dug into the cupboard while Sarah said something about Jesus. She looked at the crowd of kids at the door jostling each other for a better view.

"Y'all go on home for it gets dark, now. Party's over," Sarah said. The children moved a bit too slow for Mack.

"Get the fuck on!" he said. And they ran like lightning away.

"God forgive me," Rastus said. Benny unscrewed the cap and stuck the bottle in Maddie's mouth. Liquor dribbled down her chin as she looked up at Rastus and pushed the bottle away.

"I'm sorry 'bout Jeraldine," Maddie said.

"Fuck that guitar," Benny said. "Drink." Rastus shut his eyes and let his memory abuse him. This could have gone a hundred different ways. He could have said a hundred different things. But she had her hands on Jeraldine.

"I thought you was leaving," Benny said. The hoot owl gave Rastus his cue and he took heavy steps out of the room.

"Sorry, everybody. Happy Birthday, Luke."

Rastus shut the door.

14

Rain patted the tin roof of Maddie's place and wind whistled through the cracks in the wall. Sarah never enjoyed coming over to Maddie's and the roaches on the floor reminded her why.

Sarah never understood folks who accepted roaches as a fact of life. Like they were pets or something. Nasty ass roaches. Couldn't they see them? Sarah saw Maddie go to the ice box once and a roach climbed out of it like he was back home from work. Maddie went right ahead talking like she didn't see that thing crawl down that ice box to the middle of the floor knowing good and well nobody was gonna step on him. Sarah halfway expected her to give it a drink. When Maddie returned from the box, with the salt pork she offered, Sarah put every Hollywood actress to shame by pretending she left her stove on and had to go right now.

"Girl, you better hurry up 'fore you burn up these white folks property."

"Yeah, you right, child. I don't know what's wrong with me today."

"Run, girl."

"Okay." And run she did. Sarah dashed through the woods to put out the cold stove and vowed never to eat at Maddie's house again. If invited, she would always: (A) Have just eaten, girl or (B) Got the shits, girl.

The common excuse among folks who accepted roaches like taxes was that one couldn't do anything about them. Sarah knew that was a lie. Poor as she was, she could afford some poison from the drug store. All you got to do is put that poison down in each corner of a clean house every Saturday, or every other Saturday, and there ain't gonna be no roaches. There just ain't. And if by some miracle, a roach managed to get through, just one, Sarah would start the whole process over again.

Another excuse people used to adopt roaches as family members was that they came from the neighbors so there wasn't much a body could do. Another lie, reasoned Sarah. If the next door neighbor is that nasty, then call the white folks on 'em from Charities and Corrections. If they start some shit, then call the white folks down there at the sheriff's department.

"We can blame crackers for many things," Sarah said, "But living with roaches ain't one of them." Nope. Sarah didn't understand niggers who saw roaches as their destiny. And she never, ever would.

Tonight, she didn't have a choice, though, as she played the nurse to Maddie again. Sarah's destiny was an inability to refuse a soul in need, no matter how many times Mack called her a soft touch. She tucked Maddie into bed who put the pillow between her knees since it was both comfortable and comforting to sleep that way. She forced soup down Maddie's throat and decided it was time for them to take a month's break from each other, Christian or not.

She walked into the living area of the two room shack and saw Luke and Benny balled up asleep on the floor like puppies. They had their arms around each other and Sarah prayed for their friendship to last since she knew how adulthood could make folks hate each other.

She bent down to get Benny and rubbed her aching back that hadn't been right since a truck accident ten years ago. The pain didn't hit right away, but later, there was a tightness in the left hamstring that shot up her lower back. Standing on her feet all day didn't help and sometimes relations with Mack could be frustrating. Some days were better than others and, although it wasn't agonizing, she was ever aware the pain was there.

She rolled Benny into the crook of her arms and thrust up evenly to keep the stress in her knees. It almost worked. She took the sleeping jumble of boy and a deposited him on his feather comforter which lay in a dusty corner of his room. Bad back or not, Sarah wasn't 'bout to let this baby sleep by them spider webs. And drunk or not, Maddie oughta be 'shamed of herself. And if she didn't get her ass together, Sarah was gonna call them white folks down there at the Charities and Corrections. Got this baby down here on this nasty floor like a dog or something. No wonder Benny the way he is.

Luke woke up to see his mother wiping the corner with a dirty rag and cussing about white folks in the process. He leaned against the doorway and watched Sarah fluff up the yellow stained comforter complaining about the lumps and shaking her head. Luke was glad Sarah was his mother. He couldn't imagine life without her and was afraid to try because it might make something bad happen. He heard Job say in Sunday school that the thing he feared had come upon him. In Sunday school, Luke prayed all the time for him and Benny to be real brothers. He didn't know how that could happen but he prayed anyway. But Benny was always around, just like a real brother, so maybe that's how the prayer was being answered.

Sarah and her back reached an agreement about the best way to maneuver Benny into bed and rested him there without waking him. She stretched all the mess from the day out her bones and turned around to see Luke looking sad. She smiled and got on the floor with him. He smiled back but she could tell it was just for show. She straightened out her legs so he could lie in her lap and get his back rubbed the way he liked it.

"Now, Luke," Sarah said, "We got something very important to talk about."

"What, Ma?"

"Don't you ever eat nothing, and I mean nothing, at this house." Luke groaned because he knew what was coming.

"I mean it. Just say, "No ma'am, I just ate or no ma'am, I don't feel good. Please, son. Everybody ain't like us and they don't wash their hands. You could get sick from not washing your hands. Did you know that?"

Of course I know that. You tell me every day.

"Yes, Ma."

"Matter of fact, don't eat nothing at nobody house. If you hungry, come home, and Mama'll fix you something. It's no trouble. You hear me, don't you?"

"Yeah, Ma."

"Please, please, please, don't ever eat nothing out this house. I don't care if I'm dead and you starving. All right?"

"All right."

"Well, all right then."

Sarah wished it would stop raining so they could go on home. She had done her Christian duty and her feet still hurt. Besides, Luke needed real food in him not just cake and candy.

"I'm sorry 'bout your birthday, son."

"That's Okay." She knew it wasn't. Benny whined in his sleep and she halted her back rubbing to see if he needed her.

"Don't stop, Ma,"

"I think Benny's having a nightmare."

"He'll be all right. He do that all the time." Benny stopped and snored again. Sarah resumed Luke's back rubbing.

"How come you and daddy don't like each other no more?"

"Of course we like each other. Don't be silly."

"Then why was y'all fighting today?"

"That's grown folks business. Go to sleep." Luke jumped up in a panic.

"I don't wanna sleep in here with all these roaches!" Both Maddie and Benny stirred in their sleep and Sarah clamped her hand over Luke's mouth. She felt a deep sense of satisfaction that a mother's constant nagging had done it's work.

"Well, let's go then," she said. She was about to get some brown butcher paper out the cupboard to protect them from the rain, but decided it was better to catch cold rather than have anything from that house so close to their faces. She took Luke's hand and they tiptoed to the door. Luke wanted Benny to come with them but it didn't make a bit of sense to wake him up. Sarah cracked the door and the wind rudely pushed it open.

"You think Daddy back home from The Joint yet?"

"No. Now keep up and don't let go of my hand."

"You think Daddy gonna make Rastus come back?"

"Stay out of grown folks business," she commanded. Sarah held on to her baby's hand and together they ran into the storm.

15

*"Ain't nothing sadder; sadder than a drunk gal's
    tears.*

*Ain't nothing sadder, sadder than a drunk gal's
    tears.*

*And only God himself can understand a drunk
    gal's fears.*

Tried to tell you, baby, tell you not to go that way.

*Tried to tell you, baby, that's the wrong game to
    play.*

*Couldn't tell you nothing. Won't listen to a word
    I say.*

Oh, well.

*Ain't nothing wetter, wetter than a drunk gal's
    tears.*

That what they say. (And I believe 'em)

*Ain't nothing wetter, wetter than a drunk gal's
    tears. Mmm. Mmm.*

*Kiss the feets of Jesus. And wet 'em up with all
    your fears.*

Go head and cry, Jeraldine! Cry, gal!"

Jeraldine's pointed acoustic pain shot straight to the back and pierced a drunk gal's ears. She thought of her mama and her man. A fella with a headache recalled his bills. He might have to give up his home and start cropping. He knew that would kill him.

Mack leaned against the wall and warded off another ho which was getting harder by the second and so was Mack. He dedicated his thoughts to his family and wished Rastus would hurry up and end his set so they could talk. But Mack had his own problems. He was getting in a deeper credit hole with Braxton, in spite of being careful with supplies. Furthermore, Mack was getting tired of Sarah's mouth. She was a good mother and wife. Pretty, as well. Even though she didn't think so, which made her prettier. But she had gotten on his nerves today. So other gals looked pretty, too.

> "Drunk woman's tears on a lonely street.
> Drunk woman's tears at bad man's feet.
> Drunk woman's tears on the face of a chile.
> Drunk woman beg a man to stay a while."

Rastus swam in self-indulgence which is the worst thing a blues man can do. Yeah, he had the desired effect on the crowd. They cried, shouted, and bought more drinks. But artistically, Rastus wasn't at his best. Something he alone would notice, for now. The audience wouldn't catch on unless it went on too long. Tonight, Rastus was using art as therapy. And that ain't no good.

> "Drunk woman screaming gonna get you back.
> Drunk woman fighting back a man's attack.
> Drunk woman sanking down to the floor.
> Drunk woman holler, You don't love me no more.
> Where ya at, drunk gal?"

This Dark Skinned Diva strutted up to Mack staring at his privates without pretense. Mack's situation got profound down there and he didn't try to hide it. This was as close as he was ever gonna get to cheating so he planned to enjoy himself.

"You got a big ass dick, you know that?"

"Yeah, I know that," he said. His voice was deeper than usual.

"How come you ain't wearing your ring? Not that I give a damn."

Mack was surprised she was so observant. He lost his ring in the fields two months ago and was saving to get another.

She laughed.

"I seen you come in here a few times before. You walk up to the bar, get your little drink, and be out the door like a shot. Don't even hardly stay to see your buddy Rastus."

"Oh, I love Rastus's music. Just prefer to enjoy it at home."

"That's a married man for you. The one's still in love. Y'all close to the nest. But like I said, I don't care."

She reached down and grabbed him through his pants. Mack pushed her hand off him but took his sweet time doing it. She looked insulted and gripped him there again to show him who was boss. This time he let her rub it up and down a few times before finding the will to pry the soft hand away. It was a battle there for a second, but he ended up winning, which is living proof there really is a God. Mack's breath came heavy and he felt a little scared.

"Sorry, miss. You take care now," he said. She smiled in defeat and cussed. She eyed below his belt and walked away. Mack leaned on the wall and shut his eyes in shame. He put his drink against his head to cool the fever.

It's all right. Nothing happened.

Then he damned himself with the knowledge that adultery begins in the heart. He exhaled, opened his eyes, and saw Deacon Early looking dead at him from the bar. The Deacon shot his finger at him, the way players do, and turned back to watch the show.

Meanwhile, Rastus and Jeraldine demoralized the crowd. He cried like a fool and her rhythm was off. He always enjoyed libations before going on-stage with the pride of knowing it never affected his game. Tonight, it was. He forgot verses. Then he remembered his place and tried to fake the funk. He made Jeraldine nervous so she skipped the chorus to match his scattered thoughts. They weren't feeling each other tonight and it was evident to the now restless crowd.

"Ain't nothing deeper, deeper than… a drunk girl's grave." Jeraldine complained in discord when Rastus fumbled his stroke. Then he plain stopped playing for a minute and thought about Benny. One

whole minute. That's an eternity in stage time. He apologized to the crowd and made a lame joke. They didn't laugh.

> "Ah haaa. Ain't nothing deeper; deeper than a
>   drunk gal's grave.
> "That's what they say, (and I believe 'em)
> Make her happy, Jesus. Uh…"

He forgot the next line, which was excusable since he wrote it an hour ago, and inexcusable since he was a pro.

"Excuse me," he said to the silent crowd. The Made-up Woman was having a drink with The Pimp and watched him in worry.

"Ain't nothing sadder — " Ace Simmons had enough.

"Yeah! We know! Ain't nothing sadder than a drunk gal's tears. This drunk bitch do anything else sides cry?" Everybody laughed while Rastus stood there like a jilted groom. He had never been heckled by an audience before. Not even in his early days.

"Shut up, Ace!" Mack said. "You fucking up the show!"

"Rastus beat me to it." More laughs. Rastus had officially lost control of the crowd. So he did the only thing he could do. He jumped offstage, grabbed a whiskey bottle, and cracked Ace Simmons in the head. Ace hit the floor with blood pouring down his face.

"Is it funny now?" Rastus said. Ace's friend, Grady, grabbed Rastus from behind. Rastus wasn't ready for that one and struggled to unstrap himself from Jeraldine. He cussed himself for not thinking of that sooner and shielded Jeraldine from the scuffle. Deacon Early snapped his finger at the bouncer.

"What I pay you for? Get over there!"

Grady bitch slapped Rastus two times in front of everybody.

"I'm gonna give your drunk ass something to cry about," he said. Mack tried to help out but the yelling crowd slowed his advance. Ace wiped the blood out of his eyes and grabbed Rastus's leg. Rastus lost his balance and got slapped again. He broke Grady's hold and slipped the guitar off his neck.

"Mack!" Rastus said.

"I'm coming!"

"Catch!" Rastus flung Jeraldine in the smoky air just as Ace bit him in the leg. Rastus said a prayer for his baby and engaged in battle.

Mack pushed the Big Man out the way. He stepped on a chair and sprung into air. Two women screamed when he sailed over their heads. He caught Jeraldine and twisted just the right way to take the impact when they hit the floor.

I should have just stayed home.

The Diva held out her hands from the second story.

"Up here!" she said. Mack trusted her, for some reason, and tossed Jeraldine up without thinking. She caught her and pointed back at Rastus.

"Hurry!" Mack ignored the pain in his knee and ran into the fight.

The bouncer cleared his way though the crowd just in time to get knocked out with a chair. Ace was sorry he ever bit Rastus cause now two front teeth were missing. Grady had a black eye and bloody nose. But Grady had a cousin, Leroy, so now he was up in the mess with a busted lip. Rastus slipped in Ace's blood and Grady pinned his arms behind his back to give his cousin a chance at payback. He whipped out a knife and went for Rastus.

But Mack came from the side and tackled Leroy. Rastus stomped on Grady's foot and rammed his nose with the back of his skull. Then he spun around and gave him one straight to the mouth.

Mack and Leroy wrestled on the floor and Mack cut his hand when he snatched the knife away. But he wouldn't use the knife because he thought that was cheating. He flung it aside and they fought to their feet. Mack slung him into a table that broke in two. Deacon Early was hysterical.

"Y'all stop this or I'm gonna call the law! Somebody break this shit up! Rastus get off that nigger or you fired! Mack, stop it, god-damit, you won! I'm gonna call the law, you hear me? I'm gonna call the law!"

Deacon Early knew he wasn't 'bout to call the law with all them hos up in there.

Meanwhile, Rastus was giving Grady an advanced degree from Bitch Slap U. The woozy Ace picked up a broken bottle and crawled towards Rastus's back but Mack was alert. He kicked Leroy in the face to make sure he stayed down and got to Ace just in time. He twisted Ace's arm, made him drop the bottle, and gave him two left hooks to the side of the head. Rastus turned around as Ace flopped out and thanked Mack with a nod. Then he went back to fighting as the crowd cheered him on.

"Rastus!" He stopped at the sound of Mack's voice. "It's over." Rastus considered Mack's words. After that, he grabbed Grady's pinkie and bent it backward till it snapped. Grady screamed like he was giving birth.

"Now, it's over." Rastus didn't use guns or knives but was a real big believer in breaking pinkies. He said it helped a nigger remember.

Deacon Early ran into the middle of the devastation and shooed folks away. "All right, everybody, it's over. Y'all give us room to breathe or I'll close up early, goddamit. I mean it."

"Aw, come on, Deacon. You way too greedy to close up early," Rastus said.

"This coming out your check, you hear me? You owe me a lot of money here."

"Money for what?"

"For what? Nigger, you blind?" Deacon Early spread his arms wide. "Look at all this shit! Tables and chairs. Glasses. Injuring personnel." He kicked the unconscious bouncer. "Get your sorry ass up. You fired!" The Deacon collected himself and the bartender walked a jar of coon dick over to Rastus. "Don't give him that, dammit, that the last thing he need." Rastus snatched the drink, the bartender scuttled away, and Deacon Early stepped in close. "I invite you here to sang. Not tear the place down. Look at all the hell you caused!" Rastus sipped his coon dick and let out a sigh.

"Yeah, well. That's what they get for fucking with me."

"This ain't funny, Rastus."

"Naw, it ain't. Afraid I'm gonna have to charge you a reckless endangerment fee." The Deacon looked at Rastus like he told him Harriet Tubman sold reefer.

"A reckless what? Nigger, you must be crazy."

"Naw I ain't. And keep your mouth shut. You making my eyes water." Mack picked a chair off the floor and had a seat cause he could tell this was gonna take a while. The Diva and Jeraldine joined Mack at his caved-in table. Mack got nervous but the Diva paid him no mind. She was all into Rastus.

"I am Rastus P. Jr., mister. You lucky I'm even taking time to talk to you. I don't come in here to be harassed by low lifes. I come in here to dazzle these niggers with my God given talent and pretty ass smile."

"Well, all right!" the Diva said.

"You shut the hell up," Deacon Early said.

"Hey." Everybody turned around and looked at The Pimp sitting at the bar rubbing the Made-up Woman's leg. "You better watch how you talk to her." The Deacon got scared and The Pimp turned back to her date satisfied she wouldn't have to speak on that again. Rastus continued his tirade poking Deacon in the chest.

"I'm the biggest draw this broke down dive ever has or ever will see. Ain't like the Nicholas Brothers gonna walk up in this bitch. You s'pose to provide me with security, you cheap bastard. 'Stead of this faggot on the floor you go round calling a bouncer. You neglected to provide the necessary protection. So I had to provide it my damn self by cracking that fool in the head. These niggers coulda broke Jeraldine. Jeraldine's worth ten of y'all! And to top it all off: I'm upset. So in addition to my usual fee, which is an insult to my greatness as it tis, you owe me security costs, and a, whatchacall, uh, whatchacall that, baby, when them crackers be acting nervous and get somebody to pay for it?"

"Duress," the Diva said.

"Uh, yeah, duress. I'm all duressed! And it's your damn fault!" Rastus took a duressed breath and wiped his forehead with his sleeve. "'Course now, I can't make you pay. But if you don't... I walk. And there will never be another Rastus P. Jr." The crowd applauded. Deacon Early looked at the war torn room and tried to remember exactly how he started all this. But he couldn't fight Rastus and the fans at once.

"All right, everybody. Fine, Rastus. I... I apologize for the inconvenience and will make it up to you next pay period."

"I want it tonight, bitch."

"Fine, Rastus, fine. Don't get yourself all upset." He snapped his fingers at the bartender. "Get Rastus another drink."

"You get it. And one for Mack too. Naw, two for Mack. Fuck it, he drank all night for free. You hear me?"

"Oh, Mack, too? All right then, no problem, that's fine. But you get back up there and get to work, you hear?"

"Nigger, please. I'm on a break." Deacon Early marched off over the bouncer's body and said something about niggers and flies. The Diva arose with Jeraldine and stepped to Rastus with respect. She bowed her head and presented the knight with his sword.

"Thank you, sugar. See you later."

"You better." She turned to Mack. "Nice catch." And then she was off. Rastus sat down with Mack and laughed.

"Nigger, you look like something the Klan drugged in."

"You welcome," Mack said.

"Aw, don't get salty on me now. What you want me to do? Kiss you?"

"Naw, thanks. I don't know where you been." Rastus laughed loud and slapped him on the back too hard. Deacon Early brought the drinks and slammed them down.

"Anything else?"

"Yeah," Mack said. "Gimme a plate of ribs. Extra sauce." Mack wasn't even hungry. He just wanted to pay Deacon back for catching him in a weak moment.

"Shit. I'm hungry, too. Gimme some chicken." The Deacon walked away without a word and prayed for something real bad to happen to them. Mack kept quiet and Rastus felt awkward. "Aw, hell, nigger, you know I'm grateful. And not just for fighting with me. But for Jeraldine. You saved her, man. You know how important that is? Jeraldine's my life outside them fourteen hundred chillun I got. I ever told you how I'd be just another nigger with a complaint if it wasn't for ole Jeraldine?"

"Yeah, I think you mentioned it once or — "

"Jeraldine! Jeraldine! You the only one for me."

"Oh, yeah. Jeraldine! Jeraldine!
You got just — "

"You caused a lot of trouble today, Rastus," Mack said. Rastus stopped playing. He was shocked Mack didn't feel like hearing him sing and it scraped against the bone of his heart. Then he got mad for letting another man hurt his feelings.

"Nigger, I don't need no conscience," Rastus said.

"What you need, is your ass beat, and I probably should have let Ace and them finish the job."

"What the fuck you want from me?"

"Nigger, you a mess. You know that? What about the benefit?" Mack thought about something sad. "Ain't you even gonna ask about Benny?" Rastus tried to find something else to look at but he had seen it all before.

"What's the matter?" Mack said. "Having fourteen hundred chillun make it easy to forget about one?"

"You feeling kinda full of yourself, ain't ya?"

"You better get that bottom out your voice." They eyed each other like two frogs waiting on the other to jump. Rastus spit on the floor just as Deacon Early approached with the food. Deacon Early regarded the men with caution and put the plates down. He prayed for peace and crunched broken glass on his way back to the bar. The men ripped the meat off the bones with their eyes locked in combat; chewing like they was trying to kill each other. Rastus tossed back a drink and threw a bone on his plate.

"So how's Benny, motherfucker?"

"How you think he is?" Mack wiped his lips with his sleeve.

"Well, what he mad at me for? Thought he didn't even like her."

"You sound like a fool," Mack said. "Maddie the only family he got."

"That's a lie. Luke and y'all the boy's family. If it wasn't for Sarah, Benny'd starve to death. You said so yourself." The men ate in silence expect for tearing up them poor bones. "Still. I shouldn't have hit a woman." He looked at Mack for agreement but Mack looked away. "And I wished Benny hadn't saw me that way. And I..." His eyes got wet and Mack pretended not to notice.

"Damn. Put too much hot sauce on this chicken. Need to get some well water."

Mack knew there wasn't no well outside and there never was. Folks who wanted water drank it before they got there or waited 'til they went home. It was a bad lie. Rastus got up in a hurry. Mack watched him flash phony smiles at the fans and make quick jokes about the outhouse. The back screen door slammed after him and Mack wiped his hands on his pants and followed.

He hadn't realized how hot it was inside until he stepped on the breezy porch. Passionate couples necked on the rail and ever-present wall flowers lined Ho Row. He saw Rastus fade into the barbecue smoke and make a hard turn away from the outhouse. Mack curved around the front where he saw some loud women with laughing men. He spotted kids puffing reefers under the steps and stop whenever people walked by. He stretched in the night, looked at the sky, and recalled the last time he had that stuff. He stepped on the dirt road and walked far behind a silhouette headed for the silent cow pasture.

Rastus leaned on the post and watched the cows sleep. He took off his white hat to let his scalp breathe. He spread a blue handkerchief on the damp grass and leaned Jeraldine up on a tree. He looked at stars and heard footsteps behind him but didn't bother turning round. He knew it was Mack.

"I'm sorry for all the trouble I caused." Mack said nothing and patted his back. "He hate me, Mack. He hate me."

"Don't talk no more, man. You drunk."

"You know what, Mack?" Rastus whispered.

"What?"

"If you was to sit on that far post over there? And say what you mean in a quiet voice? I betcha I could hear every word."

"I'm sure you could, man." Rastus let out a whoop, the way folks do when the Holy Ghost come, and cried like a child gone mad. Mack looked back to make sure they were alone and gave him a great, big hug. Rastus wept deep into Mack's steady shoulder while the moon had a bird's eye view.

16

The sun woke Benny up on his dirty piece of bed and he popped up looking around the shack. He got up for a trip to the outhouse and roaches trotted off on their morning jog. Then he figured he didn't feel like walking that far and just pissed out the front door instead. His ears told him Maddie was still snoring it off and wouldn't be much trouble for awhile. Benny was starving but was embarrassed to go to Luke's for some reason. He decided to waste time checking the empty cupboard and glanced at Maddie on the way.

The trip to the cupboard was as fruitless as he knew it would be but he found himself a cold jar of water in the icebox. That tasted just right. The birds sang along with Maddie's snores and he pushed the tattered curtains aside to see what the deal was outside.

It was Saturday. No work in the strawberry field today. Folks would be racking up debt downtown getting butter, lard, pork, and supplies. He saw some kids rolling a tire and felt the urge to run out there with them but first he had to go get Luke.

Luke would know what to say and do concerning this mess. Luke would figure out a plan and make everything the way it was supposed to be. He was good at that. Benny looked at his deadbeat daddy's guitar in the corner. It looked like a baseball bat when the season was over. He lost all confidence in Luke's reasoning abilities when he stared at the guitar. He knew there were some things that couldn't be fixed. Today was Saturday. The day of the benefit. And he wasn't going to play.

What was the point of having the guitar anymore? It was time to grow up. His daddy didn't leave the thing as a sign to him and he figured that out a long time ago. What was he gonna do exactly? Be a guitar player when he grew up? A blues man?

Sure, it was nice while it lasted and The Joint was a fun house. He and Luke had everything they wanted in there thanks to… he and Luke had everything they wanted in there and made a habit out of peeking through keyholes when the working gals took in a client. It was so funny. The Pimp caught them a few times but she wouldn't do more than just shoo them away since she was scared of… since she was scared of them. So, yeah. They had their fun at The Joint, and the attention was gravy and all that. But there was no point in messing round with this guitar and the time had come to grow up. He was almost ten, after all. There was a knock on the door and an automatic entry. It was Luke.

Benny didn't know what he was gonna say to him and that hadn't changed now that he was here. Luke saved the day by speaking first.

"Mama, say come on get and something to eat." Benny was out the door like a shot. Maddie moaned and Luke went over to watch her a minute. He thought about pinching her nose to see what would happen. He and Benny use to mess with Maddie when she passed out by dropping peanuts in her mouth or pulling her dress up over her head. One time they slipped her bloomers down around her ankles. Then they climbed out the window and Benny shouted,

"Klan!"

Maddie hit the floor, face first, a little harder than gravity. The boys laughed about that one all day long. But Luke got double teamed by his folks for the prank and that time they used their hands. Maddie couldn't catch Benny and Mack wouldn't whup him. But Sarah yelled at him real good and made him cry. So instead of messing with Maddie, Luke pulled the covers up around her and shut the door on his way out.

"Klan," Maddie said. She kicked the covers off her. "Klan."

Luke saw dust floating around the bend in the road which told him Benny was at his place by now. He took his time walking since he ate some bacon before he left and wasn't hungry no more. He picked up a rock to practice his technique. Benny told him he threw like a girl. He was satisfied with his private drills but still restless about going home. Things weren't the way they should be and he wondered why God didn't do something about it.

It seemed to Luke, from Deacon Early's Sunday school class, that God used up his best miracles a long time ago. God didn't do anything useful nowadays and just watched folks die and be sad. Why didn't God stop Rastus from slapping Maddie? What's so hard about that? Why didn't Jesus come down personally and tell Maddie to stop drinking? Luke was sure that would get her attention. How come God only did stuff in the bible but no place else? Deacon Early rapped him on the knuckles for that question and the pain taught him not to ask anything about God he really wanted to know.

Where did the devil come from, anyway? How the hell could an angel go bad? Didn't God make the angels? Why would God make his own competition? Couldn't he see that coming? Why didn't God just kill the devil and get it over with? If Heaven's so great why we gotta die to get there? That's around the time Luke looked out the window more often and invented his own world instead of listening to confusing talk about the one God had abandoned.

That's why Luke thought he'd make a better god than God. He wouldn't let folks suffer under his domain. He'd go ahead and lynch the devil now. He'd give Benny a daddy and bring his mama back to life. He'd make his family rich and they'd all live in Hollywood land. Luke knew exactly how things should be.

He thought about something sad.

He drew his name in the dirt real big and remembered what he heard his folks saying last night.

Mack came home drunker than Cooter Brown and looked like he'd been in a war. Sarah screamed when she saw him and woke Luke up. Luke's room wasn't really big enough to be called a room. It used to be a big closet but was separate from the adults with a soft feather bed Mack made to keep him off the floor.

Something told Luke to stay in bed instead of running to greet his daddy like he always did. He liked being in Mack's arms and wanted to ask about Rastus. But Something told Luke to stay where he was. Something said they'd tell him to go back to bed or shut up while grown folks is talking. He'd learn more staying where he was and they wouldn't whisper or start spelling to hide stuff from him. Like he couldn't spell, for crying out loud. Something told Luke to stay, so he stayed. Luke always listened to Something.

"Don't you bring your drunk self in here waking up my baby."

Luke heard Sarah's footsteps approach and closed his eyes to fake being asleep. He knew from experience not to snore or shut his eyes too tight. That was overacting and punishable with a smack. No, just lay there relaxed and breathe kinda shallow. Turn your head towards the wall so the lantern light won't make you blink. Try to think of something pleasant so's not to get nervous about her watching. Listen to her go. Wait a minute. She might be faking herself. Now she's gone. Luke heard her walk back to Mack and scold him in whispers.

"Where the hell you been, Mack Martin? Get your hands off me. You ought to be shame of yourself. Stop it, Mack, I ain't playing with you now." Luke heard a smack that was either her hand on his face or his hand on her behind. Muted sounds. Kisses.

"I love you, Sarah. I really do."

"Why you say it like that?"

"Like what?"

"Like you in a court of law or something."

"Aw, hell, woman."

Luke heard his daddy's boots tromp across the floor. Clinks of jars in the cupboard. Liquid hitting glass and a sigh.

"That water's good and cold," Mack said.

"Look here, Mack. You can go."

"What you talking about?"

"I mean you ain't gonna use me to get some ho off your mind. I don't need you doing me no favors with a courtesy fuck." Luke pressed his ear against the wall. "I don't need you, Mack. I don't. I'm a strong woman. Had to be cause my mama was weak. I don't need you to make yourself love me and I don't need you to take care of my child. You can go, Mack. You can just go."

Luke could only hear his heart beat in the long silence that followed. He was gonna be just like Benny. A boy without a daddy. He prayed for God to do something fast but thought God wouldn't listen because he questioned Him too much. But he prayed anyway. He wished his heart would stop beating so fast. Could a little boy have a heart attack? He waited in the dark a long time for somebody to speak.

"It ain't like that Sarah. Now, I ain't gonna pretend I'm blind. But it ain't like that."

"You don't have to be blind. Long as you remember I ain't blind either."

"Why you always got to be so contrary? Huh?"

"Mack?"

"What."

"Don't fuck up. I don't know how I'd live without you but I'd give it shot."

"Okay, Sarah. Okay." Luke heard a moan and it was coming from his mama. His daddy snorted like a horse and they fell on the floor. The boy put a pillow over his ears and hummed to himself. Looked like Daddy was staying.

A couple of hours passed. He heard Sarah revert to homemaker mode and dress Mack's wounded hand. Mack whined when the iodine hit. It had to be iodine since nothing else made a man sound like that.

"You want something to eat?" Sarah said. He passed with explanations of his barbecue dinner and almost everything that led up to that.

"How's Maddie?" She told him.

"How's Rastus?" He told her the plan.

Tomorrow, they would tell Benny to come over and get something to eat like they usually did. Later, Rastus would show up to make amends. Both agreed not to force Benny to do anything in the end. But they would help out a little by locking him in there with Rastus to make sure he listened. If things went well, they'd all go to the benefit together. If not, then that would be that. Rastus would perform alone and leave on the evening train for his next town as scheduled. They both talked about how there was more involved here than the benefit and how Rastus was the closest thing Benny had to a daddy. Sarah noticed Mack sounded funny when he said that.

"Why, Mack Martin. Are you jealous?"

"Woman, you talk like a fool."

Rastus would apologize to Maddie too. They'd tell Luke everything in the morning.

"I'm sure he'll understand," Sarah said.

"He damn well better." At that point, Mack decided he was hungry after all but not for food and Luke heard him laugh real wicked like. Sarah giggled and Luke didn't get much sleep that night.

So anyway, that's why Luke was dragging his feet going home. He rounded the bend and walked across clumps of grass in front of his house. Mack was growing a small crop on the land he leased from Boss Man Braxton but it hadn't been a great year. He took time to sniff his mama's yellow, puffy flowers that kept mosquitos away. When he swung the door open, his mama fussed at him for almost making her drop the milk.

"Watch where you going, Luke. If I done told you once, I done told you a thousand times to open that door slowly."

"Yeah, watch where you going?" Benny said.

"Don't talk with your mouth full, Benny. It's nasty. And keep your elbows off the table."

"Yes, ma'am." Benny stuck his tongue out at Luke to give him a look at what chewed up biscuits looked like. Luke shot him a bird on the sly but not too sly for Mack.

"Sit yourself down," Mack said. Benny laughed but a look from Mack made him shut up quick. Mack looked at Luke like he was up to something. "Took you that long to walk back here?"

"I ain't know I was on the clock." Sarah laughed.

"You better watch your little mouth."

"Oh, Mack leave the boy alone."

"Yeah, leave the boy alone, Mack. You know he touched." Benny laughed at his own joke and noticed Luke was acting stranger than usual. "What exactly is your problem?" Benny said. Luke didn't hear him. The sky was the wrong shade of blue today and it was getting on his nerves. Mack kicked him under the table.

"Hey! Don't you hear folks talking to you? Get your head out the clouds."

"I ain't looking at no clouds. I don't never look at no clouds. Clouds don't be doing nothing. I'm so sick of folks saying that."

Mack swatted Luke's leg and faced him back toward the table with the rest of humanity. Sarah glanced back from the stove with worry. She adjusted the burgundy curtains and peeked out to see if Rastus was coming. Sarah couldn't stand folks who couldn't be on time. Everybody had a watch or access to a clock. She just didn't get it. Benny regarded Sarah transfixed at the window. He gulped his milk and wiped his mouth with the back of his hand.

"What the hell so special outside that window?" Benny said. Mack gripped the meat on Benny's arm with two knuckles and twisted. Benny hollered.

"Mack, don't," Sarah said. Mack squeezed that chunk of arm meat real hard for good measure and jiggled it a little before he felt like letting go.

"Watch your goddamn mouth," he said.

"Well, Mack, you ain't setting a good example."

"Example? Woman, I'm grown. Gimme some eggs." Sarah went to the stove and cracked two eggs into the hot skillet. Benny rubbed the knot coming up on his arm. He noticed Luke was just sitting there like a fool.

"Boy, ain't you gonna eat?"

"I ain't hungry," Luke said.

"Ain't hungry? All this good food down here? You more crazy than I accepted. That's all right, though. More for us. Ain't that right, Mack?" Mack was looking crazy and smoke filled the room. Sarah stirred black eggs and stared out the window.

"Damn it, woman!" Sarah snapped back to life and grabbed the skillet without thinking. She yelled out from the burn and made sucking sounds between her teeth. Mack jumped to her aid, examined her hand, and poured sugar in her palm. Sugar absorbed the heat of a burn better since water just made blisters. Benny thought that was funny.

"Whatcha gonna do? Eat her?"

"Shut up, Benny!" Luke said. Benny made sure the adults couldn't hear him and leaned across the table to Luke.

"I'm gonna beat your crazy ass when we get outta here." Benny was expecting a smart reply but got nothing. Mack tied a handkerchief around Sarah's hand and kissed it. She gave him a peck on the cheek and they looked out the window. Benny looked back and forth between them and decided he had enough of the Martins for one day. He slid his full body out of the chair and grabbed a piece of sausage on the way.

"Come on, Luke." Luke sat petrified in his chair.

"Come on where?" Benny rubbed his belly and clenched his butt to choke back a fart.

"Outside, that's where. Red and them out there rolling a tire."

"Rolling a tire, huh? Benny waited for him to move. "Uh, truth be told, I ain't up for rolling no tire today. Got a headache."

"Uh, huh," Benny said. "Well, I got to go to the outhouse. Bye."

"Wait for me."

"Wait for you? Nigger, I gotta shit now."

"But I'll go with you."

"What you gonna do? Wipe my ass for me?"

"Watch your damn mouth, Benny."

"Mack, you're not helping." Sarah glanced out the window her whole body relaxed. Benny had enough.

"What the hell going on outside that window?" Benny strode to the window and Luke scratched at a piece of nothing on the table. Mack and Sarah parted the way as Benny tiptoed to look out the window. Then he farted.

Luke laughed, of course, since it was a genetic response to laugh at fart. Benny looked at Luke in hatred which cut his laughter cold. Mack cussed and Sarah held her nose.

"Oh, my goodness," she said. Sarah opened the door to fan out the stench and there was Rastus P. Jr. He held a big box in one hand and fanned his face with the other.

"Gyat damn! Smell like y'all having a doo doo barbecue in here."

"Close the door, man," Mack said. "You letting the flies in."

"That ain't my fault," Rastus said. "Flies love shit." Benny ran for the door but Mack caught him.

"Let me go!"

"Now just settle down, boy."

"Mack, honey, don't hurt him. Now, Benny it'll be all right."

"Let me go!"

"I ain't gonna hurt you, Benny," Rastus said.

"I hate you!" Benny got wild. He jerked and twisted from Mack.

"Help me, Luke!" But Luke turned away. Rastus put his hand on Benny's shoulder and got kicked in the leg for the gesture.

"Ow! Fuck!" Rastus sealed his lips and moaned while he hopped around the room.

"What you doing to me, Mack? Y'all my family, not his!" Mack didn't reply and Sarah cried. "Luke, what's the matter with you? Help me!" Luke put his hands over his ears. Sarah blew her nose and got on her knees to talk to the boy.

"Benny, honey? Don't you want to play at the benefit today? You worked so hard."

"Naw! He hit my Ain-tee! Let me go!"

"But Rastus real sorry about that, son. And he's here to make it up to you."

"I don't care! Luke!"

"Now, sugar? We gonna leave you and Rastus alone to have a talk — "

"I don't want to! Y'all tricked me!"

" — but we'll be right outside. Let's go y'all. Luke." Luke ran out the door first and stood in the flowers. He leaned against the house and panted. Sarah gave Rastus a nasty look on her way out.

"Don't leave me in here!" Benny was strong for a little boy and gave Mack a time. Mack maneuvered him to the center of the room and threatened the child with death if he kicked him.

"This better work, Rastus." Mack threw Benny to the wall, ran out the door, and Sarah closed the window from outside. Benny gave chase but Mack shut the door on him. He kicked and screamed against the door while Mack held it shut. "Who got the key? Damn it, who got the key?" Sarah knew Luke had it. They gave him one to tie around his neck in case he ever had to run home and they wasn't there.

"Luke?" Sarah said. He pulled the key free from it's hiding place.

"Lock the door," Mack said. The sweat on Mack's hands caused the knob to slip and he kept having to switch grips and wipe his palms on his pants. "Damn it, can't you hear me? Lock the door!" Benny heard from inside.

"Luke! Call the white folks!" Luke stood there like Solomon at a child custody hearing. Rastus leaned on the door and lit up a reefer. He knew Sarah didn't like that shit in her house but fuck Sarah. His nerves was bad.

Sarah patted Luke's back. "Give me the key, son."

"No, Ma. It wouldn't be right. I'll do it."

"Then do it already, God damn it!" Mack said. His nerves was bad too. Benny heard the key enter the lock and knew he had lost. He sat on the floor and cried.

"Luke! I thought you was my friend, man."

"I am." Then Luke locked the door. His mama held him while he cried.

"About time," Mack said. He wiped the sweat off his face with his shirt. Rastus listened to the bawling of one child from inside and one from without. He knocked on the door.

"Uh, look here, folkses. If I wanted to listen to a bunch of crying chillun, I'd go home. Why don't y'all take Luke somewhere and buy him a ice cream or something." Sarah put her face to the door and screamed through the cracks.

"We taking a walk down to the creek and then we'll be right back! I suggest you have this mess, don't cry baby, have this mess finished when we get back because I plan to take possession of my home! And don't forget about Maddie. I'm ashamed of you Rastus P. Jr. Just ashamed as all get out." It was Mack's turn.

"And let me tell you something else, nigger!" Rastus took a toke off his reefer and put his fingers in his ears. "You'd best not lay a hand on that boy or I'll hunt you down and kill you. Hand to God!" Rastus didn't hear any more sound through his fingers so decided it was time to talk.

"Uh, huh."

"My wife is injured out here and we need to be inside my house to take care of her."

"You right."

"My little boy out here traumatized and it's all your fault."

"Uh, uh." Mack paused.

"Nigger, you listening to me?"

"That's right." Mack kicked the door and clunked Rastus in the head.

"You better make this right! I'm telling you that right now! Hitting a woman. There's more important things in life than a goddamn guitar!"

"Nigger, you sound like a fool," Rastus whispered.

"Whatcha say?"

"You right."

"Let's go, Mack. Let's just go." Luke untangled himself from his mama's embrace and pressed his face against the door.

"Bye, Benny."

"Fuck you!" The Martins took a walk to the creek.

Rastus watched Benny weep for a minute. He sat down by the box he brought and fanned himself with his hat.

"I'm sorry, Benny. I'm sorry I hit your Aintee. I ain't the type of man go round hitting women. Ain't my style. Ask anybody. I just, I don't know, went a little crazy that day. I apologize."

The boy didn't respond and Rastus closed his eyes. "Now I'm gonna go down to Maddie, after we get through here, and these people come back and unlock this door. I'm gonna make it up to her too. I'm gonna apologize, or maybe get on my knees, proba- bly buy her some liquor, give her some money, anything 'cept fuck that bitch. And I'm gonna mean it. I'm really gonna mean what I say. And we both knows how important that is, now don't we?"

Benny said nothing.

"Now, I wasn't kidding when I told you I'd make you my son if I could. You believe me, don't you?"

Benny said nothing.

"Now look here, motherfucker. We both know I ain't got shit wise to say. So here." Rastus kicked the lid off the box with the tip of his boot and that's when Benny saw it.

The big, brown back was shaped like a woman. Curved on top, narrow in the middle, with a shapely bottom.

"I ain't buying your ass no case." The rosewood soaked up sun through the window and the grain created illusions of new light within.

"The blues ain't nothing to fuck with, boy." The long, black neck jutted out from the curve and stood straight up like a pillar of song.

"Not that long ago, when niggers was slaves, they'd sing 'bout how fucked up life was in the fields." Rastus flipped the instrument to show it's front. Six steel stings stretched and ready to talk.

"Sometimes, they just wailed and that was called a field holler. After while, field hollers gave way to gospels and gospels broke off to this other thing."

It was shiny like a Christmas toy. Not that Benny had any frame of reference for that. The smooth cherry face had a hole in the center deep enough to echo the meaning of life.

"Then, one day, a nigger picked up a guitar. He did a call-and-response mixed in with the holler. He'd sing a line, his guitar would answer. He'd sing another line, and the guitar would answer. Mostly started down there in the Mississippi Delta. Cause that's where crackers worked us to death on them levees.

In prisons, convicts sung work songs 'bout the warden and the chain gang. Folks made up their own songs or learned from another. And that's how the blues was born."

It was a limited edition Gibson guitar. Benny never had anything new in his life.

"I love you, Rastus."

"Yeah, motherfucker, I bet you do." The guitar was a bit big for the boy but Rastus knew he'd grow into it soon. The deadbeat daddy's guitar had been tuned, re-tuned, re-strung and shined but it was time to put it down. Truth be told, it was never that good in the first place. It was a testament to Benny's talent and Rastus's training that they made the thing sing at all.

"What I'm gonna do with my other guitar, Rastus?"

"Just like the nigger who left it behind, it ain't worth shit no more."

Rastus sat Benny in his lap and together they went over the chords as if he never played before. Rastus positioned his hands over Benny's fingers and soft-sung the scale while the boy strummed the match. He received little tips about intonation.

"Just don't hit the strings; make the whole thing ring like a bell."

He explained how, even though this was juke joint music, it was also the sound of loneliness and slaves. Benny was charged with learning his history and remembering where he came from. He always had to be true. Whether serious or funny, he had to make a point. He had to know how to tell a story. If it was serious, he had to have something to say. If it was funny, he'd better damn well make people laugh. He had to strive for perfection. Not cause he had to, but cause he wanted to. He had to be better than the day before. He had to be a Soldier for The Blues.

"You know what integrity is, boy?"

"Nope."

"Well, look here. In-teg-ri-ty usually mean being morally straight. Upright. But, that ain't what I'm talking 'bout. Not the morals of church folks or something like that. Shit, I get some of my best reefer and best blow jobs from members of the gospel choir. Naw, the kind of integrity I'm talking 'bout is how you handle yourself when folks ain't looking. When I say integrity, I mean being honest. Especially in regards to your music. Being whole. Being fearless. Being every last part of yourself. If you can't do that, then the music won't work. You can make some money off it, but it won't be the blues. A lot of folks won't understand our kind of integrity but fuck 'em. Cause Jesus hung around with swindlers and hos and said the sick need a doctor not the healthy folks. Niggers gonna talk about you but we don't care what they think. Folks you don't even know gonna hate you just because. We gotta be every last part of ourselves. In-teg-ral. Whole. And if we end up being wrong, then I'll save you some ribs in Hell. Now, Benny? Do you want to be a man of integrity?"

"Yeah."

"Then say so."

"I want to be a man of integrity." Rastus didn't seem convinced. Benny thought for a second and rephrased himself.

"I *am* a man of integrity."

"There you go." Rastus gave him a hug. They sat there doing that for a while and then there was a knock at the door. The Martins were back. Mack made a production of tinkling the key in the lock before he opened the door. Everybody saw a calm Benny in Rastus's lap with a beautiful guitar.

"Oooh," said Luke as he rushed to the duo. He was about to touch the guitar but stopped himself. He knew Rastus and Benny traveled in places he couldn't go and he didn't want to appear presumptuous. Benny felt a little funny since Luke had betrayed him. But he was happy and didn't feel like being mad at nobody today. He took Luke's hand and put it on the guitar.

"Rastus, gave it to me." Luke looked at the thing like God had finally done something right.

"It's pretty, Rastus," he said.

"Thank you kindly, Luke." Sarah started straightening up and was ready for these folks to leave. It had been a rough morning and she still had shopping to do. Mack went over and rubbed the guitar, too.

"That's nice, Rastus. Damn nice. Almost as cute as Jeraldine."

"Nigger, you talk like a fool." They laughed and went out to the yard for brandy. Sarah called them alcoholics. Benny and Luke were left alone with the thing.

"Man, that's the prettiest thing I ever saw."

"Yeah."

"So you gonna play in the benefit now?"

"Yeah. Guess I got to now."

"Don't you want to?" Benny thought about something sad.

"Yeah. I do." They sat there not knowing what to say for a spell while Sarah pretended she wasn't listening.

"Well, look here, man," Luke said. "I'm sorry 'bout earlier but you was going crazy up in here. Just like Dr. Jekyll."

"Who?"

"Dr. Jekyll."

"Nigger, I don't never know what you talking 'bout." Luke explained how he saw this picture show at the Bijou Playhouse one time about this cracker who went crazy on purpose. His name was Doctor Jekyll, but when he took this special moonshine that he mixed up himself, he became this po' white trash named Mr. Hyde. Mr. Hyde just didn't give a fuck and did all the things Doctor Jekyll was scared to do. But even though Mr. Hyde was a free soul, he was always messing up Doctor Jekyll's life. So one of them had to go. Mr. Hyde went crazy one last time before the sheriff's department came along and put a bullet in his ass. But when Mr. Hyde died, the part that was free, he took Doctor Jekyll with him.

"So anyway, you was acting like Doctor Jekyll. You had to be put down."

"Naw, I ain't no Doctor Jekyll nothing. I'm Mr. Hyde. I'm the part that's free and do as I please."

"I'm free too. I do as I please myself."

"Naw, you think too much. You Doctor Jekyll."

"Naw, you Doctor Jekyll. I ain't scared of nothing."

"I ain't scared of nothing neither, nigger. I'm Mr. Gyatdamn Hyde. I ain't playing with you now."

"I'm Mr. Hyde!" Luke pushed Benny and Benny pushed him back. Sarah put down her skillet.

"I don't want no more foolishness in this house today. Both a y'all come here." Luke and Benny traded thumps to the ear, heels to the foot, partial trips, real hard pinches, and elbows to the ribs on the unnecessarily slow walk to Sarah. "Now boys, I didn't mean to pry but I couldn't help but overhear your conversation. It seems to me that Doctor Jekyll and Doctor Hyde — "

"Mr. Hyde, Ma!"

"Okay, baby. Mr. Hyde... it seems to me that each fella needed the other. One just couldn't do without the other one. Doctor Jekyll was a man who wanted to be free, too. That's why he made up Mr. Hyde in the first place. And then, when Mr. Hyde died, oh my goodness, do you know what that did?"

"What?" said the boys.

"That made them incomplete. Poor Doctor Jekyll couldn't live without Mr. Hyde. And even though they made each other so mad sometimes, and wanted the other fella to disappear, you know what?"

"What?"

The free part couldn't live without the smart part and the smart part couldn't live without the free. And both parts were real brave for trying something different. For fighting to live and refusing to die."

"They was two parts of the same whole!"

"That's right, Benny," Sarah said.

"You hear that, Luke? Together, wees got integrity!"

"That's good, Benny. See? You're smart, too." Benny blushed. Luke didn't know what they were talking about. But having integrity with Benny seemed like a good way to go. He shook his buddy's offered hand like a man. But he was still Mr. Hyde.

17

The one colored school in Braxton, Alabama followed the Jim Crow rules to the tee. It was both separate and shitty. One classroom, with one teacher, doing the best they could with disgraceful supplies, in a place crammed with children of different ages. Some folks didn't even know why they bothered.

Them schools that the colored college boys in the next county went to wasn't gonna recognize this broke down school in Braxton as no proper preparation for University. These kids would have to go to a real school someplace else to be considered accredited. And if they could do that, then their families wouldn't sharecrop in the first place. Teacher's didn't know why they bothered, either. Sometimes you got a teacher who gave a damn about the kids, but mostly, you got these recently graduated colored folks who saw Braxton, Alabama as a penance they paid until they went on to greater glory. Kinda like a soldier waiting to be decommissioned. They would serve their time there, 'bout a year and a half, then they could say they taught some poor nigger children in such and such a place, write a social studies paper with a lot of big words in it, present it to some white folks for a grant, or to get published, or to get a way better job in a way better place. And then they was gone, child.

Every now and then, the kids got a teacher who invested in them instead of using them for a step up the ladder of success. One such woman was Ms. Debbie Coleman.

Ms. Coleman was a short little thing and most of the kids were taller than she was. She was pretty as hell with big, kind cow eyes and the clearest, blackest, prettiest skin in the world. She spoke in a high, gentle voice that sounded like a lullaby except when she had to tell you something more than three times. Discipline was like baseball to Ms. Coleman. And three strikes meant the switch. Ms. Coleman knew how kids could pretend the switch hurt 'em when it didn't. So she always hit them right in the center of the palm in front of the whole class. Can't nobody fake the pain of being hit in the palm with a switch in front of everybody. That would usually be enough for the offending student who wouldn't act up again until school was almost out.

Besides, Ms. Coleman was the type of teacher you just wanted to be good for so you wouldn't disappoint her. Nothing made a child feel more like nothing than the look of disappointment in Ms. Coleman's eyes. So everybody left the nonsense outside and came to her class to learn.

Ms. Coleman actually cared. She was raised on a steady diet of Frederick Douglas and W.E.B. by her upper middle class parents in Atlanta. She was affected by racism and the times just like everybody else, but because she was the kind of woman who was used to having something, and had seen her parents get along just nicely, and was aware of the accomplishments of colored folks who had it rougher, she didn't believe in laying down and giving excuses.

Ms. Coleman's parents were horrified that she would turn down an internship at Howard University and go to Braxton, Alabama, which to them, was the asshole of the Universe. Mother cried and recollected her labor pains. Father threatened disinheritance. But Father threatened disinheritance every three months or so and the labor pain thing didn't get to her like it used to.

Ms. Coleman cried on a field trip to Braxton that she took as a college student, for some reason or another. She couldn't believe these beautiful Negro children, who were naturally smart, couldn't get a decent education if they wanted to. Ms. Coleman wasn't stuck up or anything but she was a twenty year old woman who had been sheltered, as much as possible, so stuff like that was truly a surprise to her. Towards the end of her senior year at Spellman, she took to reading in the library more about all these separate but so called equal schools. She ignored her sorority sisters, in AKA, and they gossiped behind her back about if she was truly aware how lucky she was to be an AKA given how black she was. Ms. Coleman didn't give a damn, though. She never had a problem making friends and the dull ass bitches ain't never had shit to talk about no way.

Ms. Coleman was fine as hell, but except for the occasional date, she didn't pay boys no mind. Mother reminded her, for the fifth time that day, that when she was a senior at Spellman she was already engaged to Father by then.

Ms. Coleman loved Mother but wished she wouldn't go on so about marriage. Ms. Coleman believed if God was running her life, and she had faith He was, then the right person would be presented without her running around like a chicken with her head cut off looking for a man. All of Ms. Coleman's time was taken up maintaining her straight "A" average and researching poor schools in the South. She was determined to be of use to children. Not cause she had to but cause she wanted to.

After graduation, she tried to make Father understand The Talented Tenth had a responsibility to reach back to the underprivileged. Father said that was bullshit. Father was a good man but he was tired of everybody thinking he should give away his money just to prove how black he was.

"Nobody ever gave me anything and these poor niggers hate you more than the white folks do."

Ms. Coleman couldn't argue with that. She herself had been the target of less privileged folks with ugly minds no matter how much she tried to be nice to them. They always thought she was trying to be white. Nevertheless, she couldn't get these kids out of her mind. There was a picture of two of them in a newspaper one time. One had a guitar and was leaning with his friend against a strange tree that grew crooked out of the ground.

Ms. Coleman could have easily taught at one of the poor colored schools in the Georgia area. However, she had been spoiled, in a good way, all her life and needed to get away from her parents. So that was that. But not quite. Father told her,

"I will cover all your living expenses for one year. The minuscule salary you make down there in Butt Fuck Egypt can be used for soda pop money. After the allotted time is over, and you get this Sojourner Truth shit out of your system, you are expected to return home, accept the job at Howard, and get married like a normal woman."

Ms. Coleman was a saint but she wasn't crazy. Free living expenses sounded like gravy. It wasn't that much of a salary, after all. But she made secret plans to disobey Father and was sure he would understand after he saw all the good she would accomplish. Colored folks were the first people on earth in the richest section of the planet. Ms. Coleman never let herself forget that. She knew she could do it. Father gave her one last lecture and some traveling money while Mother cried.

Things were a little rocky when she got off the train to Braxton. Atlanta was the South, of course, but Ms. Coleman grew up on Auburn Avenue and wasn't used to white folks treating her like nothing. That was just the kind of stuff she read about.

There was no real board of education in Braxton, per se, at least not for colored children. About a dollar and forty-six cents was earmarked for the education of each child. The county sent them some books, when the white children were done with them, and had somebody with a clipboard come down, on occasion, to take notes about the dilapidated facilities they weren't gonna do nothing about no way. Because there was no administration for the colored schools that counted, Ms. Coleman was greeted by a leader of the community named Deacon Early. She thought of how appropriate that was since colored churches were always the first meeting posts of anything important dealing with social change. When Deacon Early dropped her off at the boarding house in town, which he also owned, he grabbed her titties and stuck his tongue in her ear.

Father used to be a boxer back in the war and taught his girl a thing or two about a balled up fist and where to point it. Ms. Coleman didn't believe in kicking a fella in the nuts because she thought that was cheating. So Deacon Early left out her room pinching his nose and holding his head back so the blood wouldn't get on his shirt. He later told his fourth wife he fell.

Deacon Early fell a lot.

Poor Ms. Coleman wanted to call Father and Mother but knew that would be a passport home. She thought about the fact Deacon Early had a key to her room and wedged a chair up against the door knob to keep him out. Now, Ms. Coleman ain't never had to use a chair for nothing in her life besides sitting in it. So she didn't know if she was doing this thing right or not. She pulled on the door a few times, and it seemed to hold, but she didn't feel completely safe. That's all she needed. To get raped and killed down here in Butt Fuck Egypt so Father could say he told her so. She cried herself to sleep that night.

Next morning wasn't much better. The boarding house served something that was supposed to be breakfast and Ms. Coleman realized she took Mother for granted. She planned to write a lovely note telling her so. Ms. Coleman understood her parents weren't bad people, but just two hard working Negroes who didn't strive to ensure her an easy childhood, just so she could turn around and have a difficult adulthood. She poked her fork at some stuff the waitress called grits and forced herself to eat it. This was the only place in town a colored woman could get a meal and Ms. Coleman had to keep her strength up. She wiped away tears and thoughts of Father and Mother. Her first day of class would be later that week and she had many things to do.

Some Big Man, who smelled like liquor, and called himself the custodian, drove Ms. Coleman out to the school so she could get a look at the place. Lord have mercy, it was worse than she expected. She asked the Big Man to help her clean it up and he looked at her like she was crazy.

"Now, see here," Ms. Coleman said. "There are things here that need to be cleaned. You're the custodian. Who the hell should I call? The plumber?" Almost getting raped and having a bad breakfast was getting on Ms. Coleman's nerves. "Don't you have any children? Do you honestly want them sitting in this filth?"

"Lady, I gots five boys and they too busy working the fields 'stead a messing round with school."

"Messing around? Sir, your children need an education."

"Naw, my chirren need to have they ass in the fields so we can have a roof over our heads. You ain't gonna let us live in this school, is you? Didn't think so. But I'll help you clean up if it'll shut you up."

Ms. Coleman forced herself to get over the fear of being alone with another local man and accepted the cold offer. She couldn't be afraid of these people if she was going to help. As she began to mop, and the Big Man moved desks into the yard to hose them down, Ms. Coleman was struck with doubts.

Why am I here? Am I trying to prove something by making life more difficult? Am I embarrassed to be a rich, little colored girl? So I come down here to prove how black I am? Maybe some of that teasing got to me more than I realized. Do these people even want my help? If this man doesn't care about his children's education then why should I? I don't have any children. And, according to Mother, I never will at this rate.

She wrung out the dirty mop like an amateur and continued her monologue in the Garden of Gesetheme.

What am I doing here? If the parents won't make the children come to school then what am I supposed to do? Maybe it's a waste of time. What's the use of learning about a bunch of things that have no practical application to these children? Who cares if Columbus discovered the world in 1492 if you have to pick strawberries in the morning? Am I arrogant? Who am I to think I can come down here, like a little white missionary, and change people's lives? I need to let them see me. That's it. I need to let these people see who I am.

Ms. Coleman won that round with the devil and decided to go to revival that night. Even if it was at that horrible man's church. She continued her fucked up job of mopping and thought of a few of her favorite things.

That night, Ms. Coleman put on one of her many pretty dresses that Mother ordered from New York City. She got a ride from another girl staying in the boarding house who was passing through Braxton to meet her fiancee in Troy. Ms. Coleman briefly wondered why that made her jealous. Then she got in the Oldsmobile and chatted on the way to church.

When they arrived, the future bride went off to say hey to some folks she knew from this juke joint on the edge of town. Ms. Coleman wondered what a future bride was doing in a juke joint but reminded herself it was none of her business. When the girl left her alone, which Ms. Coleman thought was quite rude, all the coloreds stared at the newcomer, like they was crazy, which coloreds will often do. Ms. Coleman waved to the Big Man who she saw with his five boys. He waved her over and she practically ran to his pew since she was relieved to see a somewhat friendly face. She was introduced to the Big Man's wife and each of his boys. The boys looked at her with their mouths open and smiled when she smiled at them. The Big Man informed his boys that this was their new teacher and they'd best not give her no trouble. Ms. Coleman was shocked.

"But I thought you said — "

"Yeah, well. Here's the thing. They can't all come on the same day. And sometimes all of 'em gonna miss some days. 'Specially round harvest season. You gotta get that through your head right now."

"Oh, yes! Sure. I mean... I'll do my best."

"I'm sure you will. We'd invite you to sit down but there ain't no room."

"Oh, of course! Don't worry about it." Ms. Coleman looked around the crowded church and didn't see anyplace to sit at all. The future bride had forgotten about her and was sitting over there with Deacon Early and some laughing men.

"You can sit with us," Sarah said. Ms. Coleman turned around and there they were. The two little boys from the newspaper article about the strange tree. She thought it odd one boy still had a guitar and wondered if he was with the choir. They were sitting with a kind looking woman, an attractive man, and a woman who looked hung over. Ms. Coleman stared at the boys in wonder.

"Uh, Miss?"

"Oh, Lord! I'm sorry," Ms. Coleman said. "Forgive my manners. I... I just... I just... I just..." The family looked at Ms. Coleman and waited for her to tell them what she just was.

"You're new, child. I get it. Sit down," Sarah said. Ms. Coleman regained the use of her mouth and introduced herself to the group who returned the introductions.

She relaxed for the first time since she got to Braxton and settled in to enjoy the revival. The Deacon opened the service with a prayer. Ms. Coleman grunted, which Sarah couldn't help but notice. The preacher, who was a guest from another church in Montgomery, looked kinda cute to Ms. Coleman. But she was convinced she would instantly land in the crack of Hell if she lusted after a man in a pulpit. So she cut that mess out.

The choir sang a rousing song about Daniel in the lion's den and all the folks stood up and clapped. Two people got the Holy Ghost for real and a few others got it for show. Sarah couldn't stand folks who faked the Holy Ghost. She just didn't get it.

Don't these fools know God the wrong one to play with? Ms. Coleman enjoyed the choir and, when they finished, the Cute Guest Preacher got up to talk. He had a deep voice that was unexpected coming from a fella that young.

"Nigger's voice deeper than mine," Mack said. Ms. Coleman laughed and Sarah kicked Mack in the leg. Benny dropped a quarter and got down on his knees to find it but Ms. Coleman coulda sworn he was looking up her dress. She saw Mack do something to Benny's arm out of the corner of her eye and the boy found his quarter all the sudden. Now she could concentrate on listening to the Cute Guest Preacher and keeping her own thoughts pure.

The Preacher began by shocking the crowd with how the Story of Job never made any sense to him whatsoever. Folks dropped their jaws and started looking crazy. Deacon Early scowled and looked around to see how much this would affect donations. The choir clutched their bibles and looked at the fella sideways. Sarah was shocked but wanted to see where this thing was going. Mack was just waiting for this thing to be over. Maddie woke up. Ms. Coleman just listened. The Story of Job never made any sense to her either.

The Preacher continued in confidence, though. He didn't do a lot of hollering, for the sake of hollering, and playing around with his voice in the pulpit. Sure, he had soul, but he also had a point. He knew the best way to get folks whooping and hollering was to talk straight to their hearts instead of trying to show off.

"Basically, in the story of Job, God and the devil make a bet one day. Devil say, 'Hey, Lord I betcha I can make that Job fella hate ya if you give me half a chance.' Job ain't done nothing to nobody, now. But God said, 'Take your best shot.' So the devil does all these things to Job but he still won't turn on God. His friends was no help cause they were telling Job he had to have done something wrong or God wouldn't be messing with him like this.

Job didn't turn on God but he was angry and cursed the day he was born. And I know good and well, down here in Braxton, Alabama, at least one or two of y'all have felt the same way."

"Amen!" said half the folks.

"Well!" said the other. Deacon Early said nothing.

"But even though Job didn't turn on God, he really did want to know why all this stuff was happening to him. At the end of the story, God appears to Job in a whirlwind and basically says, "I'm God. And I can do what I feel like doing. You human. You gotta deal with it."

Deacon Early stood up. "That's right!" he said. Most of the church applauded Deacon Early who sat back down looking smug.

Ms. Coleman worried about the Cute Guest Preacher. But the Preacher was heavily endowed with the Spirit and wasn't about to let a tough crowd worry him.

"But don't you see? Even though Job was restored for his trouble, that's no answer to a very good question. Now, I ain't trying to blaspheme here but God gave me a brain and I intend to use it. When you can't find no work, does it make you feel any better to say it's the will of the Lord? When you can't pay your bills, and you hear about another lynching, or your kids are sick, or you hear about a woman having three miscarriages in three years, does it truly make you feel any better, or help you understand, by hearing somebody say, 'Oh, well. That's the will of the Lord?'"

Nobody said nothing.

"Me neither. But a story that actually does make sense in the bible, when it comes to suffering, is the story of Joseph. Joseph was a special and wonderful child who made other folks around him feel jealous."

"Well!" Sarah said real loud.

"Joseph's brothers threw him down a well one day and told his daddy he was dead. Now, he didn't deserve that. Joseph was sold into slavery. Didn't deserve that. Joseph went to prison. Didn't deserve that either. Even helped folks in prison who was supposed to get him out when they got free. And they forgot all about him. Don't you just hate it when folks lie to you?"

"Amen! Well!" said the whole damn church.

"Chunk that ball, Reverend. Chunk that ball!" the Old Man said.

"Joseph suffered several other things in slavery. If you want to look them up, they somewhere towards the end of Genesis. I ain't bring my bible today, and it ain't like I got the whole thing memorized." Everybody but Deacon Early laughed. Ms. Coleman laughed longer than other folks did.

"But things started looking up for ole Joe. He became valuable to the Pharaoh. He made the best of what he had from where he was. Pharaoh noticed his hard work. Got a few more promotions. Got advancements in life."

"Well, all right!" The Big Man said.

"Then one day there was a famine that Joseph saw coming cause he was close to the Lord that way. Everybody in the land had to come to him for food because he knew how to plan. Even his own brothers, who threw him in the well, had to come a crawling to him. And after Joseph had a little fun at their expense... ain't nobody perfect, you know." The crowd laughed.

"After he had himself a little fun... he saved his family from famine by inviting them to live in the Kingdom."

"Amen!" said some folks from the choir.

"He saved the family that was house of Israel! The genealogical bloodline for the Son of God Himself! (You better preach!) Naw! Joseph didn't deserve his suffering! (Well!) Yeah! He got a raw deal! (Amen!) Naw! He didn't understand what was happening! (Go head, now!) But instead of being a pawn in the hands of fate, and calling that the will of the Lord... Joseph could say 'If I wasn't in this place... at this time... my family would have starved to death — "

The whole church shouted.

" — and *ev-e-ry-thing* would have been in vain. (Yes, Father!) Did he enjoy what happened to him? Course not! But at least he could see that God had never really abandoned him. And there was some type of *point* for everything he'd been through! And you know — "

Everybody heard a woman scream. It sounded like a holler from another time. Right then, right there, out of nowhere, Ms. Coleman got the Holy Ghost. And Sarah could tell it was the real deal. Luke and Benny got scared and scooted close to each other since the pretty lady in the nice dress was acting crazy. But kids don't know what they're looking at when they see the Holy Ghost.

They don't know the Holy Ghost is a gift from God that can't be faked. It's either there or It ain't. It's the very spirit of God Herself pouring into a human vessel. It only comes when a person realizes a truth. And the reason why folks look crazy when It comes, is cause they ain't used to all that love and power coming at them all at once. They just don't know how to handle it. Ms. Coleman was gone, child. Mack got hit in the face by one of her arms as he struggled to hold her down. Sarah, who had the Holy Ghost a few times herself, softly fanned Ms. Coleman and spoke comfort in her ear. The whole thing completely blew Maddie's high. The locals, who thought Ms. Coleman was stuck up before, looked at her with new respect.

"Who that?" somebody said.

"Oh, that's the new school teacher," the Big Man said. "She gonna be teaching all five of my boys."

"When?"

"Day after next. Didn't you know? This school season, nigger." Other folks made immediate plans to enroll their children in that school tomorrow. The Cute Guest Preacher looked down in the pews at the sight of an angel gone wild. Deacon Early's fourth wife snapped the choir to attention and got everybody singing Jesus on the Mainline. Maddie thumped Benny on the ear.

"Since you love that guitar so much, why don't you go up there and play with the choir?"

"Sorry, Aintee. I only work for the blues."

The church nurses took Ms. Coleman to the back and Sarah followed with her purse. The Preacher praised the Lord and lusted after Ms. Coleman. The Deacon thought this was an excellent time to pass the plate and he was right. It was the most lucrative take in revival history. Deacon Early never missed a trick for a man of God.

"So anyway," the Preacher concluded in a rush, "That's why I hate the Story of Job. God bless." And he was off that pulpit so fast and in that back room with that bawling school teacher it was a pity and a shame. Everybody said so. Folks thought it was just disgraceful. Ms. Coleman had been in town five whole minutes and she was now an inspiration and a scandal. This guaranteed a full class on the first day of school.

When Ms. Coleman woke up, from wherever she had been, she saw the smiling faces of Sarah and the Preacher. Ms. Coleman was disoriented and a little bit scared. Sarah explained to her that she had just received the Holy Ghost.

"I assure you that's impossible," Ms. Coleman said. "Father and Mother are both Methodists." Sarah just smiled. The Preacher reached down and held her hand.

"I guess God told you something you really needed to hear," he said.

"Well," said Ms. Coleman, not quite knowing what to say, "Thank God." Then right there, in front of Sarah and the nurses, the Preacher leaned down and kissed Ms. Coleman dead in the mouth! And do you know that slut kissed that nigger right back? Probably faking the whole damn thang. Running round here acting like she got the Spirit. The nurses ran out and told everybody with ears but Sarah just assumed it was the will of the Lord and invited them over for dinner sometime. Child, that school was so full on the first day of class some of them babies had to sit on the floor. Ms. Coleman had arrived.

Ms. Coleman was happy doing what God put her here to do and made the most of what she had. Sometimes, she got frustrated all the kids couldn't come to school every day but the classroom was never empty. The Preacher courted Ms. Coleman proper and even painted the school bright red just for her. Donations came in from around the community of chairs, paper, pencils, and a used bell from the church that was getting a renovation.

Ms. Coleman got in trouble with the white folks at the county cause she sent back some second hand books one time. When the white man with the clipboard came by to ask why, Ms. Coleman said they weren't good enough for her students. She reminded him of the law of separate *and* equal and let him know who her family was and all the lawyers they knew. The white man with the clipboard left in a huff but next week there was a box full of brand new books.

Maddie told Ms. Coleman she better watch her ass before the Klan come a calling. Sarah praised her for her bravery and dedication. Ms. Coleman and the Preacher came to the Martins for dinner and were thrilled to meet the legendary Rastus P. Jr., who had just started Benny's lessons a month earlier. The Preacher loved blues and enjoyed hearing Rastus talk about the history of the music.

"You know Robert Johnson, Mr. Rastus? I love his music, too."

"Yeah, I know him," Rastus said. "Nigger owe me money."

One time, the Preacher and Mack got into it about his sermon.

"So what you trying to say?" Mack said. "About Joseph and the Pharaoh? Be a good slave so master will notice and everything'll work out fine?"

"Lord have mercy," Sarah said. "You'll have to forgive him."

"Forgive me? Woman, I'm grown."

"You got it all wrong, Mack," the Preacher said. "I'm saying bad stuff is going to happen so we might as well make the best of it. And even though we don't like it, one day, it'll all make sense."

Mack grunted, Rastus laughed, and Sarah offered everybody more tea.

Luke and Benny had a big crush on Ms. Coleman and would always fight if the other fella said he was gonna marry her. That was around the time Benny started coming to school more regular. Between Ms. Coleman at day, and Luke at night, he finally learned how to read just fine.

Sarah made curtains for the classroom and Ms. Coleman was always drawing pretty pictures to hang up in class and give the kids something to think about. She'd write little slogans about success and determination with the art supplies she spent her own money on. All the kids would come home and tell their folks what they learned in school that day and most of the parents saw the point in an education. They were proud to have their kids knowing something more than they did.

Father and Mother were a little concerned when Ms. Coleman wrote she accepted a proposal of marriage from some nigger she met down there in Butt Fuck Egypt. But when they met the Cute Guest Preacher for the holidays, and found out his family had left him various properties in Maine, and that he graduated from Howard University; well then they warmed up to him just fine. In addition, Mother was very happy her daughter loved a man as much as she loved Father. That's every good Mother's fondest hope.

Father's one year deadline had come and gone but it really didn't matter anymore. The Preacher had volunteered for the NAACP when he was vacationing in Washington last summer. They remembered him and were so impressed with his personality, he was offered a good paying job. Ms. Coleman was in a state.

"I don't know why you can't take a job in Braxton. You know how much I love my children."

"Baby, there ain't no NAACP in Braxton. This is a great opportunity for me. For us. Washington has kids too."

"But not these kids. How can you be so selfish?"

"How can you be so silly?"

"Silly?" They had an awful fight about it and she screamed the wedding was off. She ran to the Martin house and cried in Sarah's arms for a good long time.

Luke was thrilled. He never liked that Preacher anyway and now he could have Ms. Coleman for himself. But when he saw she really had a broken heart he wasn't happy anymore. He got on his knees and prayed for the Preacher to come back. There was a knock at the door and there he was.

"How come you can't answer no other prayers that fast?" Luke said.

They made up in front of the Martins and Ms. Coleman agreed to follow her man to Washington. Father and Mother would be so happy. Now she'd be married like a normal woman.

The church threw a going away party and folks cried a lot. Red cried louder than anybody there but Luke and Benny decided not to make fun of him about it. All the kids gave her gifts of apples, pies, loving notes, and other pretty things their families could afford. Ms. Coleman made a speech she couldn't complete since she broke down in front of everybody there. The Cute Guest Preacher rubbed her neck while everybody formed a farewell line. The Big Man hugged her hard and wept.

"I thanks you kindly for what you did for my children."

"Thank you for helping me clean the school." Ms. Coleman promised everyone an invitation to her wedding in Atlanta. Nobody but Deacon Early could afford to go and he probably wouldn't be invited. But folks appreciated the gesture, just the same, and they continued to hug and kiss her good-bye.

The next day, Ms. Coleman and her Cute Guest Preacher died in a plane crash on the way to Washington. She wanted to take a car but he was determined to show her the best.

The town was destroyed. Luke didn't get out of bed for three whole days no matter how much his mama pleaded or his daddy threatened. But Mack was just talk. He wasn't gonna whup the boy at a time like that. Benny would come over and play him a song then curl up on the bed with him before falling asleep himself.

Benny never went to school again.

The teachers that followed were by the book and substandard. Deacon Early renamed the school, The Coleman Learning Academy, and wrote Father and Mother that he had done so.

The Cute Guest Preacher was right. The Story of Job is a fucked up tale.

So anyway, that's why this benefit was so important. The Coleman Learning Academy was being dedicated today. Rastus and Benny had to be better than great. They had to be Soldiers for The Blues.

Because this was a woman who lived and died for children. She didn't fit in with the locals but they adopted her as their own. She came into womanhood in their town. She fell in love in their town. She received the Holy Ghost in their town. She made life better in their town.

This benefit was for Ms. Debbie Coleman. And it had to be the best in the world.

18

Folks got there early. The moon was out, the church was full, and a cool breeze made the summer night tolerable. It was one year ago tonight Ms. Coleman came to revival in Braxton.

"She had just got through talking to me," the Big Man said. "I said you sit down now, sugar, cause the service 'bout to start. See, folks got to be ready for the Holy Ghost. You got to be in a sitting position, so when you get knocked on your ass, you'll be already there. I said, you sit down now, sugar. And she did. Sure 'nough. She sat right down. My five boys was her first students, you know. Mmm, hmm. Yes, sir. All five. Yes, indeed. Cause I say, Ms. Coleman, these chirrens need to get up in that school and get a education and you gots to get that through your head right now. Didn't I say that, baby? Mmm hmm."

Folks piled into the church that smelled of new paint. Deacon Early used some money from The Joint to renovate the church for a tax write-off. It worked like a charm and now Little Bethel was just as big as the white church which hadn't gone unnoticed by Boss Man Braxton. He spotted Deacon Early on the way to the benefit and frowned at his brand new suit.

"Early? Come here a minute, boy."

"Yes, sir, Mr. Braxton, what can I do for you, sir?"

"You always talk like a congressman or something, you know that, boy?"

"Yes, sir, Mr. Braxton, I knew that, sir. Is there anything else?"

"Y'all getting together for that colored gal from Atlanta tonight, boy?"

"Her name was Ms. Debbie Coleman, sir. And the answer to the question is yes." Braxton hated it when Deacon Early answered questions like that. It wasn't that he was disrespectful but Braxton could tell that he didn't respect him. Deacon Early wasn't confrontational like Mack but he had his ways.

"That church almost big as the white one, boy."

"Twenty square feet bigger, sir, begging your pardon, but I'm sure God can fit into both places." Deacon Early chuckled while Braxton gave him a half smile.

"Waste of money, you ask me. Y'all nigras ain't up to nothing funny in that church, is you? Heard your Ms. Coleman's fiancee was working for that N double P P."

"That's right, sir. And we were double proud of him. At any rate, sir, the good white folks of Braxton have nothing to fear from the denizens of Little Bethel."

"Ain't nobody said we was scared of y'all, boy."

"I'm sure I didn't hear that, sir. And why should you be, sir? We do the same things in our church that good white folks do in theirs."

"Like what, boy?"

"Why pray, of course, sir. Just pray."

"Uh huh. And exactly what do nigras pray for these days?"

"Just the usual, sir. Nothing to concern an important man like yourself. I'm sure you'll still be here in the morning. Good day, sir."

Deacon Early strutted into Little Bethel right up to his reserved seat. He shook plenty of hands while "Precious Lord" rolled out of the organ and was reverently introduced to the Colemans. They all settled in and waited for the program to begin.

Backstage, Benny was nervous and Rastus was high and Luke was walking around like a manager or something. He made Benny get up and do jumping jacks to work off his tension. Benny complied even though didn't feel like it. Rastus noticed Benny usually did whatever Luke told him to do. After the exercise program, Luke made Benny sit down and drink some juice and close his eyes. Benny wanted water but Luke said juice was better so that was that.

Rastus stood up and stretched. He tuned Jeraldine and tried to block out the Little Angels youth choir who were out front butchering, "Go tell It on the Mountain."

"Can kids go to hell for fucking up a gospel song?" Rastus said. Luke and Benny laughed. "It ain't funny. It really ain't." He plucked Jeraldine's chords and twisted her frets. Benny's guitar had been tuned by Rastus earlier, but because his hero was messing around with Jeraldine, he figured he'd better do the same to... to...

"Hey!" Benny said. Luke and Rastus jumped from the yell and folks in the congregation turned towards the back room to see what was going on. Rastus rushed Benny and yanked him by the arm.

"You little fucker, why you scream out like that?"

"Don't you know folks can hear you, Benny?" Luke said.

"I'll handle this, boy." Luke sat down somewhere. Rastus knelt down so he could look Benny in the eye. "Now let me tell you something, boy. I am Rastus P. Jr. I'm a drunk, a reefer head, and a scene. But damn it, I'm a professional and there's just some things I ain't gonna tolerate. Don't you ever yell out while there's an act on-stage. You hear me? I will slap your little ass so hard you'll start giggling. "

"Sorry, Rastus."

"Now what the fuck is your maladjustment?"

"My guitar ain't got no name. You got Jeraldine. I got a guitar." Rastus pondered a minute. He sat by the window and realized he was out of reefer then remembered what he was supposed to be thinking about.

"Come here, boy." Benny came over and sat in Rastus's lap with the nameless guitar. Grateful applause could be heard from the pews as the Little Angels ended their torture. "You know, Benny... uh, Luke, come on over here so you ain't over there by yourself looking crazy." Luke ran to Rastus and jumped in his lap. "Ow! God damn! Don't dive on my nuts like a drunk squirrel. You crazy?"

"Sorry, Rastus." Rastus thought about what he wanted to say and Deacon Early got up to make a speech about Ms. Coleman.

"You know, Benny, naming your guitar's a very important thing in a man's life. She's your calling card. She's your weapon. She's your — "

"Why it gotta be a she?" Luke said.

"Nigger, don't question me. Who the star round here? It's a she cause I say so. It's always a she. What the hell he look like stroking a man on-stage? It just ain't done." Luke didn't see the point in that but decided to let it ride.

"Now it's gotta be a woman who's important to you, boy. Who's changed your life in some way. You got a little girlfriend or something?" Benny and Luke laughed so he took that as a no. "Well, it ain't gotta be a girlfriend. It could be any woman who's important to you. What about your mama? Be a nice tribute." Benny didn't really warm up to that idea. He didn't even know his mama. Then his eyes brightened up.

"What about Ms. Sarah? She like my mama in a way."

"All right, now!" Rastus said. "Benny and Ms. Sarah. Got a nice ring to it."

"Uh-uh," Luke said. "I don't want nobody stroking my mama on-stage." So they let that ride.

"Hey, I know," Rastus said. "I'll be generous and give you one of my bitches. How's about Linda? Ole gal I used to fuck in St. Louis. One breast was bigger than the other. When I fucked her sideways, it looked like a titty fight." Nobody said nothing. "Oh, I know, I know," Rastus said. "Queenie. Big bitch I used to fuck in Tennessee. Don't never turn down no big bitch, boys. Pussy so hot we used to have a weenie roast. Benny and Queenie. Sound good, don't it?" Nobody had much to say to that either. "I got it, I got it now. Kay Kay. Sweet bitch. Mouth big as the Nile as twice as wet. Mama of my two twin boys in California. Fine woman. Always liked her." Nobody was into Kay Kay. Luke felt it was safe to say something again.

"I know. Lucille. That's a nice name." Rastus rolled his eyes.

"Now, Luke, what the hell a blues man look like with a guitar named Lucille? Ain't no future in that."

"Yeah, Luke," Benny said. Luke thought Lucille was a fine name for a guitar but decided to let it ride. Time passed and the fellas listened to part of Deacon Early's speech about being the first to take Ms. Coleman in his capable hands.

"Well, shit. I'm dry," Rastus said after while. "Name your own damn guitar. I named mine." He shoved the boys off his lap and

Deacon Early's speech ended. Father and Mother were introduced to a standing ovation.

"Who's Jeraldine named after, Rastus?"

"Luke, my boy, there's some things a man oughta keep to himself." Rastus finished tuning Jeraldine while Benny looked at his no name guitar. The adult choir got up and sang "Soon I Will Be Done."

"Don't worry, Benny," Rastus said. "A fine name will come to you one day. Don't force it."

"Yeah, giving something a name ain't nothing," Luke said. "Adam named all the animals."

"That's a lie," Benny said.

"It ain't a lie. It's a story. There's a difference," Luke said.

"It's still a lie. How Adam gonna name all the animals in the whole damn world? Don't make no sense." Luke forgot he questioned God's logic all the time and got mad. He liked bible stories and didn't want anybody trashing them.

"It does too make sense. He had to name the animals cause God told him to. God made all the animals in the world to come to Adam. They did, and he named 'em one by one."

"Shit, that sound like it took all day," Rastus said.

"Probably did," Luke said. "Who cares? The point is he named the animals."

"Nigger, please," Benny said. "If I was a lion and I came up on Adam, and he said, Okay. You look like a lion. I'd say, Okay. You look like dinner."

"You so goddamn stupid, Benny," Luke said.

"Hey now, hey now," said Rastus. "Chillun don't need to be cussing in the church. Y'all wait till y'all get outside."

"Name your own stupid guitar."

"I will, nigger. Talking 'bout Adam named all the animals."

"He did, bitch." Rastus was through.

"Now, look here, motherfuckers. I'm gonna name you 'Foot Up Your Ass' and you 'Teefs On the Floor' if yall don't shut the fuck up like I told you to." The boys shut up. It had been a long day and nobody wanted a foot up their ass or their teeth on the floor. The audience applauded the choir who began the second song, "Were You There When They Crucified My Lord?" Luke peeked around the wall to see what was going on. "Get your little ass away from there!" Rastus said. "Now look here, Benny. I figured we'd start off with — "

"Oh, uh, I didn't tell you? Luke wrote us a song already. Wees gonna sang that."

"Oh, wees is? Where the fuck Luke get off writing a song? Why y'all didn't tell me? Who the star round here?" Luke looked at the ceiling.

"Luke can write real good," Benny said.

"What the fuck Luke know? He thank one nigger named all the animals." Luke looked hurt and Rastus felt an unfamiliar feeling that might have been guilt. "Aw, come on, now, Luke. You know I'm playing with you."

"No, you ain't."

"All right, I ain't. Now stop pouting. If I wanted to look at a pouting child, I'd go home. Your little ass don't know nothing 'bout writing no song and I do and that's that." Benny walked up on Rastus and stood with a slant.

"Now, look here, motherfucker. If we don't use Luke's song? I ain't going on. And that's that."

"Boy, I just bought your broke ass a new box. You can play it here or the hospital. Take your pick."

"Just forget it. Forget the whole thing," Luke said. He went to the window and got that far away look. Benny put his hand on his shoulder.

"How you gonna say no if you ain't even looked at it?" Benny said.

Rastus cursed himself for forgetting his brandy and made a vow it would never happen again. "What so important about this song?"

Benny waited on Luke to answer.

"One day Ms. Coleman told us to write a narrative poem," Luke said.

"Uh, huh. A narrative poem, huh?"

"Yeah. A narrative poem is a poem that tells a story."

"I know what a narrative poem is, little fucker."

"Oh. Well. Anyway. I wrote it. Ms. Coleman liked it a lot. She made me read it in front of the whole class. I didn't want to at first but she told me I should never hide my light under a bush."

"A bushel," Rastus said.

"Right. So. I did. Everybody clapped real loud. I liked that. I liked it a lot. When everybody left, Ms. Coleman kept me after school. She said she didn't want to say nothing in front of the class because she didn't want to play favorites. But she thought I had a great ca... capacity for storytelling. She said I should always look at things the way I do no matter what nobody say. The next day, we had the party for her and then..."

And then Luke didn't get out of bed for three whole days. Benny pretended he was looking at a picture on the wall.

"So what this narrative poem about, anyway?" Rastus said.

"It's a story about a boy who sells his soul to the devil so he can be the greatest blues man in the world."

"You calling me the devil?" The end of the choir's song was met with applause and amens. A ten minute intermission was announced and folks went outside to get refreshments.

"I ain't calling you the devil. It's just a story, that's all. I started writing it and then it's like... I wasn't writing by myself no more. Something took over and the story started telling itself. Like it had a mind of it's own. I didn't hardly have to erase or nothing." Luke stopped speaking while the other two watched him. He was in his own world again and would be back in a minute. "When I was finished, I just looked at it and read it over and over 'til I was almost tired of it. Then I read it again. It was about us but not about us. We was in it but we was like... like..."

"Like building blocks," Rastus said. "The story is way bigger than you are and demands to be told." He looked out the window and held Jeraldine to his chest. "It'll come through you or some-body else but it's gonna live. Just like water gonna flow. But could go through a river or a stream. Just like the wind gonna blow. Through a windmill. Or a sail. Or a pretty gal's hair. The story gonna be told and there ain't nothing gonna stop it. And it uses you. Like a farmer use a mule. That's what a story does."

"That's right," Luke said. "That's it." Benny was quiet. Luke and Rastus were in a place where he couldn't go and he didn't want to say something stupid.

"Let me see this thing," Rastus said. Luke pulled the folded sheets of paper out his pocket. Benny already knew the words but they still had to compose the music. Rastus didn't know the words and only had a few minutes to learn them. Piece of cake. He just had to make sure it was worth his time. He wasn't about to let sentiment mess up his show. He scanned the pages. Laughed a little. Laughed a lot. Nodded his head. Shook his head.

He took out a chewed-up pencil and scratched some things out. Wrote some things in. Luke got mad about that but kept his mouth shut.

"Benny, get over here," Rastus said. He gave him a bass line. Benny absorbed it. Rastus hummed a little. Benny sang the hum. Then they put their heads together and talked. Luke sat himself down somewhere. The story didn't belong to just him anymore and he had to get out of the way.

19

"Well, here we are," said Father. "Butt Fuck Egypt. Population? Pathetic."

Intermission took place under a huge tent the Big Man and his boys erected earlier that morning. The tent was left over from a traveling colored circus that came to Braxton three years ago. The circus was chased out of town by the Klan on account of a trapeze act, with two muscular black bucks, swinging a white gal through the air with the greatest of ease. And it looked like she was enjoying herself. The next night, a cross burned at the entrance of the tent so the colored circus dropped everything and hightailed it out of town. The Big Man didn't see the point in disposing of such a nice thing and kept it stored in the church basement in case it was ever needed. Deacon Early thought it was stupid. When the hell would they ever need a circus tent? Tonight, however, confirmed the Big Man's foresight.

A spread of food cooked by local ladies sat upon cloth covered tables on both sides of the entrance. Flowers from Sarah's garden book-ended the delights: Thick slices of roast beef covered with gravy, hot cornbread with melted butter, yellow potato salad with speckles of relish, barbecue ribs dipped in hot sauce and honey, smoked chicken seasoned with lemon and pepper, hot pots of greens with a ham hock flavor, five apple pies, four peach cobblers, three lemon meringue pies, and one strawberry pie.

But Father wasn't hungry. Mother ate some chicken, just to be polite, but didn't believe in eating just anybody's potato salad. She refused the offer from a local lady who walked away rolling her eyes at her friends. Sarah approached the Colemans, trying to be nice, but sensed her presence made them uncomfortable. She reminded herself these people were still grieving and left. Deacon Early tried to engage Father in conversation and was treated a bit better since he flew them in. Still, it was an awkward chat so Deacon lied about having things to check on.

"My God, how do these people exist in this heat?" Father said. He patted his brow with a monogrammed handkerchief.

Sarah asked Mack talk to them but he refused. Mack believed the Colemans should at least fake a better attitude, grieving or not. Sarah got mad at him and forced herself to talk to Maddie who was drinking lemonade that smelled kinda strong.

"So how you feeling, Maddie?"

"Oh, girl, I'm feeling fine." She swayed on her feet and Sarah grabbed her elbow to steady her.

"Getting started early, ain't you?"

"Oh, girl, leave me alone. Rastus brought me some white folks gin to apologize. Couldn't insult the man by not drinking, now could I? Can you see it?"

"Keep your voice down, Maddie."

"Well can you see it? That's what I wanna know."

"Yeah, I can see it if you keep poking your head at me like a fool. But if you just act natural, like you got some sense, then naw, I can't see it. Hold still." Sarah examined the make-up job she did on Maddie's bruise. She wore a veil and most of the swelling had gone down. "You could use a little touch up. Come on." They walked out back for some privacy.

"I ain't mad at him, Sarah, so don't you be either, all right?" Sarah dug in her purse for make up. "I said it's over, girl. You hear me?"

"Whatever you say, Maddie. Take off the veil." Sarah closed the back flap of the tent.

Inside, Charlie geared himself up to meet the parents. He used to see Ms. Coleman at church and drove supplies to the school in his truck. She was always so appreciative but he didn't think it was a big deal since he passed the school every day. Ms. Coleman always made folks feel that ordinary acts were special. So, out of respect for her, he figured he should go speak. He tried to get Mack to go over there with him but Mack said,

"To hell with them stuck up niggers." Charlie made a reserved approach.

"How yall doing?" Charlie said.

"Fine, thank you. Yourself?" Father said. Mother nodded.

"I'm Charlie." Father introduced himself with a strong handshake. Charlie couldn't stand fellas who tried to break your hand when they shook it. What did it prove? "Your daughter was a fine woman. Fine woman. I see where she got her looks from, Mrs. Coleman. If Mr. Coleman don't mind me saying." Charlie laughed.

"No, I don't mind," Father said. "Not really." Charlie stopped laughing. He looked back to Mack for reinforcement but he was sitting over there with his arms folded.

"Yeah. So. What kind of business you in, Mr. Coleman?"

"Both my wife and I are retired school teachers."

"Oh, yeah?" Father didn't respond. He despised answering the same question twice.

"Well," Charlie said. "Guess it runs in the family, huh?"

"That's a fair assumption," Father said. He checked his watch. Mother tried to help out this dismal demonstration of the art of conversation.

"So, what kind of business are you in, Charlie?"

"Oh, I'm a sharecropper just like every other nig… uh… colored nig… uh, person round here. Except Deacon Early. And the HooDoo Woman. And the Pim… this dik… uh, this lady we all knows and, uh some of her employees."

"Oh, really?" Mother said. "A woman entrepreneur? How inspiring. And what does she do exactly?" Charlie felt a desperate need to be invisible.

"Oh, well, you know."

"No," Father said. "We don't."

"Oh, well, you know. She arranges for, uh, parties, and stuff like that."

"Like a hostess?" Mother said.

"Yeah, that's right," Charlie said real fast. "A hostess." Mother was confused but Father wasn't.

"A professional hostess?" Mother said. "In this area?" She realized how that sounded and wished she could stuff the words back in her mouth. Charlie just looked at her.

"Just drop it, dear," Father said. Mother finally caught up with the program and her back stiffened up like she smelled something on her shoe. Charlie's desire to be invisible returned with a new wish to die.

"But Ms. Coleman never met her. That's why she ain't here. The hostess, I mean. Not Ms. Coleman." Father and Mother didn't even bother helping out. "Sure is hot, huh? Well. We sure did love us some Ms. Coleman, I tell you that right now. And y'all sure did do a good job with her, I tell you that too. And. Well. We sure is sorry."

"Thank you," said Father.

"Thank you," said Mother. Charlie went to pour himself a drink.

Father tolerated other town folks who got up the nerve to form a greeting line despite the gossip floating about like fog that it was a really bad idea. And it was. Father was just awful. Mother did her best to deflect his disdain but she didn't have the flow. Every time she opened her mouth, it became more evident, along with her pearls and cultured posture, that she had nothing in common with these people. So the condolences just got down to, "Sorry 'bout, Ms. Coleman." Then a quick handshake and a nod to Mother. Mack was over there chewing roast beef when Sarah and Maddie reappeared.

"Where y'all been?"

"Nowhere," Sarah said. She wiped gravy off his chin and looked at him with concern. "What's the matter with you, Mack Martin?" He put his plate down on the table and held her hand.

"People who don't do nothing but take up space live 'til they ninety-nine years old. Good folks die when everything's going right. Just don't make no sense." She touched his face.

"You right. It don't." Maddie put down her lemonade and wrapped her arms around them both.

"Maybe, like in the Story of Joseph, it'll all make sense one day," Maddie said.

The line thinned down to three sacrificial lambs for Father's contempt. He embarrassed Mother but she understood. This was the place that killed Debbie. The place they never wanted her to go. But she admired Debbie for following her own mind. Mother was never like that as a girl. At least Debbie got to love who she wanted and do what she wanted. Most people go a lifetime without that happening. So Mother forgave Father's unforgivable breach of etiquette. After all, Mother loved Father.

Deacon Early came back out of the church ringing a cow bell.

"Ladies and Gentlemen, your attention. Your attention, please. We have one more presentation before the dedication of the Coleman Learning Academy." Mother felt pride hearing the official name. "We have a special song by none other than Rastus P. Jr." Folks went crazy with hooting and hollering which offended Father. Mother clapped along as Father whispered in her ear.

"I've never seen such bad taste. These hicks act like this is a hoot in-nanny or something."

"Really, dear. Why don't you try showing a little grace?" Mother said through a smile.

"Grace?"

"Yes. This is all for Debbie. Or don't you know that?" Father scowled and the applause continued.

"Well who the devil is this circus act they're bringing out?"

"It's not a circus act. It's the blues."

"You've heard of this savage?"

"Honestly, dear. Everyone's heard of Rastus P. Jr." The tent got quiet and Deacon Early continued.

"So, let's all finish your lemonade, or whatever you got in that cup, Maddie…" Everyone, including Maddie, laughed while she shot Deacon Early a bird. Mother giggled and Father was disgusted.

"… and get back up in this church!" Folks guzzled their drinks and swallowed their food. The church matrons fussed at people about putting their trash in the garbage pail. Deacon Early parted the line that formed out of the tent on his way to get Father and Mother.

"Right this way, Mr. and Mrs. Coleman," Deacon Early said.

"I think we've seen enough."

"Excuse me?"

"We're done," Father said. "We're going home. Now. I mean, honestly. First, we have to sit through all these choirs. What were you people thinking? Don't you know that makes us relive the funeral?" Mother was mortified. Deacon turned to check the line, and sure enough, folks were pretending not to listen. "All that wailing was depressing. And those children. My God, man. Were those Debbie's students? What was that? Revenge for too much homework or something?" Deacon Early got hot.

"Now, see here, Mr. Coleman, it's not like these kids are professional singers. It's the spirit that counts."

"What a dull cliché," Father said.

"But, I believe you'll find that Rastus P. Jr. never disappoints. Your daughter and her fiancee were quite fond of him."

"Debbie never knew what was good for her!" Nobody bothered pretending they weren't listening anymore and just plain turned around and looked.

"Please, dear." Mother grabbed Father's arm. "Don't do this." Father shook her off and pointed at Deacon Early.

"You killed her." He turned to the crowd. "You all killed her!" Everyone whispered. "I told her and I told her. To leave you dumb ass geechy niggers to yourselves. But no."

"Honey, stop it! Please, forgive him. He doesn't know what he's saying."

"The hell I don't!" His voice echoed to the top of the tent. Maddie stepped forward and put her arm around Mother.

"Now, you listen to me, Mr. Coleman. Wees all upset. Wees all miss Ms. Coleman. But you just need to settle down, now. Think about your wife here. My nephew's in this show with Rastus and they'll make you feel better. Now just settle." Father flat out laughed at Maddie. Everybody looked on as he laughed and laughed and laughed. Mother put her face in her hands.

"Woman," Father said, "You're a drunk and a fool. One condition can be corrected. The other cannot." Maddie quivered in humiliation. Mack stepped up to the plate.

"Nigger, you crazy or something?"

"Oh great," Father said. "It's John Henry."

"I ain't no John Henry but I can still drive a spike up your ass." People laughed as Deacon Early pushed Mack away from Father.

"Mack, don't you start none of your foolishness on church grounds. I'm telling you that right now." Sarah ran into the church.

"I'm all right, Deacon, I'm all right." Mack moved Deacon Early aside. "Now, let me tell you something, mister. You see all this food out here? Well, we don't eat like this everyday. This out here for y'all. Even though you don't think it's good enough for you. We can't afford to feed our own children like this while you running around claiming we killed your daughter. We got to crop them berries tomorrow, mister. And the cracker we work for don't give a damn 'bout Ms. Coleman. But we do. That's why Deacon Early named a whole school after her. Now, I know you messed up 'bout your little girl. Who ain't? But you need to start acting like a man, nigger." People cheered and Deacon Early looked at Mother with regret. But Father wasn't going down that easy.

"You ignorant hick. You presume to talk to me like that?"

"I presume to slap the black off your ass if you got any left." Father took off his jacket and threw it to Mother who began to cry.

"I might not be black enough for the likes of you. But I was a boxer in the war, John Henry. And I'm black enough to beat your dumb ass."

"Well, come on with it, Cary Grant! Bring it on!" Charlie got there just in time to hold Mack back while Father assumed the boxing position. Mother screamed.

"Beat his ass, Mack!" yelled Maddie. She took another sip of lemonade. The crowd gathered around and said pretty much the same thing. Deacon Early spoke to the heavens.

"I've said it before… and I'll say it again… My people. My people."

Just then, everybody heard music and spun around to the entrance of the tent. Rastus and Benny were armed with guitars. Luke and Sarah stood behind them.

"I know y'all ain't started the party without me!" Rastus said. "Well, since y'all don't feel like coming to us, we decided to come out here to you."

He crunk up the bass and approached like a snake charmer. Benny joined in. Rastus got up on Mack and Benny stepped into Father. Jeraldine called and the no-name guitar responded. No-name called and Jeraldine responded.

"How everybody doing tonight?" Rastus said. A few people halfway answered. "I say how y'all motherfuckers doing tonight!" Mother felt faint. The crowd answered louder and Deacon Early leaned his head against the tent pole and prayed. Rastus hummed a little gospel and ascended Jeraldine's pitch. Benny maintained the beat. "Hey, Mack! What up, nigger? Mack Martin, ladies and gentlemen! Give him a hand!" Folks clapped in confusion. "Give it up, God damn it or I'm leaving! Mack Martin, motherfuckers!" The applause went up.

Luke cheered loud for his daddy but Sarah pinched him real hard so he cut that out. Mack looked at Rastus like he wanted to kill him.

"I declare, I declare. Mack a crazy ole nigger, ain't he?" A few folks giggled. "Y'all know it's true. Shit. This nigger would arm wrestle Jesus at the Last Supper." Everybody laughed, even Sarah. Rastus changed cords and matched Benny's riff. "No, sir. I don't fuck with ole crazy ass Mack. Nuh-uh. Mack so mean snakes won't bite him. I ain't lying." Charlie bent over in a chuckle and pointed at Mack. Sarah smiled, waved him over, and he walked to her like a bashful child. "Yeah, that's right. Get on over there with your woman. Sarah, see if you can train that nigger." More folks laughed and a few patted Mack on the back. Rastus took this time to look Father up and down.

"You ain't the revenue man, is you?" Father was not amused. Especially when he noticed Mother wobbling under stress. Rastus noticed too. "Lady? I'm sorry. But you've had enough." The no-name guitar underscored the hoots and hollers from the crowd. Deacon Early hid in the shadows.

"Now, see here," Father said. "I don't think you're very funny. My wife doesn't drink."

"Oh. Well, that's the problem." That brought the tent down. Folks slapped their legs and elbowed each other then formed a circle around Rastus, Benny, Father, and Mother. Once again, Jeraldine made the call and, once again, No-name answered. Rastus smiled at the Coleman's, showing them just how white teeth can get. Mother made eye contact with Rastus and relaxed a bit. Rastus winked at her and gave Father a nudge.

"I'm just playing with you now, just playing. Go stand over there in the crowd somewhere." Father hesitated. "Go head now. You fucking up the show. And take that drunk woman with you." Mother screamed in shock and laughed with the crowd. It was her first genuine laugh since she got there. Father led his wife to the sidelines with a firm grip.

"All right, folkses. Here we go. We all know why we're here. For a very special lady who was taken away too soon: Ms. Debbie Coleman." Everybody applauded and Mother's smile faded. Father noted the tears of both children and adults while the applause went on long and loud.

"Let's take a moment of silence to ask God why."

The guitars broke the silence.

"All right, then. Debbie Coleman was a woman who thought every kid was special. She encouraged the chilluns. One such boy was Luke Martin. Come on up here, Luke." Mack and Sarah exchanged looks as Luke stepped between them into the circle. Everybody looked at him and wondered what the hell he had to do with this. Benny whistled support for his buddy in the middle of playing. "Luke Martin was one of Ms. Coleman's prize pupils." Luke spotted Father looking at him and looked away. "He wrote a narrative poem in her class one day and tonight we gonna set it to music. Now, for all you niggers who ain't in the know; a narrative poem is a poem that tells a story."

"Oooh," a bunch of folks said.

"And thanks to Luke; we got ourselves one hell of a story to tell. Tell the folks the name of your poem, boy!" Luke looked at everybody looking at him. Rastus encouraged him with a nod.

"The Devil and the Braxton Blues," Luke said.

Sarah led the applause and all but Father joined in.

"All right, all right!" Rastus said. "He a cute little thing ain't he? Nothing like his daddy. Get out the way there, Luke." Luke took his place by his parents in a great deal of discomfort because hadn't expected to be introduced. Adding to the anxiety was the fact that Rastus made a few *changes* and Luke was standing right next to his mama. "But Luke Martin ain't the only special boy among us tonight. In case y'all ain't noticed; me and Jeraldine ain't up here alone. Making his premiere debut to the coloreds of Braxton, is my protégé', Benny Raye!" Benny smiled, bowed, and turned around so everybody could get a good look at him. He showed off with an elaborate flourish on his instrument. "Benny Raye and... his guitar!" Benny narrowed his eyes during the ovation and Rastus chuckled at him.

"I'll get you for that," Benny said.

"You ready?"

"I been ready."

"Good. And, Benny? Whatever you do?"

"Yeah?"

"Don't fuck up."

Jeraldine took off and No-Name sped to catch up. Together, they formed a funky freight train of string carrying a cargo of blues. Mother stared at Benny while the crowd bounced to the beat. She remembered him from that picture Debbie couldn't stop talking about. Those boys. These people. The last ones to see Debbie alive. The music raced through the tent. Deacon Early tipped out the shadows. Luke's heartbeat matched the rhythm. "And now, Ladies and Gentlemen," Rastus hollered, "The Devil and the Braxton Blues!"

Rastus:
The Devil was drinking moonshine in this juke
joint made of fire.
Giving working gals some tips on how to be a liar.

Mack and Sarah looked at Luke. Mother clutched her pearls.

Everything was going gravy in the hell raising
place of Hell.

But there was only one thing wrong: There was no
   soul for sell.

Benny:

Business was good for that wicked soul.
Crackers getting richer and niggers in the hole.
But a certain situation made the Devil just yell.
The situation was: No souls for sell.

Rastus:

The Devil took out a crystal ball and knew just
   what to do.
He spied on every black boy, every white boy,
   every Jew.
Then all the sudden, he let out a shout. And, Lord
   what did he see?
Just a lonely, little colored boy crying by an Old
   Crook Tree.

Benny:

Look out, Braxton! Now he's here!
A laid off angel with nothing to fear.
Know any prayers? Better say you some.
Here he come, Braxton! Here he come!

Rastus:

He came to the boy at the Old Crook Tree saying,"
   What's the matter, child?"
When the boy looked up and saw who it was he
   just about went wild.
He didn't bother running cause he figured he was
   through.
He said, "Well, Mr. Devil, sir, I can't play the
   blues."
Take it, Benny!

Benny:

Went to the club with my pappy's guitar,
With all kinda plans 'bout being a star.
But when I started playing all the folks said, "Boo.
Get your ass off the stage, nigger, we hate you."
Got ran out the club by a pimp with a knife.
Right in front of everybody running for my life.
All the men started laughing and the women
*   laughed, too.*
Passed a cow in a pasture and the cow said,
*   "Boo."*
I gotta lot to sing about. Don't you see?
The blues is my life and my life's in me.
My mama been dead and my daddy ran away.
When it come to the blues I gots plenty to say.
I'm just a little colored boy wanting it good.
Wanna live like the rich folks in Hollywood.
Gonna have a full belly. Gonna have a full heart.
But the niggers down in Braxton won't let me start.

Folks started looking crazy and murmured amongst themselves. Luke looked straight ahead to avoid his parent's eyes. Father tapped his foot.

Rastus:

With a nod of his head the Devil said, "That's a
*   sorry tale, all right."*
With an evil gleam in his eye he said, "I'll fix you
*   up tonight."*
With a wave of his hand he said, "My powers will
*   help you reach your goal."*
With an evil, cackling laugh he shouted, "But
*   you'll have to sell me your soul!"*

Benny:

Devil reached in his overalls and pulled out an ax.
Took a swing at the tree and then he hit it like that.

Rastus:

After two hundred years of standing free,
That was the end of the Old Crook Tree.

Benny:

Then the Devil picked up a fat, green worm.
And laughed right at it and watched it squirm.

Rastus:

Then the Devil squeezed the worm and the guts
*   came out.*
Then he threw it on the wood and he turned
*   about.*
Yanked the boy by the hair plucking out a few
*   strands.*

Benny:

Took a dead turtle shell and then he cut him on the
*   hand.*
Put the blood on the wood and the child felt sick.

Rastus:

Broke a little piece of shell and said, "Use it for a
*   pick."*
Then they both jumped back when the lightning
*   struck.*
And the fire blazed up on the now dead trunk.
And the hair spread out making guitar strangs.
Devil blew the smoke off and said, "Play that
*   thang!"*

Benny:

Look out, Braxton! Here he come!
Boy playing blues with a loaded gun.
Boy playing blues with a story to tell.
Stroking on a music box straight from Hell.

Rastus:
When our boy showed up at the club that night,
the people laughed and said,
"You can't handle what we dish out. Go home and
go to bed."
But when he stroked that Hell box, and he started
to hear the call,
He wasn't holding nothing back. He let 'em have
it all.
Go, Benny!

Benny dropped to his knees and played like a nigger possessed. Possessed by a talent nurtured with belief and drilled past endurance. Encouraged before an audience of cows by a mentor with a big heart absent of pity. Tutored in the ways of rhythms and rhymes borrowed from ancestors heavy in chains. Fueled by rage masking the pain of neglect. Guided by a mind on the quest for adventure. The mind of a child. A child who knew the score.

Maddie was awed by her nephew's display and wished she had something to do with it. Father was mesmerized by the boy's fluid moves. Luke looked at Benny in admiration, thrilled at the sound of his poem coming to life. Mother got over her initial shock and clapped in approval. Everybody followed her lead and wildly applauded Benny's solo. The applause blended into the beat and Benny took his bow. Rastus looked at his pupil like a proud papa bird watching baby bird leave the nest. If it wasn't show time, he probably would have cried. But it was show time.

Rastus:
Told a tale of broken hearts and coloreds got the beat.

Benny:
Told a tale of broken dreams and coloreds tapped
their feet.

Rastus:

*Told a tale of broken homes and coloreds clapped
their hands.*

Benny:

*Told a tale of broken backs and made the coloreds
stand.*

Rastus:

*He played that magic guitar, man, like nothing
you ever seen.*
*All the men said, "Go head now!" And all the
women screamed.*
*And when the show was over, then the boy was
idolized.*
*The pimp who tried to kill him even came and
apologized.*
*Well, our boy was walking home that night, feel-
ing like the best.*
*Feeling the satisfaction of really knowing he
passed the test.*
*About that time, the lightning flashed and made
the hoot owl cry.*
*And just two seconds later, he looked the Devil in
his eye.*

Benny:

*Our boy said, "Thank you, Mr. Devil, for being oh
so great.*
*But I don't wanna sell my soul. I wasn't thinking
straight.*
*I never thought this possible. I never thought this
real.*
I see I'm gonna need this soul to tell how good I feel.

Rastus:
The Devil laughed his head off saying, "I could
not care less."
He picked his head up off the ground, said, "I
made you the best."
He screwed his head back on and said, "I say this
onto you:
Better gimme what you owe me, or you'll really
sing the blues."

Now it was solo time for Rastus. His rough hands slid down
Jeraldine's neck and she descended to a threatening bass. Thick
notes beat against the crowd and a vibe ran down their spines.
The crooked sneer of ownership erased his smile. He owned their
minds and the ears to their hearts. He owned their topic of tomorrow's conversation. He closed his eyes and laughed at a private
joke; then he flung Jeraldine in the air. The music stopped, heads
went back, and she flew to the top of the tent. She hung there a
second, floated down with a flip, and landed back in his hands.
Screams pierced the tent as Rastus demonstrated his nimble
touch. The touch of a man who paid his dues. The touch of a man
who played the blues. The touch of a black man who knew the
score.

Benny:
Then, something grabbed the Devil and it shook
him mighty hard.
It bent him like a horseshoe and he crumbled like
a card.
And standing above the Devil very tall and very
lean,
Was the biggest, strongest angel any man has ever
seen.

Luke jumped into the center and joined the party while his parents reacted in surprise.

Luke:

*To the Devil he said in a mighty voice, "You'll
take no one's soul.*

*Gonna teach this boy a lesson, so you go back to
your hole.*

*Now I know you had a bargain, so here's what
I'm gonna do:*

*The boy will give back every bit of his blues man
power to you."*

Luke touched No-Name's neck with the tip of his finger just as
Benny stroked a riff that faded. Sound was absorbed into the
angel's body who twisted round slowly like a man made of clouds.

He hypnotized the crowd with his silent ballet and stretched his
other arm to the sky. His fingers descended to the devil's guitar
that twanged with the return of it's dubious blessing.

Luke:

*To the boy he said in a mighty voice, "You have
been a fool.*

*The blues ain't nothing to play with, boy, and life
shoulda been your school.*

*You were too scared to try again. Too weak to reach
your goal.*

*You wanted it all so lightning fast you were will-
ing to sell your soul.*

Benny:

*So, the boy learned a valuable lesson about work-
ing for your dreams.*

*When we put our mind to the problem, then it
ain't as hard as it seems.*

*And the Devil went back a cussing in that juke
joint down in Hell.*

*But he had one major problem: There was no soul
for sell.*

Rastus, Benny, and Luke:
Look out, Devil! Better run!
When God get mad, it ain't no fun.
Got the Holy Ghost now and I'm hard to catch.
And our business is concluded in the strawberry
patch.

Rastus and Benny ended with a diddle and Luke did a split in the grass. Folks went crazy. Sarah and Maddie jumped up and down hugging each other while Mack whistled with two fingers in his mouth. He pushed through the crowd that swarmed the performers and picked Luke up with a hug.

"You did good, son! Real good!"

"Thank you, daddy." Sarah pushed Mack out the way to fuss over her baby. Some local ladies passed her by on the way to Rastus.

"Quite a boy you got there, Sarah," the lady said.

"I've always said so," Sarah said without looking back. She covered Luke with kisses and he whined.

"Not here, Ma."

"Oh, hush, now. I don't care if your little friends make fun of you or not. You're my baby and I want everybody to know it. Luke Martin, I am so proud of you."

"Thanks, Ma." Luke saw Benny trapped in Maddie's bawling bear hug. Benny didn't want to hurt Maddie's feelings so he let himself be suffocated to death. Rastus came to the rescue.

"Now, Maddie, you gonna make me jealous, gal. Come here." Maddie released Benny who fell to the ground in relief. All the kids came over to him and asked to touch his guitar but he told them to go to hell. Maddie took Rastus's face in her hands.

"I thanks you kindly for what you done for my family." For once, Rastus was at a loss for words. He answered by hugging Maddie and giving her a kiss. Luke finally made it to Benny and for a second there was nobody in the world but them.

"We did it!" Luke said.

"Yeah!" Benny said.

"You was great!"

"I know!" Luke laughed and they shook hands. Deacon Early pried his way through the thick jam of people.

"Excuse me, please. Pardon me. Whew! I declare. Hot as Hades, ain't it, boys?"

"What's Hades, Deacon Early?" Luke said. Deacon Early laughed and patted him on the head.

"Such an inquisitive child, ain't he? Mack. Sarah. You should be proud. The brightest child in my Sunday School class."

"Then how come you always rapping my knuckles when I ask a question?" Deacon Early laughed quickly to defuse the funny looks from Mack.

"Hades is another name for Hell, my boy, but I'm sure you won't have to worry 'bout that for quite a while. Benny! Benny Raye! I declare, I declare. All that talent in such a little man. God is good, ain't he?"

"How the hell would I know?"

"Watch yourself," said Maddie.

"You're quick, Benny. I like that. Benny, my boy, how would you like to headline at the club after Rastus leaves town? Hmm? You can have the gig until he gets back."

"Yeah!" Benny said.

"Careful, Benny." Rastus said. "The boy needs to be paid with money, Early, you know that right? Not five magic beans."

"Rastus, believe it or not, I'm gonna miss you."

"Oh, I believe it." Rastus and Deacon laughed and hugged. Maddie was thrilled.

"My nephew. Taking over for Rastus P. Jr. Lord have mercy. Well, what do you say to the good Deacon, Benny?"

"When I get paid?" Everybody laughed except Luke which didn't go unnoticed by Benny.

"Oh. What about, Luke? "Benny said.

"Yeah, what about Luke?" Mack said.

"Well, what about him? I mean, no offense, Luke was good. Real cute. But I need a guitar man who can sang. Now, Luke, you don't play the guitar, do you?" Everybody waited in discomfort for Luke to respond. Rastus eyed the Deacon like he might hit him but knew this wasn't the time or place. Luke stared at the guitar in Benny's hand then up at the waiting Deacon.

"Naw, I don't play no guitar. But I never wanted to." That last part made Benny get a little knot in his chest but he didn't know why.

"But I wrote the song. I told everybody where to stand in rehearsal. I'm the one who knows how things s'pose to be."

Sarah grabbed Mack's hand. Nobody said nothing for a spell and the crowd hushed a little to listen.

"Yeah," Benny said. "Luke know everything, all right." Rastus squinted his eyes at Benny. Luke got a knot in the center of his chest but he didn't know why.

"So, you wrote that song?" Father walked through the still crowd from the back of the tent with Mother right behind. He took a look at Mack, got down on his knees to Luke's level, and hugged him. Luke was comfortable in Father's embrace and patted him on the back. Father faced him with tears in his eyes.

"What a wonderful song, young man. What a joyous, rambunctious poem."

"What's rambunctious mean, mister?" Luke said.

"Rambunctious means a hell of a lot of fun." Everyone but Benny laughed so Mother tapped him on the shoulder.

"You were good, too," she said. Benny halfway smiled. "Oh, Mr. Junior. My word. Your reputation is no exaggeration."

Rastus tipped his white hat.

"Which reputation is that, ma'am?"

"Now that'll be enough of that," Father said. Everybody laughed except Benny and Luke who were looking at each other funny for some reason. Mother caressed Luke's lovely face.

"And you?" she said. "You did my daughter proud. Oh, Debbie." Mother broke down while everyone remembered what they were doing there. Father extended his hand and Mack shook it cause that's the kind of fella Mack was. Father turned to address the crowd.

"I'm sorry about my behavior earlier. I'm just…" He turned to Mother who took over.

"We just want to say thank you. Thank you so much for this splendid benefit. Thank you for what you've done for our daughter."

"You're welcome, Mr. and Mrs. Coleman," Deacon Early said. "And now, we shall walk down to the school yard to dedicate the new Coleman Learning Academy." Applause.

"I'm afraid that won't be possible just yet, Deacon Early," Father said. The crowd tensed up.

"And why's that?"

"I'm starving. You people have anything to eat around here?"

20

Later that night, Rastus and Benny sat on two fence posts and chunked rocks at cows. A campfire had been built and Rastus used the firelight drama to tell the boy ghost stories.

"Nuh-uh."

"Uh-huh."

"You lying, Rastus."

"Naw, I ain't. If you don't believe me ask the HooDoo Woman."

"I ain't going over there. HooDoo Lady don't bother me, I don't bother the HooDoo Lady. But you still lying."

"Naw, I ain't."

"Yes, you is."

"Naw, I ain't. And that's how she got a reputation."

"Man," Benny said. "Ain't that something?"

"Yes, it is." Rastus was tired of hitting cows and Benny was out of rocks. They unpacked their kerchiefs loaded with roast beef sandwiches Sarah had made. Both of them smacked real loud just to make the cows nervous.

"I'm thirsty, Rastus." He gave Benny a flask of never-ending brandy. The boy took a shot and jiggled his head from the burn.

"You getting good at that."

"Thank you kindly. You know what, Rastus?"

"What?"

"I want a reputation too. Like you and the HooDoo Lady. I want folks to know I'm coming before I get there. I want everybody to know my name. I want 'em to know I'm the wrong one to fuck with and I can damn sure play this guitar."

"They already know that."

"But I want more people to know. Everybody. I want to be the best blues man in the whole wide world.

"You willing to sell your soul?"

"Quit playing."

"I ain't playing nothing. You got to give up something to get something, boy.

"What's gonna happen to me when you go away, Rastus?" Benny startled Rastus by sounding like a child.

"Ain't nothing gonna happen to you."

"Oh." Rastus realized he gave the wrong answer. Benny threw the rest of his sandwich to a cow who sniffed at it and walked away.

"Boy, what you doing? That cow ain't gonna eat no beef. That coulda been that cow's mama for all you know."

"Yeah, I guess." Benny studied the ground while Rastus studied him. "Thank you for my guitar."

"You welcome, boy."

"I don't miss the old one at all."

"Who would?"

"Take me with you, Rastus. Please."

"Come on, now, Benny."

"Take me with you!" Benny grabbed Rastus and refused to let go. "I'll be good. I swear I'll be good. I ain't no baby. You know me. I can take care of myself. We can play together, Rastus. Just you and me."

"Benny, Benny — "

"And I can help out, too. You know like how we do at The Joint. When you don't feel like being bothered with a gal? I'll come over and cry and say mama want you to come on home now."

"Benny, we done talked about this. I wish I could take — "

"I'll be good, Rastus." Benny broke down in his arms. "You said you wished I was your son. You said so."

"And I meant it, boy. But — "

"Then make me your son, Rastus. Please!" Rastus felt warm tears soaking into his shirt while Benny yelled into his chest. "I'll be a good boy!" Rastus felt his lips curl into a painful grimace and he cried too. He shook Benny hard to get him quiet.

"Stop!" The wood in the campfire popped. "Please, stop." The cowbells jangled in the dark. "Please."

But Benny wouldn't stop.

Rastus picked the boy up and carried him to The Joint. He had Jeraldine slung across one shoulder and tried to make Benny hold No-Name. But Benny kept dropping it in the dirt on purpose. Rastus didn't have the strength to get mad at him. Instead, he kissed him on the cheek and told him he was breaking his heart. The bouncer opened the screen door for him as he made it up the steps out of breath.

"What happened to him?" the Bouncer said.

"He fell." The Bouncer looked at Rastus's swollen eyes.

"What happened to you?"

"I fell too, motherfucker, now move out the way." Rastus was grateful the place was empty. He dropped into an unsteady chair with his burden and sat there for a moment trying to get it together. Deacon Early walked up with his apron on.

"Good show tonight, Rastus."

"Yeah, I know." Deacon Early looked at Benny.

"What happened to him?"

"He fell," the Bouncer said.

"Gimme a drink," Rastus commanded. Deacon Early mumbled something and walked off. Rastus propped Benny's limp body on his knee to wipe his face with his handkerchief and make him blow his nose. He caught the Bouncer looking at them but really didn't care. After while, the Bouncer had the taste to find something else to look at. The Dark Skinned Diva swayed on over with Rastus's drink in hand.

"Here ya go, Ras... ooh. What happened to him?"

"I bit him. All right? Y'all happy now?"

"Don't get shitty with me, Rastus. I ain't in the mood."

"All right, all right, just, just, just sit down or something. Lemme think." And so she did. Rastus grabbed his drink and rubbed it across his forehead. Then he guzzled it down so fast he coughed all over the place.

"I declare," said the Dark Skinned Diva as she patted Rastus on the back. She took this time to check out Benny. She saw dried tears on his face and thought of her own boy she left behind in Tuskegee but that's a long story. She rubbed Benny's face in a motherly fashion.

"What's wrong with the little man today? Hmm?"

"Nothing," Benny said. He turned away from her and nuzzled Rastus's shoulder. And then she understood.

"He's not the only one gonna miss you."

"Gal, please. You know can't nobody throw that thang like you do."

"Aw, shucks, nigger. You gonna make me cry."

"I'm trying to pay your ass a compliment."

"Uh huh."

"I'm serious now. You 'bout to hurt my feelings. I done tole you a thousand times you'd… make…" Rastus looked at Benny. "…a… man… forget…." He stared at the Diva who raised an eyebrow at him. "… the world… was… ending." Rastus smiled and the Diva dropped her jaw but he reached across the table and closed it shut. She pushed his hand off her and slapped his arm.

"Now look here, Rastus — "

"Aw, bitch please. You gonna get holy on me now?" He slammed some money on the table. "What about now?" He slammed more money down. "How 'bout now?" The Dark Skinned Diva sighed and looked up to the second story.

"How old is he?"

"Almost a man."

"You must think I'm crazy. I got eyes, don't I? That boy can't be no more than ten or eleven."

"Well, in nigger years, that's almost a man." Rastus stretched forth his hand and cash fell like leaves to the table.

"You never could hold on to money."

He shrugged and smiled. "A man wants the best, he gots pay for the best." She smiled back at him. "You know, darling…" He slid Benny off his knee. "… I always say people like us provides a service. Like a doctor or a hoodoo man." He watched her stuff the money in her satin bra.

"Well, Rastus, I never thought of it like that."

"Well, that's your problem. One of many." He turned to Benny who was still out of it. "Now, Benny? I wants you to go upstairs with the nice lady. All right?" Benny panicked and grabbed him.

"You trying to trick me! You gonna run away when I ain't looking!" He started crying again. Deacon Early and the Bouncer looked over from the bar. New pains shot through Rastus's heart and the Diva decided to take control.

"Oh, hush now," she said, "You just hush all this foolishness right this minute." She stroked his head and he eased off Rastus.

"Now you know Rastus wouldn't play a dirty trick like that on a fine young man like you. Rastus loves you. And you know what? I love you too."

Benny reached up and touched her scar from The Pimp. She extended her hand and he took it. They ascended the stairs while the men looked on. Benny looked back at Rastus who gave him a nod.

They reached the second story and she opened the door.

"What's your name, lady?"

"You can call me Bertha."

Bertha shut the door.

21

Even though Luke was a grown man now, technically, this was his first date. Not that he was a virgin. Both he and Benny had been through more hos than Santa Claus. Local gals learned about the Martin reputation by the truckload. So many, in fact, that Sarah asked Mack to give Luke the speech.

"We too old to be raising babies. You better hurry up and marry one of these gals. And quit acting like a child in a man's body. You wasn't raised like that and you know it."

That type thing.

But as long as Luke pulled his weight around the house, he felt he could do as he pleased. Neither Mack nor Sarah ever asked him to leave and Luke liked living at home. He just hated the town. Benny still lived with Maddie and Red brought Willa to Ace's place when he married her, so it wasn't unheard of and no shame in it. More hands in one place meant more food in one house. Besides, Luke was the kind of man who needed to be around his family. Even if he hardly paid them attention, he needed to know where they were. Now he needed to know where Mary was too.

Luke took Mary to the Bijou Playhouse the night before the baseball game. Benny spent all afternoon teaching him how to drive the truck. He bugged Mack for one of his clean shirts because Mary had seen all his clothes before. Mack also gave his son some cologne he had since his honeymoon and a shave.

"How old was you when you got married, daddy?" Mack wiped the shiny straight razor and looked into space for a memory.

"Don't remember." He held Luke's head to the side and scraped the razor from cheek to chin. "Hold still fore I nick you."

"You don't remember when you got married?"

"Course I do. Just don't remember my age. One or two things have happened to me since then, you know." Mack wrapped Luke's face in a hot, white towel. "Now just sit here a minute. Gonna give you a professional touch." Luke enjoyed the wet heat soaking his face. But comfort soon turned to boredom in his little cocoon and he had questions to ask. He peeled back a corner of cloth so he could see.

"Daddy, that don't make no sense. All you got to do is start from the age you is now and count backwards as long as y'all been married. Now how long y'all been married?"

"Can't rightly say."

"Huh?"

"Fifteen, twenty, twenty-five years. Something like that. I always remember our anniversary, April 16, so I don't expect to be harassed about stuff like that." He shoved Luke's head down and put the towel back in place. Luke sat there as long as he could take it and uncovered his mouth.

"Daddy, I'll never understand you."

"Look who talking."

"How a man gonna forget something as important as that?"

"It don't bother her, why the hell should it bother you?"

"But — "

"Look, son. Your mama has always been a part of my life, ever since we was kids. We watched each other grow up. She saw me turn into a man, I saw her turn into a woman. We been there for each other in every good and bad time. I don't know what life would look like without her. Just seems to me she's always been there. Just seems to me I always loved her. I can't be bothered with the math."

Luke covered his mouth back up.

Later, Sarah helped Luke get ready too. She added a flower to his lapel and wiped away the extra grease Mack caked the boy's hair down with. She got close enough to tell him it might be a good idea to brush his teeth again. He did and with that he was out the door waving at his folks as he went down the row to get Benny's truck. Sarah cried for some reason and Mack didn't shush her for it. He just waved at his son and watched him disappear around the bend in the road.

Meanwhile, at Mary's place, she had been running around doing her best to look just right. Mary's mother had long been taken by consumption so she didn't have a feminine influence to tell her if those bangs made her look like a school girl or if that dress made her look too fat.

She asked her daddy and eight brothers but her daddy said she was pretty no matter what she wore which was sweet and useless at a time like this. Her brothers told her they don't look at their sister that way which Mary thought was both stupid and unnecessary to say. She begged her daddy to get them out of the house so she could have time to herself for female issues. Her daddy didn't know what that meant but it spooked him enough to get out the house and push the army of brothers outside with him. Mary didn't have any female issues except the need to be alone in a family of men which was an issue onto itself. She just needed to sit there for a minute and looked at the stained white wall behind the potbellied stove.

"Girl, it's only a movie," she said. Her brothers looked up from the engine they worked on in the yard to see who Mary was talking to. She slammed the shutters on them and rambled on attacking invisible hairs and picking transparent lint. It didn't help she was a little ahead of schedule. It didn't help she was nervous as hell and it damn sure didn't help she was in love with Luke.

It's only a movie. If he hadn't proposed marriage at the end of fornication, why would he do it after a movie? She got the feeling she was the first female he had taken to the Bijou. He never came out and said it but men say a lot when not talking about anything specific. He often related how he enjoyed being the only one in the theatre. He mentioned how overwhelmed he was as a child when his father first took him there. It was one of the few times they did something else together besides work the fields. He brushed over the devilment he and Benny got into when Deacon Early caught them throwing popcorn at the screen and made them clean up the place as punishment. When they were cleaning the projection room, he looked through the pictures on a reel of film. He couldn't understand how something so separate and still came alive. He mentioned this and many other things about the Bijou but never another woman. As if he would. But he still seemed nervous about asking her to go so Mary reasoned she was the first. There was a knock at the door. She jumped from her chair and made herself slow down.

She was determined to show him she wasn't easy in spite of what already happened between them. Luke might have been her first but so what? She reminded herself it was only a movie and opened the door. Luke stood there, crowded by suspicious men folk, with flowers from Sarah's garden in his big hands.

"Hey, Mary."

"Hey, Luke. Them for me?"

"Uh-huh." She took the flowers inside while he dealt with the family.

"How you doing today, Mr. Lewis?"

"Oh, I'll do I guess. How Mack?"

"He fine."

"How Sarah?"

"She fine too."

"That's good." Four of Mary's crazy brothers dug around under the hood of the truck with a wrench they used as a hammer. Luke couldn't tell exactly what they were doing to the thing. JJ, Mary's oldest brother, wiped green grease on his undershirt.

"What y'all doing to that engine, JJ?" Luke said. JJ was annoyed by the interruption of his delicate operation.

"We fixing it." He looked at one of his dim brothers and who nodded at him.

"Well, I can see that. What's wrong with it?" JJ looked at his other brother like that was the dumbest question he ever heard.

"Well damn, Luke. Won't know 'til we fix it."

"Mary, you ready?" Luke said real fast. Mary had been ready but hid in the doorway praying not to pass out and that her family wouldn't embarrass her. She was halfway grateful for God's fifty percent success rate and forced herself into the open.

"All ready."

"You look real pretty, Mary."

"Thank you."

"So where y'all going and what time y'all getting back?" Mr. Lewis said. He checked on his still and waited for an answer.

"We going to the Bijou Playhouse, sir. Be back in a couple of hours or so."

"Well, make it a couple and leave out the so." He tested liquor from a wooden cup and all the brothers came begging like a litter of piglets. "You hear me?"

"Yes, sir."

"And by my calculations, a couple mean two. Two hours. Starting now."

"Well, it's gonna take us a minute to drive there."

"Two. And don't think I can't tell the difference."

"Yes, sir."

"So what picture show y'all going to see?"

"Body and Soul. It's a Oscar Micheaux movie."

"Uh-huh."

"Got Paul Robeson in it."

"That right?"

"He was All-American at Rutgers, you know."

"Yeah, I know."

"Oscar Ma-who?" JJ said, all snide like. Mary gave him a dirty look.

"Mi-cheaux," Luke said. "Oscar Michauex. He a colored picture maker. Make pictures 'bout colored folks. Adventure pictures. Romantical pictures. Political pictures. Any kind of picture you can think of. Just like the white folks." JJ rolled his eyes and elbowed one of the brothers.

"A nigger making movies 'bout niggers. Who the hell wanna see that?"

"Niggers, I guess," Luke said. Mary laughed and kinda leaned on Luke and Mr. Lewis smiled at that.

"Well, y'all best be off now. Take care of my girl, Luke."

"Yes sir, Mr. Lewis. I always will."

"I'll hold you to that, Luke. Y'all have a good time." They walked off holding hands with Luke avoiding looking at the brothers lining the way. JJ grabbed him by the arm.

"Just don't take too good a care of her or we gonna beat your crazy ass, cloud boy." Cloud boy. Cause he had his head in the clouds. Luke wondered how long it took JJ to think that up. He looked down at JJ's dirty hand on his daddy's clean shirt and felt his face get hot. But he knew fighting with JJ would be a lousy way to start a date.

"Boy, quit acting like a fool. Daddy!" Mary said.

"Boy, if you don't let go that boy, you better," Mr. Lewis said. But JJ didn't relent. He wanted to see how bad Luke was without Benny to back him up. Luke was cool, though. All he did was flex. He just flexed that arm, thick with muscle, two solid, separate times. Luke's head might be in the clouds but his arms were in the fields and JJ felt with a quickness he was no match for him. He figured he'd best back off since getting his ass beat by company would be a source of a teasing that would last until Armageddon. He patted Luke on the bulge in his arm.

"Aw, boy, you know I'm just playing with you." JJ laughed and Luke laughed back for different reasons. He led Mary to the truck and opened the door like a gentleman. He hopped in the driver's seat and then they were off. Later, the truck jerked into a parking spot at the theatre. Big Flooty saw Luke jump out and got her mouth all set for a reunion. When she saw him run around the passenger side, though, and hold his arm out like a debutante man for some knock-kneed bitch with a fourth grade hairdo, well child, Big Flooty was through. Who was this nappy headed heifer? And why was Luke acting like that thing was the belle of the ball? A blind man could see she wasn't used to going nowhere. Probably didn't even know what a movie house was. Probably one of them niggers who start running when Tarzan chase elephants towards the screen. Country ass bitch. And where the hell she get that dress from? A toy store?

"Hey, Luke. Long time, huh? A big ole long time."

"Two, please." Luke didn't have time for this. He only promised her the present and now that was past. Flooty slapped the tickets on the counter like a losing hand of cards.

"So, who's your friend?"

"Mary Lewis Big Flooty, Big Flooty Mary Lewis." Luke hurried to get the money out his slacks. He wasn't used to wearing anything but dungarees and these fancy pants had pockets within the pockets that were hard to dig change out of. He got two fingers wrapped around the coins but dropped the tickets. He got down on his knees with a curse and a gust of wind blew them away. Luke and Mary laughed while Flooty looked back and forth between them.

"Flooty, can you give us two more?"

"I'm sorry but there will be other customers. I can't commit such an infraction." Luke didn't want to fuss with her in front of Mary and ran down the sidewalk after a brief apology. The women were left alone. Flooty smiled a like a wolf with a baby lamb.

"Love that dress, girl. Made it yourself, huh?" Mary didn't respond and Flooty kinda chuckled. "Yep. I can always tell when they make 'em themselves. It's cute though." Luke won the game of tag with the tickets and was headed back to the booth while Flooty looked him up and down. "Mm, mm, mm. That's a whole lotta man. What you think, Miss Mary? Ain't that a whole lotta man?" Mary watched Flooty apply lipstick to her wet mouth. Luke was back and a bit embarrassed.

"There now. Got it. Sorry 'bout that, Mary."

"Oh, that's all right," Mary said. She squeezed his muscle. "Whole lotta wind around here."

"Well." He smiled and brushed her bangs out of her eyes. "I guess we'd best be going in."

"I guess we'd best. Luke leapt ahead of her to open the door and Big Flooty eyed them both like a serial killer.

"Have I told you how pretty you look in that dress?" Luke said. Mary stopped at the entrance and twirled around.

"What? This old thing?" She looked dead at Flooty. "I made it myself." And with that she sashayed through the door.

Mary walked around with her face towards the ceiling letting all the wonder pour into her eyes. Luke didn't rush her and stood back to watch. He knew they had time because the newsreel was playing and it wasn't nothing but bad news, so who cared? He got a kick out of Mary being wowed by the place. And that's when he knew he loved her. He loved her so much it made him insecure.

Mary "oohed" and "ahhed" at the relics of entertainment that occupied every corner of the lobby. Other patrons bumped into her as she stood there like a fool rubbing the plush carpet back and forth with her foot. When Luke took her arm, the static electricity shocked them both. Mary hollered and giggled with Luke. She swatted his arm for laughing at her and turned to see how many people were staring at her. A few folks were looking, but they smiled at her too. The Old Man waved at them from the concession counter.

"Nothing like young love," the Old Man said and gave them a wink. This caught them by surprise but neither bothered to correct him.

"How you doing this evening," Mary said.

"No better, no worse, young miss. Take it easy." The Old Man left with his popcorn giving Mary a full view of the delights behind the glass. She wanted licorice sticks, them black balls of chocolate filled with caramel cream, a big cup of fountain soda with plenty of ice, her own man-sized box of fresh popcorn, extra butter, some hard candy to suck on, the purple ones, one of them fresh baked pretzel things, and a napkin.

Luke said he'd have the same.

He was worried about money but didn't want to look cheap. He dug around in the hidden compartments of his pants hoping for luck.

"Hey, take a look at that wax statue of Nat Turner, baby. Look like he'd kill you right now, don't it?"

"Ooh," Mary said. She bounded away from the concessions counter where a long line formed behind Luke. He leaned in to talk to the ticket taker who had grown into a middle-aged man with thicker glasses and promoted to concessions.

"Uh, look here, man…"

"Don't worry bout it, Luke" the Concession Man said. "You been at the Bijou almost long as me. Just don't tell Deacon Early." Luke shook his hand like a man buying a car.

"Thank you. Thank you kindly," Luke said. "I'll pay you back. Hand to God."

"All right then," the Concessions Man said. He didn't quite believe him. Luke scooped the goodies into the cardboard horn of plenty and took a look at his reflection in the counter. He called Mary over who still walked about bumping into brand new people. They went up the chipped golden staircase, under the doves, under the stars, and right down the center walkway to Luke's favorite aisle seats. No matter how many people came to the Playhouse, his aisle seat always waited on him like a friend saving his place at the bar. Mary didn't really like sitting so close but this was her first date and she didn't want to act country. She tilted her head back and her eyes dilated to the last story of the newsreel about the Harlem Renaissance.

"Oooh, Luke, look. That's Zora Neal Hurston. Lord, look at that hat. Oh I wish I could be like her."

"You way prettier than she is, Mary."

"That ain't what I'm talking about. I mean be like her. A writer. Up in Harlem. With all those new Negroes. Starting something special."

"You already is special, Mary." He put his arm around her.

"What about you, Mr. Martin?"

"What about me?"

"Don't you want to be a New Negro? Change the world?" Luke laughed.

"I'm serious. I remember you used to want to be a writer, too."

"I ain't never wanted to be no writer, Mary." Somebody shushed them so she lowered her voice.

"Yes, you did. When we was kids. You wrote that poem at the benefit? That's when Benny first sang for everybody."

"Yeah, well. That turned out just great for him."

"You sound jealous." Luke looked at her funny and she thought he was mad at her.

"'Course I ain't jealous. When this damn movie gonna start?" They ate in silence as the newsreel showed a brief scene about life at Tuskegge Institute.

"Don't you think it's strange y'all ain't heard nothing from Braxton yet?"

"Mama had a talk with Mrs. Braxton and bought us some time. We'll probably be leaving next week."

"Probably?"

"We will be." She looked at the screen not really paying attention to the news. "I was gonna tell you later. I just wanted us to enjoy ourselves." She sipped her soda and told herself she'd better not cry.

"So where y'all going?"

"Probably Talapoosa. Daddy can't stop talking 'bout the SCU and there's a man there knows a lot about it. Maybe you can come with us."

"Come with you? What are you saying?"

"I don't know."

"You don't know?"

"Mary, I can't be bothered with the math."

"Huh?" Several people shushed them and they were shamed into silence. He held her hand and she felt a strong heartbeat through his fingers. The newsreel ended and the theatre went black. The curtains on the screen closed and opened again to signal the main event.

22

Benny made a mental note to never pray again.

What kind of world is this gonna be
Where a man can't exist without penalty?
What kind of world is this gonna be
Where a man can read about it but can't be free?
What kind of world is this gonna be
When people like you hate people like me?
What kind of world is this gonna be?
Mack Martin's swinging dead from The Old
    Crook Tree.

The first thing Benny saw were the hoods. Like rows of dunce caps except there was nothing funny about it. And guns. So many guns. Dunce caps and guns. They rode onto the field without a word in casual formation with Braxton in the lead. The coloreds of Braxton watched the man himself ride to home plate and shoot The Umpire dead. Women screamed and men hollered but another shot from Braxton in the ground shut that up. He looked at The Umpire's body and said,

"If it's one thing I've seen enough of, it's niggers with guns. Now where's Mack?"

"There he go," Ace Simmons said. All heads turned to Mack. Sarah grabbed his hand and Luke made a move forward.

"Don't, son. Just let me handle it."

"We can do this together, daddy."

"Do what together? It's over. Let me handle it."

"But — "

"Luke," Mary said. "Don't make it worse." Maddie put her hand on Luke's arm and shook her head. Sarah gave him a look.

"We ain't got all day, boy!" Braxton said.

"I'm coming." Mack tried to walk away but Sarah held on.

"Let me go."

"I ain't never let you go before. You think I'm gonna start now?"

"Damn it, let me go."

"I ain't never listened to you either." Mack gave up. He and Sarah walked on past the Big Man, past the Old Man, through the crowd, hand in hand. They ignored Ace Simmons and stopped right in front Braxton on his horse.

"Well, well. The great Mack Martin. This don't concern you, Sarah. Get back over there."

"The hell it don't." The crowd was still. Benny held his bat. "This concerns my husband so this concerns me."

"Suit yourself."

"Mrs. Braxton said we had 'till next week to get out of here," Sarah said.

"Bitch, I don't pay no nevermind to what a woman said to me."

"Don't you talk to my wife like that." Then there was a sound. Like firecracker or a pop. And Mack went down. That was one shot too many for the nervous town folk and they scattered like a herd of cattle. Luke and Mary were separated in the panic.

"Mary!" But she was swept away. Luke ran through the crowd to help Mack. And Benny just ran. "Benny! Come back!"

> *Benny dropped his bat and ran.*
> *Told himself they'd understand.*
> *Told himself he's just one man.*
> *Benny dropped his bat and ran.*

"I'm coming, Daddy!" The bullet went clean through Mack's leg. He was shot by a fella named Bob; a pudgy piece of poor white trash with no chin and a hairline that started and ended at his ears. Bob was always trying to make an impression on Braxton to be a part of his inner circle. So he figured shooting Mack was the best way to do that. Luke dove on his daddy to shield him from the storm of people. The Ku Klucks chased folks about for sport and swung whips at every black face on the ground. Maddie screamed for Jesus and ran from a horseman close behind her.

"Ma!" Luke held out his hand to Sarah but they were separated by the tide of bodies. "Ma, get over here!"

"I'm trying!" She was batted about like a ball in her attempt to reach her men. Braxton's horse reared up in all the confusion just as Sarah was pushed to the ground. Then the horse's hoof landed smack in the middle of her back. Pain spread like hot gravel trapped under her skin and dribbled down the sides.

The massive beast stumbled off her but she didn't move. She could only lay there, stiff with the trauma of it all, and grunt in shallow breaths.

"Ma!" Luke leapt up and knocked Braxton off his horse. His fist were jackhammers on the boss man's nose and crunched broken bone into his face. Braxton tried to shield himself but Luke swatted his arms out of the way and went for the sunken nose again.

"Luke, stop!" Mack said. He pressed his hand on the bullet hole but blood sneaked between his fingers. He ignored the pain and shouted through the commotion. "Take your mama and get out of here! Sarah!"

Sarah was right in the path of the Big Man and his family running from a night rider. The rider swatted the back of the Big Man whose escape was hampered with his grandbaby in his arms. Luke spotted Sarah trying to move without success and ceased beating Braxton down.

"Ma!" He jumped off Braxton and zigzagged through horses. He scooped her in his arms just in time and ran to the clearing. The Big Man's tragic parade sped by.

"Get 'em," Braxton said. "Get 'em both! Bring 'em back here!" Most folks escaped to the woods but the Old Man was too slow and got beat up by the bleachers. Braxton got off the ground and wiped the blood from his face with a plaid, wrinkled handkerchief. He stood over Mack and kicked him in his wound. The hurt spread from Mack's leg, crossed his bowels, and went straight to the top of his head. He fixed his eyes on Luke running into the woods with Sarah.

Luke was always a good runner but he was no match for the horses he heard barreling down on them. Guilt made him aware every move was violent to Sarah's back. He saw her eyes shut tight to block out the agony. The horsemen were on either side of them now. One fella threw a rope to the other and they pulled it taut to trip them.

Run, Luke, run.

The horsemen shouted ugly things about what they would do to them both. He felt the rope touch his back. In a few seconds they'd make him fall. Nothing to do now but run and pray.

Then; *ffwip... ffwip.* The Klansmen dropped the rope in a tangle and joined it on the ground while their horses rode past Luke and Sarah. Two blades wiggled in their windpipes and blood soaked the hoods of their yellowed sheets. The Pimp wasn't lying. She always had some spares.

"Come on," The Pimp said. Luke looked around for her but couldn't tell where the voice was coming from. "Over here."

There she was. In the bushes. Luke ran over there and lay Sarah down while The Pimp pulled the loose horses into hiding. Luke parted the branches and saw Braxton and them yank Mack to his good leg and bind his hands.

"Can you talk your way out of this one?" The Pimp said. Luke bent down and checked on Sarah.

"Ma? Ma, you all right?"

"My back." Her voice trembled when she spoke. Each syllable took maximum effort. "My... back."

"Can you walk?" Her silence answered the question. His heart broke to see her weakened to an ordinary thing. He heard the rallies of the Klan all around him.

"Woowee!" they shouted. Then rifle fire. He looked at the sky. He looked at the sky and did what he did best. He used his imagination.

"I want you to take one of these horses and get my mama far away from here. I'll catch up... we'll catch up later."

"We?" The Pimp said.

"Me and my daddy." The Pimp looked through the bushes and saw one of Braxton's boys tailoring a custom made neck tie just for Mack.

"Think about your mama. Don't let her lose a husband and a son in one day."

"You ain't listening. I want you to take Ma and get out of here while you still got a chance. Please."

"I always knew you was touched." The Pimp loaded Sarah belly down over the back of the horse with Luke's fretful help. He peeked through the bushes and saw them put Mack on a horse by the Old Crook Tree. They slipped the noose around his neck.

"Hurry up." Sarah moaned in protest and reached her feeble hand out to restrain him but he brushed her away and tied her to the horse with rope from the saddle bag. The Pimp jumped on the steed and held Sarah steady. She looked around to make sure they had a clear getaway. Looked like all the Klansmen were gathered at the tree.

"Good luck," she said. She kicked the horse in the ribs and galloped away at a pace that wasn't good for Sarah's back but necessity overruled comfort. Luke stood there by himself and cussed Benny for running away. Everybody ran, of course, so who could blame him? Luke could. That's who. They were overwhelmed and outgunned so what could Benny have done?

He could have stayed. That's what. He could have stayed here with me.

Luke put thoughts of Benny in the back of his head and dashed out to drag the dead Klansmen to the thicket. He stripped the robes off one and slipped them over his clothes. He put work gloves on to hide his black hands. He wore the mask lopsided so the eye holes wouldn't betray him and tucked it under to conceal the blood. He blessed Sarah, damned Benny, hoped for Mary, and hopped the horse.

"Giddy up!" He rode into the action.

Meanwhile, at the Old Crook Tree, Mack was all trussed up and ready to swing but Braxton wasn't through messing with him yet.

"How's it feel, Mack?" He slapped him. "How's it feel now, huh?"

"How's the nose?" Mack said. He spit in the boss man's face. That wasn't the smartest move in the world and got him a couple of rifle butts to the head. Braxton took out a knife and held it at his privates.

"Wouldn't it be sad if I cut off your dick and stuck it in your mouth? Wouldn't it? That's the way my daddy use to do it, God rest his soul."

"Know what would be even sadder?" Mack said. "I'd still be the bigger man." Braxton laughed and looked at him like a buzzard who could see the future.

"Put him on the ground," Braxton said.

"But we just put him on the horse," said one of the boys.

"I said put him on the ground!" They gave the noose some slack and slammed Mack on the ground just as a Klansmen with a lopsided mask rode up.

"Cut off his clothes," Braxton said.

"But, sir," Bob said. "There's ladies present." And so there were. The families had arrived. There hadn't been a lynching in a good five years. Little Linford, Bob's boy, tugged his mama, Nancy, along on the dash to the Tree.

"This here's bigger than fireworks on the Fourth of July! Ain't it, mama?" She laughed and stroked his blonde hair. "Oh boy, there's the picture man!" The Lopsided Klansman turned to see who the picture man was. A photographer rode up in a car and unloaded his equipment. "Can I get a postcard, mama, please?"

"I ain't got fifty cents," Nancy said.

"Aww."

"Set it up over here," Braxton said. He stepped on Mack's face. "Congratulations Mack. Your death is gonna be a means of correspondence. Maybe we'll send it out to recruit for the SCU."

He smiled at Mack's look of surprise.

"Oh yeah. Red Simmons told us all about that." The Lopsided Klansmen gripped his reigns hard. "We gonna put your corpse on a postcard, boy. So other niggers know not to get out of line." He leaned down to him. "And on that postcard? Guess what it's gonna say. Gonna say, 'Pulled a gun on a white man.'"

"How's about, 'Commie Nigger?' Bob said. "Everybody knows them unions is full of Reds. Or it could say, 'Red, Black, and Dead.'" Everybody laughed and Bob enjoyed being the center of attention.

"That's a good one, Bob," Braxton said.

"How'd you know it was me, sir?"

"Recognized your voice, stupid. 'Sides, you the only one out here who tucks his sheet in his pants." Little Linford watched everybody laugh at his daddy. Bob blushed under his hood and looked away from his wife. The photographer was set up now.

"All ready?" The Photographer said.

"Sure, sure," Braxton said.

"Shouldn't you have that nose looked at, Mr. Braxton?" The Photographer said.

"Nonsense. It'll keep. It's my Purple Heart for the cause." They applauded him. "Somebody stand this nigger up." Bob pushed a couple of Ku Klucks out the way in the rush for the job. He grabbed Mack by his bonds and pulled him to his feet. At that point, Mack checked out. He refused to show pain, or hatred, or fear. He checked out. He didn't quit. He just refused. He stared into the camera and dared it to tell the truth.

"All right, here we go," The Photographer said. "A little to the left. That's right. Scrunch your head down a little, Mr. Braxton. That's it."

"Daddy, I want to be in the picture too," Little Linford yelled. The other mothers complained it wasn't fair to their children.

"Enough!" Braxton said. "The other kids'll get a turn when he's dead. Hurry up, Little Linford."

"Oh, boy!" He ran to the group who stood around Mack like fisherman with a trout.

"Much obliged," Bob said. He pumped Braxton's hand with too much vigor. "Much obliged indeed, sir."

"Yeah, all right, Bob." Braxton wiped Bob's sweat on his pants and stood smiling by Mack.

"How come you're not in uniform, Mr. Braxton, if I may be so bold?" The Photographer said.

"Them damn sheets give me a rash." Everybody laughed while Mack stayed focused on the camera.

"All right, all right," Braxton said. "Enough fun and games. Let's get this over with. You too, fella." Everybody looked at the Lopsided Klansman and wondered why he didn't move. "Hey! I'm talking to you! You deaf?" Still, he didn't budge. They all just looked at him.

"What's the matter with him, daddy?" Braxton had enough of this nonsense and stepped out of the pose to go over there. The Lopsided Klansman moved his horse to the group.

"Finally. Get the pig shit out your ears."

"Okay, you're going to have to get off that horse," The Photographer said. "You're too high." Lopside moved too slow for Braxton.

"Oh, for Pete's Sake." Braxton strode to Lopside and pulled him off the horse. "This ain't that hard." He pushed Bob out the way and stood Lopside next to Mack. "What's the matter? Don't you like pictures?" He stood on Mack's other side and smiled. The Photographer squeezed a ball in his hand and the flash exploded in light and smoke.

The light. The smoke. That's when the Lopsided Klansman remembered that The Umpire had a gun.

Lopside looked at Mack but he just kept staring through the camera. "Okay. One more. And hold it." Lopside wanted to touch him, to hold him, to let him know… Poof. More light. More smoke.

I gotta get that gun.

"All right, Mr. Braxton. I got what I need. Hey. Can I interest you in a moving picture?"

"How's that?"

"A moving picture. You know. Like in the picture shows, sir. You'll be immortalized in motion."

"That right? And how much does immortality cost?"

"Oh, I'm sure we can work out a fair price, Mr. Braxton. Just take me a minute to get the other camera. You'll love it."

"Well, we're tired of standing around. Wanna get this thing over with. I'm hungry." Lopside looked at The Umpire's body. And sure enough, there was the gun laying right next to him. Nobody bothered to get it in all the excitement.

"But that's the beauty of it, Mr. Braxton. You just go on doing what you do. All the better. And I'll catch it, in motion, on film, as a testament to what you men do to protect our women and way of life. I'm telling you, it'll be outrageous."

"Well, I don't know."

Mack laughed. He laughed like a man who needed to.

"A picture show," Mack said. "That's a good one." He continued laughing at life's little joke while Lopside found it hard to breathe in his mask. Mack's laughter made Braxton want to kill him even more.

"What the hell's so funny?"

The illogical glory of Black Male Pride told Mack to laugh harder. So he did.

"Go get that camera," Braxton said. "Let's stretch this nigger's neck."

"I'll be right back." Braxton's boys put Mack back on the horse while he laughed like a loon. Lopside wandered closer to the gun. Little Linford poked Mack with a stick and dared other kids to do the same.

Just a little bit closer.

"Bob, make sure the other end of that rope's secure so it won't slip when the horse leaves him dangling." Bob obeyed with gusto and Lopside now stood over the gun. The Umpire's eyes were still open. The Photographer came back with the motion picture camera and put it on a tripod.

"Woowee!" somebody said. They all looked to see what the fuss was about and there was Thomas, Bob's smart assed brother-in-law, giggling on his horse like he had a secret. Lopside's eyes grew big under his mask. For behind Thomas, bound by the necks and tied to his saddle, were Mary and Maddie. They had to run to keep up with the trot of his horse. Maddie was half naked and sported a busted lip. She moaned with the fatigue of a soul dry of tears. Mary was all bare and bled from her rectum. Her strong body covered with the marks of resistance. Blisters like plums on her neck and legs. One side of her face was so swollen her head had an odd, distorted look. Like God was making a woman and stopped in the middle of His work to make a man instead.

Mack screamed.

The Photographer let it roll.

And The Lopsided Klansman died inside.

> When something pretty breaks, when it breaks,
>   do it make a sound?
> When something pretty breaks, when it breaks,
>   do it make a sound?
> My pretty heart is broken but was quiet when it
>   hit the ground.

"What in Sam Hill is this?" Braxton said.

"Exactly who the fuck is Sam Hill?" Thomas said. "Ever wondered?"

"Don't you sass me."

"Don't you talk to Mr. Braxton like that, Thomas," Bob said. "You out your fool mind?"

"Tell me, Bob, is there air up Mr. Braxton's ass or do you have to provide your own?" Everybody but Little Linford laughed at Bob while Thomas dismounted his horse. He looked back at Mary and bowed. "Excuse me, sugar. I'll be right back."

The Lopsided Klansman picked up the gun.

Thomas bounded up to Boss Man Braxton and gave him a sock in the arm.

"Miss anything?" He looked at Mack. "My lord. Y'all caught a big one." More laughs.

"Thomas, what am I gonna do with you?" Braxton said.

"Hang this nigger so's I can get back to my date." He kissed Braxton on the cheek and patted his rump. "Woowee!"

"Woowee!" They all said.

"If you catch something from them niggers, it'll serve you right," Nancy said.

"Oh, come on, Nancy. We can't all be married to a stud like Bob. I gotta get it when I can." He rumpled Little Linford's hair and regarded the camera on it's stand. "What's all this?"

"This here event's being recorded with moving pictures. You'd a knowed that if you'd a been here on time."

"Take it easy, brother Bob. Now is the time. And here I am." He slid out of his hood and smiled into the camera. He had red, curly hair and dead, green eyes divorced from his playful manner. His gapped teeth were stained with the habit of snuff. A droopy mustache hung from under a nose keen enough to cut glass. He wore a permanent sneer and scratched his bump covered face with his dirty nails. "Make sure you get my good side."

"I'll do what I can," The Photographer said. Thomas didn't think that was cute.

"You getting smart with me?" Little Linford drew close to Bob. He could tell when Uncle Thomas was about to blow. The Photographer peeped from behind his camera. "Answer me, you som-a-bitch! You getting smart with me?" Thomas drew his gun and pointed it at him.

"Please." The Photographer raised his trembling hands. "Please don't." Thomas put the gun to The Photographer's temple and steered him in front of the camera.

"Now won't this make a pretty picture?"

"It won't work if I don't turn the crank," The Photographer said.

"Shut up! Now let me tell you something you som-a-bitch. I will shit down your throat and wipe my ass with your tongue. You think I'm joking?"

"No!"

"Yeah, you do."

"Easy, Thomas," Braxton said.

"You think I'm joking, don't you?"

"No, I don't. Mr. Braxton?"

"Don't talk to him. Talk to me! You ignoring me?"

"No! I'm not."

"Thomas, you are embarrassing the fuck out of me," Bob said.

"You don't take me serious, do you?" Thomas said. The Photographer tried his best to speak.

"I… I…" Thomas aimed his pistol and shot Maddie in the head. Blood splattered on Mary's face. Then Maddie's body dropped in the grass.

"Maddie!" Mack said. "Naw! Naw! Naw!"

"Well, what about now?" Thomas said. "Huh? Bet you take me serious now! Don't you?" Little Linford clutched Bob's robe. Lopside had his finger on the trigger but didn't know where to point the gun. If he took out Thomas, they'd shoot him anyway and still kill his daddy and his girl. Mary shivered in the heat of the sleepy sun and stared at Maddie's twitching leg. She wouldn't let herself look at anything else. She felt herself being watched. She glanced

212 / THE HOLLYWOOD COLORED

up with fearful eyes at a Klansman staring her down. She looked at the leg again.

Mack looked at the whole body, though. There was nothing else to look at. Nothing else to think about but Sarah and Luke. He prayed they got away. He prayed for a quick death. He feared one of these prayers wouldn't be answered.

Lopside looked at the thing that used to be Maddie and willed himself away from a telling reaction. There was no way he could win this. It was stupid to try. For the first time in his life he realized imagination wouldn't be enough. What he needed was —

"Thomas! Get control of yourself and I mean now!" Braxton said.

What he needed was a hostage.

"Well, he was messing with me!" Thomas said.

"Nobody's messing with you, you dang fool. Now give me that gun!"

"Oh, come on."

"Give it here." Thomas sulked and threw the gun to Braxton. And then he began to cry. Nancy sighed and the families whispered to each other.

"Sorry 'bout that Mr. Braxton," Bob said. "He's always been wound up tighter than a virgin on his first night in jail." Bob laughed at his joke alone.

Lopside cocked the gun and started his walk to Braxton. Surprise him from behind. Make him cut daddy down. Get Mary out of here. And then what?

Don't do the math.

Little Linford titled his head to discern if Thomas was safe enough to talk to yet. He didn't like seeing his uncle cry. Thomas caught the boy looking at him. He wiped his tears, smiled at Little Linford, and turned to The Photographer.

"Jesus. I'm sorry."

"N-no problem," The Photographer said.

"I just didn't think you were taking me serious. I hate it when folks don't take me serious."

"I take you serious, Uncle Thomas." He spread his arms wide for Little Linford who ran from behind Bob and jumped in his embrace. Bob didn't like that but The Photographer loved it and thanked God for the distraction. He practically tip-toed back behind that camera. Thomas nuzzled Little Linford's cheek.

"You understand," Thomas whispered. "Don't you?"

"I think I do," Little Linford whispered back.

"Cowards," Mack said. Everybody looked at him, surprised he spoke. "All of you. A bunch of crazy ass crackers who never got over losing the war. Playing dress up in your mammy's sheets. Raping girls, killing unarmed women. I hope you all go to hell and devil's a nigger. You hear me?"

"What he say?" Thomas said. The Photographer ran to his car. Lopside passed Thomas on his way to Braxton. "What that nigger say to me?" Thomas strutted to Mack with Little Linford in his arms. Braxton and the others crowded in.

"You know what, Mack? I think we've had about enough." He turned to the families. "What y'all say? Ain't we enough?"

"Hell, yeah," Nancy said. "Hang that nigger high!"

Braxton stepped beside the horse and prepared to give it a swat.

"Y'all ready for the main event?" he said. The crowd screeched obscenities in the affirmative and even children joined in with bile of their own. Little Linford wiggled free of his uncle and ran ahead of Lopside to join his friends. He stopped to pick up a rock and threw it at Mack. It gashed him in the forehead and blood poured into his eyes. Bob cheered his son and Lopside picked up the pace. But so did Thomas. His shrill voice pierced the rowdy crowd.

"What'd you say to me?" Mack blinked back blood and met Thomas's wild gaze.

"I say you a coward!" Thomas drew his pistol and Mary closed her eyes. Then, the Lopsided Klansman grabbed Little Linford and jammed the gun against his skull.

The cheering stopped.

"What in Sam Hill?" Thomas said.

"Drop the gun."

"Uncle Thomas?"

"What the fuck?"

"Drop the gun."

"Daddy?"

"Drop the gun."

"Little Linford?"

"Drop the gun."

"What he say?"

"Drop the gun. Drop the gun. Drop the motherfucking gun! Everybody!" Nancy screamed and ran to her son. Lopside smacked the boy in the head and made him cry so Nancy stopped in her tracks and screamed again. Other mothers joined her. Bob stood there unable to take it all in. Braxton and the boys looked on in confusion. Mack and Mary didn't know what the hell was going on. Thomas was so scared he had to concentrate to talk.

"I'll... I'll kill you if you — "

"Hey. Guess what? I ain't taking you serious. Now drop the goddamn gun. 'Fore I spill this boy's brains like you did Maddie's."

"You know that nigger?"

"Shut up, Thomas!" Bob said. "Okay, mister. Okay. Y'all heard him!" Bob threw his gun down and slapped Braxton's weapon out of his hand. The boss man looked at him hard. "It's my boy, sir." He snatched off his hood and exposed his tearful eyes. "It's my boy." Braxton gave a nod to the others.

The soft thud of metal hitting grass mixed with the whines of Little Linford. The hoot owl began his evening song while the sun took the red eye down. Thomas was the last one to drop his weapon.

"Now get over there. By the Tree. But cut her loose first." Mack and Mary woke up from a painful dream. They recognized the voice. And so did Braxton. Thomas took out his knife and kept his eyes on his nephew while walking to Mary.

"It's okay, Little Linford," Bob said. He smiled as best he could. "It's okay, son." Little Linford cried some more.

Mary shook when Thomas touched her hand to cut the rope away. She quickly covered her breast since modesty was the only thing she had left.

"Give her your sheet."

"I can't believe this shit," Thomas said. He got out of his robes and handed them to her. She looked at the sheet like it was something from the outhouse and walked buck naked away. Lopside allowed himself to smile as she took her place by his side. He hadn't planned to reveal himself this soon. Visions of Zorro still danced in his head. But he couldn't let his woman just stand there like that.

"Hold this." He gave the gun to Mary who held it on the hostage. Lopside's mask hit the ground and two white women followed. He shed the shroud of the enemy and draped it across Mary like she was a queen. He kissed her wet cheek and took back the gun.

Now Mack. Then Thomas.

"Cut him down," Luke Martin said. Thomas went to the Tree yearning for just one of the rifles that littered the ground. But what about Little Linford? Braxton considered how easy it would be to pick up his gun and just start shooting. There was no way Luke could kill them all. But what about Little Linford?

So? What about him?

Braxton watched Bob snivel. He never liked him and never would. He watched Thomas cut Mack's hands free. Thomas was all right but he was nothing but trouble and always would be. This whole thing was their fault. Mack would be dead by now and Braxton could have been at home, tending his nose, getting ready for supper, if not for pathetic Bob and his ridiculous, inbred family. His nose. That nigger broke his nose. And now this? He looked at Little Linford.

I don't even like children.

He made his decision.

Luke gazed at the camera.

"Mary, take the gun."

"What you doing?"

"They wanted to film our weakest moment. Now, I'm gonna film theirs."

Mary took the gun and pointed it at the boy as Luke knelt down behind the camera. He peeked through the viewfinder at Thomas going for the noose. He had to climb on the horse with Mack to reach it.

Luke turned the crank.

"So this is how they do it," he said. "This is how they make movies."

Braxton started a silent countdown.

Three.

Braxton narrowed his eyes at Luke.

Two.

Thomas cut into the rope. Mack thanked God.

One.

Braxton swatted the horse's rump. Thomas hit the ground in shock watching Mack kick and gag above him. Mack tucked his chin but it was just no use. His weight conspired with the rope to crush his neck and he could feel every last second of it.

"Daddy!"

Luke jumped from behind the camera and snatched the gun from Mary. He grabbed Little Linford and put the gun to his head.

"I'll kill this boy! You hear me? I'll kill him! Cut him down! Cut him down now!" Mary watched Mack swing and listened to Luke's voice. She could tell he wasn't gonna kill that boy. And in a few more bluffs, absent of bullets, the Klan would know it too. Bob ran to Mack's side and grabbed his legs. He lifted him just enough to give the rope slack so Mack's raw throat could hack new air. Nancy pretended not to notice other women scalding her with stares. That was it. Their name was mud in Braxton, Alabama.

"Let him go, Bob," Braxton said.

"He's got my boy."

"Let him go!"

"Fuck you!" Bob adjusted his hold on Mack and lifted him higher. "Thomas, cut him down." Thomas looked at Braxton who shook his head. "Thomas! He's got Little Linford! Cut him — " Braxton kicked Bob in the gut and down Mack went again. The second time hurt even more than the first. His air shut off like somebody turned off a faucet as he jerked and twisted against the pull of the earth.

"I'll kill him!" Luke said.

"Go ahead," Braxton said.

Thomas looked at Braxton to make sure he heard that right. He saw Mack's face begin to bloat and blood drool over his swollen lip. Then Thomas made a decision that would change his life forever. He grabbed Mack's knees, lifted him high, and listened to him inhale. He kicked at Braxton like a crazy man when he made a move against him.

"Get back! Cut him down!"

"This ain't like you, Thomas!"

"Hang another nigger!"

"This the one who pulled a gun on me. This the one who dies! Whose side you on?"

"I'm on Little Linford's side!" Luke didn't like where this was headed.

"Mary. Get on the horse and ride away. Go."

"I won't leave you, Luke."

Nancy was hysterical but none of her neighbors offered comfort. Little Linford got mad when his mama cried. He cut his eyes at the gun by his head. And then at Luke. He noticed Luke was busy watching Mack and wasn't paying him much attention.

Braxton rallied the knights.

"Are we gonna let these nigger's make a fool of us? Are we?" The Klan looked back and forth between Mack and Little Linford.

"Don't listen to him." Thomas said. "He's gonna kill my nephew. Somebody just cut him down!" His arms were getting tired.

"Are y'all gonna listen to me?" Braxton said. "Or to nigger loving poor white trash?"

"We ain't no nigger lovers," Thomas said. "Y'all know me."

"Y'all know me too. And let me tell you a little something 'bout poor white trash — "

"Mr. Braxton, don't," Bob said.

" — I've done shares with them too over the years."

"Our family's been off shares for years," Nancy screamed.

"But not that many. They worked alongside niggers. Got to know niggers — "

"Mr. Braxton — "

" — chose niggers over us. Now! In these crucial times! Times like these! That need a Klan! Are we gonna save the child of a nigger-loving family?" Braxton's face got red as he ranted on. "Or are we gonna uphold our Confederate flag? This nigger pulled a gun on me! You could be next! Think about your families! Choose!"

The Klan was still. Thomas held Mack and prayed. Then Little Linford grabbed Luke's hand.

"Stop it!" Luke said.

And the gun went off.

Bob and Nancy screamed. Thomas watched Little Linford fall in the grass. And then he let Mack go.

Mack didn't have the strength to fight it this time. He swung there and saw the Klansmen pick up their guns. He saw them take aim at Luke and Mary. It was the last thing he ever saw.

Mary looked at the hole in Little Linford's face. Luke dropped to his knees and shook the boy. There was a white hot flash. And that's the last thing she saw.

Luke watched Mary hit the ground. He screamed when the bullets tore up his body.

He saw a rusty truck.

He saw Benny with a gun.

And that's the last thing he remembered.

23

"Luke!" Benny shot at everything wearing a sheet. He wondered if Maddie got away and then he saw her body. He cussed God and kept firing into the mob.

"Mack!" Charlie unloaded his twenty-two from behind the truck's door he used as a shield. Bloodied up three sheets right quick. "Mack!" He wept and fired, wept and fired. A second truck pulled up.

"There she go," JJ said. "Cover me!" His army of brothers rose out the back with full rifles and let it rip. Mr. Lewis looked at his little girl, naked and bleeding in the dirt. JJ ran to a tree and let it block bullets while he cocked his Winchester. They were still outgunned but had the element of surprise. The Klan was more concerned with retreat and getting their families to safety. Only Bob ran to recover Little Linford but Thomas knocked him out and dragged him behind the Tree. He stared at Mack's corpse as bullets whizzed past their heads and listened to shouts of wounded men. Nancy and the families crushed dry leaves running to the woods, to their cars, and free horses.

Boss Man Braxton stole somebody's pinto and beat it to a speedy escape. Benny had him in his sights as the horse splashed through the creek. He fired. Braxton fell and turned the water red around him.

JJ reached Mary and pulled her body behind an oak.

"Get Luke, too!" Benny said. But JJ ignored him. Two of Braxton's boys rode into the creek to retrieve him.

"No, you don't!" Charlie said. He dropped the empty pistol, cocked his rifle, and blew a big hole in the henchman's chest. The other fella let out a scream so high only dogs could hear it and Charlie squeezed the trigger and opened his chest as well. Braxton watched the other body drop right next to him. He kept still in the muddy water and closed his eyes. The creek continued to bleed and he continued to breathe; playing dead while others died instead.

"Benny!" Charlie said. "Get Luke and let's get outta here!" JJ ran back to the truck with Mary in his arms and loaded her in the bed while the brothers had his back. More Klansmen dropped. Then JJ got it in the shoulder. Mr. Lewis jumped out of the driver's side and returned the fire. JJ slipped under the tarp with Mary and reassured his brothers with a painful face.

"I'm all right," he said. "Keep shooting!"

Benny was clear to reach Luke but his heart skipped a tick when he turned the body over. Luke wasn't moving. Benny felt the world fade along with Charlie's pleads to hurry. Thomas took advantage of Benny's daze and picked up a gun in the grass. He aimed it and cocked the trigger but Bob woke up.

"Little Linford!"

"Shut up!" Too late. Thomas ducked behind the Tree and Benny fired.

He dragged Luke to the truck by his torn shirt, shooting while running backwards. Luke woke up a little and thought himself dead. He didn't feel that he was moving but the world moved instead in dusty swirls of snapshots frozen in his heavy eyes. Like the crooked trail of blood his body leaked. And Mack so still on the Old Crook Tree. So still, the rope he hung from seemed like a pole. And the motion picture camera. With the little bit of strength that he had left, Luke flung his hand out and grabbed the camera off it's stand. Benny couldn't believe it.

"Uh, nigger, you see anything else you want out here? 'Cause Lord knows we got the time." He pulled Luke to the side of the truck as Charlie fired his last shots. Luke passed out again but his arm locked around the camera like it was built into him.

"What that he got there?" Charlie said.

"Ain't no telling." Charlie huffed around the truck with caution and helped Benny toss Luke in the back. Mr. Lewis and the brothers sped off. "You welcome, motherfuckers!"

"Come on, Benny." Charlie puffed back behind the wheel of the truck and took one last look at Mack. He jammed his foot on the pedal and they was gone.

Bob freed himself from Thomas and ran to Little Linford. He put his mask on the boy's damaged face to hide the gruesome sight. Then he wrapped his arms around him and rocked. But Thomas didn't look at Little Linford. Other things were on his mind besides grief. He stepped into the creek and sloshed on over to Braxton. He grabbed him by his soaking wet collar and pulled him close to his razor sharp nose.

"I knew you was faking," Thomas said.

"Help me." Thomas dunked Braxton's head in the water and held it there until the bubbles stopped. Then he yanked him back up and watched him suck air. He waited with patience for him to stop coughing. Bob ceased rocking and was about to say something but a glance from Thomas changed his shattered mind. He looked around the empty field and held Little Linford closer.

"We... we got to stick together, Thomas," Braxton said.

"Stick together? With poor white trash like me?"

"Thomas. I'm... begging you."

"Request denied." Thomas held Braxton underwater and waited for the bubbles to stop again. Then he waited some more. He wasn't sure how long he stayed there mashing the head into the mud but after awhile he heard Bob cry and remembered where he was. He waddled out of the creek and passed Bob by still refusing to look at the source of his tears. He came to the Tree, a bit out of breath, and sat on the Crook with a smile. He looked at the remains of Mack Martin and said,

"I'm gonna get those niggers. No matter where they go. No matter where they hide. I'm gonna get those niggers."

*   *   *   *

Charlie's truck could go about fifty miles per hour but he was doing eighty. He had his foot all up in the gas tank, putting that truck through it's paces like hell was behind them.

"You see anybody back there?" Charlie said.

"Naw," said Benny. He looked at his reflection in the dirty windshield and saw a man crying. "They got Maddie." Charlie didn't know what to say. They rode on in silence as Benny thought about Bertha. He didn't have time to get her when he was rounding up the cavalry. Couldn't go home now. Home was the first place the sheriff would look who was probably under one of them sheets in the first place. They had to get out of Braxton, Alabama.

"How's Luke?" Charlie said. "He alive?" Benny took a look.

"Just about." He tapped his heel and shifted in his seat. "We gotta get outta here, man. Get Luke to a doctor."

"Don't you think I know that?"

"Well what we gonna do, man? Where we gonna go?"

"Benny, calm down. It'll be — "

"Look out!" Charlie saw her just in time and cut the steering wheel hard. The truck slid to a stop two inches from her body and she waved the dust away from her face in irritation.

It was the HooDoo Woman.

She went to the rear without a word and put her foot on the bumper to climb in back. Benny and Charlie rushed out to assist her, ignoring her angry protest she wasn't that old. She settled down with Luke and spread out a cloth of sundry herbs, feathers, and vials.

"Drive to the train station," she said. Charlie didn't understand but knew from experience to trust her.

"Come on, Benny," he said.

"I'm staying back here." Charlie took a short cut to the train yard while The HooDoo Woman doctored on Luke. Benny held on to steady himself from the rough and rushed ride. The wind whipped his hat off and the HooDoo Woman caught it and gave it to him without even looking. He slowly put his hat back on and inched away from her some. The unpaved road didn't bother her at all. She was one with her balance like leaves on smooth currents. Her fingers dug deep in the bloody wounds as if looking for something dropped in warm dough. All the time she went,

"Mm mm. Uh-huh." Benny watched her knuckles sink under the flesh, bulging up like worms searching for a way out. A wave crossed his stomach like he dropped a great distance. She tilted back her head and sighed till the air all but left the bottom of her lungs. She withdrew her slimy fingers from the open flesh and let the bent bullet fall to the bottom of the truck. It rattled and rolled from one end to the other while she repeated the procedure from legs to chest.

The sun went in for the night so Charlie turned the headlights on. Slim, dead trees with skinny branches scratched Benny's neck when they pulled into the yard.

The HooDoo Woman whispered in Luke's ear with the intimacy of somebody who knew him pretty well. She picked up a vial of clear liquid and squeezed his mouth open with her thumb and finger. She poured the stuff down his throat and whatever it was tasted nasty enough for him to make a face. His wounds bubbled and boiled with a frosty fizz. His body stiffened up and he mumbled for Mary. She fanned feathers round to chase troubled thoughts away.

"You won't see Mary for a very long time," The HooDoo said as she patted his head. He called for his mama. She closed her eyes. "Drive to the third car from the back," she told Charlie.

"Where we going?" Benny said.

"West."

"West where?"

"Did you practice today?" He remembered Luke used to ask him that when they were boys. But childhood was far away this night. He looked at the sky and hoped whatever Luke found there would do something for him. But it wasn't working. He thought of his aunt. They had their problems but she loved him as much as her crippled heart allowed. She deserved way better than what she got. And Mack. Lord have mercy. They killed Mack.

So Benny looked at the ground at the broken glass and discarded metal. Only things of the earth caused him pain or pleasure and looking at the sky didn't mean a damn. He took his flask of never-ending brandy out his pocket and took a full swallow. That didn't work either.

"We don't know nobody out west."

"But everybody gonna know you. Then you can pay me."

"Say what now?" She grabbed his hand with the strength of a man and said,

"West is the land of hopes and dreams.
West ain't always what it seems.
But to have your revenge and pass this test,
You gotta go, hafta go, will go West."

Benny pried his hand away and rubbed it while she laughed. The truck stopped at the third car from the back and Charlie killed the lights. Just then, there were new lights from a Terraplane so clean the paint job gleamed in the moon. It came to a stop and out stepped Deacon Early. But he wasn't alone.

"Bertha!" Benny said. He jumped out of the truck and snatched the case from the Deacon without greeting or gratitude. He hugged her like a sweetheart and laughed in the night. Deacon Early, however, had an attitude.

"Now you listen to me, you heebee jeebee bitch. I don't work for you. You got that?"

"Look like somebody forgot what it felt like to limp," the HooDoo Woman said. Charlie looked at Deacon's leg and noticed he was over the accident. But Deacon Early shrugged her off.

"All the power of the mind."

"Well, mind your ass on over here," she said. She told Charlie and Deacon Early to open the boxcar door. "Benny, you get Luke." Benny tried to take the camera away from Luke but the HooDoo Woman said, "Leave it be. Y'all gonna need that."

He carried Luke to the box car and slid him into the wide, wooden space. Charlie struck a match. A group of hobos, huddled in the corner, shied away from the light.

"This here's our car," one of the hobo's said.

"Y'all don't mess with them, they won't mess with y'all." Charlie said.

"I can't hang around here all night, you know," Deacon Early said. "Don't need no crosses burning in front of The Joint." He looked around to make sure they were safe.

"Do what you're good for," The HooDoo Woman said. Deacon tossed Benny a fat money clip. He caught it with one hand and stuffed it in his pocket. This didn't go unnoticed by The Hobo in the corner. The train whistle sounded and steam hissed from the engine.

"All aboard!" They heard from the front.

"You ain't coming, Charlie?"

"Naw. Gotta get my lady. Gotta do right by Mack. And I'll take care of Maddie, too."

"Thanks, man. But be quick about it and get out of town 'fore somebody recognize you. Hear me?"

"It's the will of God that I wasn't there," Deacon Early said. "Don't need to be getting these white folks riled at me. Still got a business to run, you know."

"Somebody need to find Miss Sarah," Benny said. The HooDoo Woman pinched his arm.

"Somebody need to get on this train!" Benny jumped on board rubbing his arm as the train lurched to a grinding roll.

She threw him a black velvet bag. "Use that to deal with Luke. He gonna be real sick but that'll keep him alive." The train pulled away.

"What we 'spose to do when we get there?" Benny said.

"Do what you always do."

"How we 'spose to get in touch with y'all? How long we gotta stay there?"

She said something Benny couldn't hear and the train left her further behind. Charlie, Deacon Early, and the HooDoo Woman disappeared in a veil of steam. Benny stared at the black bag and put it in his pocket."Benny…"

"I'm here, buddy. I'm here."

"Where… are we?" He got the shakes and all the bums glanced at each other.

"It's ok, buddy. I got you." Luke tried to make sense of his new surroundings.

"Where we going?" Benny thought for a second.

"Wees going to Hollywood."

Luke blacked out.

Benny dragged him to a corner of the box car and took Bertha out of her case. He got as comfortable as he could and plucked his baby with love. The soft, sad music filled the car, caressing the bums.

A strong, cool breeze came through the door and a wide shaft of moonlight shined on Benny. He gazed into night and recollected the day. The bums watched in confusion and he flashed a sad smile.

"It's a long story, fellas."

Then Benny played the blues.

Is Benny about to be a star?

Is Hollywood all Luke dreamed it would be?

Are Mary and Sarah still alive?

Whatever became of Rastus, P. Jr.?

And what role has HooDoo in Hollywood Land?

Discover all the exciting answers in:

**THE
HOLLYWOOD COLORED
BOOK II**

www.warewordpublishing.com
1-888-350-7644
for ordering information.